Anguish and Absurdity in Medicine

More than 50 medical stories and as many insights

Douglas Halford

Contents

Dr Starling's case book

Living with disability

Medicine and society

At the fringes

Introduction

As a junior medical student I sat one evening in the viewing gallery of one of the hospital's operating theatres, watching a radical mastectomy operation. In the roads around the building people were making their way home to the suburbs, perhaps doing a little shopping or having a drink on the way, while here inside was something extraordinary, and on the face of it, barbaric: an unfortunate woman was having a breast cut off. But the surgeon and his team were performing their task quietly and efficiently. The anaesthetist, relaxed and chatty, was holding the patient's life in his hands. There was no drama, except in my head. It was another day at the office – normal for medicine.

I became a doctor more or less by accident. In the VIth form I chose to study physics, chemistry and zoology because they interested me. I had no career in mind. Later, I realised these A-levels could get me into medical school. My friends assured me that such a career choice was not on the cards for a poor duffer like me.

'Doug, your dad will have to buy you a practice.'
'You don't speak Latin, Doug.'

The view was that a person from my background doesn't become an important person like a doctor. At that time the three GPs in my suburb – Drs Norman, Lorimer and Dyas – were universally regarded as pillars of the community, a race apart. They were seen flashing past in their big cars on their way to home visits. Social inertia meant that medicine as a career was still largely taken up by those with medical or professional parents and who were, in the main, privately educated. In fact there was nothing tangible to stop this grammar school boy from below the line joining them if I could get my A-levels.

Eventually, I scraped into medical school, finding myself with some clever and seriously posh colleagues, many of whom had a medical background. I thought, 'You're probably the thickest person here. You're going to have to pull your finger out to keep up with this crowd.' I studied day and night and, to my

1

amazement, at the end of the term I found myself close to the top of the heap. This unexpected success was such a pleasant novelty that hard work became a habit and has stayed a habit. Now, I'm a sad case: I can't stop. So I'm writing this bloody book! Medicine is a vocation like none other save, perhaps, nursing. You are in a privileged position of trust. You get to learn intimate details of people's lives that, perhaps, they don't even share with their nearest and dearest. They trust you to examine their bodies, to prescribe dangerous medications and to operate on them. You tell them the best news and the worst. You advise them about matters of life and death. You may be with them when they enter the world, and when they leave it. You witness their first breath and their last.

In what other trade do you meet a stranger, ask him a few questions and then stick a gloved finger up his bum? Outrageous! But normal for medicine. Let's be clear - I am not mentioning this as a perk of the trade, but simply that it singles out medicine from, say, accountancy or bus driving, though not always from the priesthood.

I am fortunate that the career I chose by accident has been a lifetime interest. I was thrilled at the outset when I bought my first medical tomes – *Gray's Anatomy*, Samson Wright's *Applied Physiology*, Cunningham, Ham and Leeson – and a skeleton in a wooden box. But medicine is not everyone's cup of tea. Of students starting at medical school, approximately ten per cent give up in the first year. It's hard work and often disturbing: you tend to believe you've contracted all the awful diseases you are studying, and there is a great deal to learn and keep up with. My career took me into research and teaching as well as caring for the sick. I worked in the UK and abroad. Later I did medico legal work.

Humour is never far away. You have to laugh otherwise you might cry. Doctors and nurses tend to be a crude and irreverent bunch in the worst possible ways.

2

In the gynae clinic:

> *Doctor: Madam, what sort of contraception do you use?*
> *Patient: Er, my husband uses his head.*
> *Nurse: Doesn't it hurt his ears?*

I have written a collection of anecdotes and stories, many of them none too serious, gleaned from a lifetime in medicine. Many relate to events from decades ago, but I believe they are no less interesting or relevant for that. Times have moved on and some of these stories describe actions and attitudes that would rightly be considered unacceptable today. I have not attempted to sanitise them.

Some of these tales are straight accounts of patients and colleagues, anonymised where appropriate, but to convey other ideas I have resorted to fiction. All these stories are based on my experiences and observations. Some feature a mythic Dr Starling, the senior physician. He's not me: he's too clever, too dedicated, too wholesome, and too much of a 'good egg' to be me, I assure you.

Medical Life

Wake up Nursie!

Of all the philanderers to have walked the wards at St Ethelburga's, none was more notorious or perhaps more successful than Dr Andrew Andrews. As well as having the inclination, Dr Andrews possessed the personal and material qualities necessary to make an impression. Admittedly he wasn't tall, dark or strictly handsome, but he compensated for those deficiencies by being, or seeming to be, rich, aristocratic, and suave. He had inherited advantages that the rest of us lacked and he revelled in them, oozing an air of arrogant superiority. He had the charm of a gynaecologist and the arrogance of a neurologist, which didn't make him popular with his male colleagues in the doctors' mess, who were understandably eaten up with envious disapproval.

In his defence, it is difficult for a single male junior doctor with healthy appetites not to let it go to his head and stray, however briefly, from the straight and narrow. For years, this mutt had been a downtrodden student, trailing behind crusty old consultants with a taste for ritual humiliation.

'Andrews, tell me the twenty-seven branches of the maxillary artery, or perhaps you could manage one or two of them.'

'What artery was that, Sir?

He had been at the bottom of the pecking order, a flatworm on the evolutionary tree of medicine, and there were doubts as to whether he would make the grade. He was even bullied by nurses and midwives who treated his status with contempt while envying his prospects.

Then, with a bit of luck and after a few harrowing days in dusty examination halls, everything changed. He emerged from his dried pupal case, inflated his wings and took flight. Perhaps he was a little nervous and tentative for his first few days but soon he had shaken off any such feeling. He walked the wards with a livelier step and new authority. He was in demand, for he had acquired relevant skills and knowledge, though no one was

5

more surprised about that than he. He was needed to write up patients' drugs, to put up drips, to do the lumbar punctures, to write up notes and to make clinical decisions, particularly when his seniors had retired to their private consulting rooms, to their clubs, to their wives or mistresses.

From that moment, the nurses had been inclined to give him a second look and allowed their heads to be turned by his charm. They noticed, perhaps, how diligent he was, how clever and knowledgeable, or even how compassionate and tender. Perhaps, too, they noticed his glances and tried unobtrusively to be there when he needed help or information.

'Maybe I could help you with the drip, doctor.'

And when the curtains are drawn round the bed of the unconscious patient, who knows what delightful exchanges and intimacies may occur?

This transformation in prospects occurs with all, and even the least attractive male may reap its rewards. Those to whom nature has been kinder can enjoy a plentiful harvest, if so inclined, for females numerically dominate these institutions. And few were as inclined as Dr Andrew Andrews MBBS.

In previous ages there had been talented and enthusiastic womanisers but war, social norms, fear of pregnancy and venereal diseases had curbed their excesses. But this was the Sixties, and there was the pill, penicillin, promiscuity, and permissiveness. Came the age; came the man!

Dr Andrews' conquests were numerous and varied. He was chronically sleep deprived. In addition to stirring up envy amongst his colleagues, he was resented by the many females he had discarded or overlooked. Malice and spite roamed the corridors of the Nurses' Home. Ministering angels fought over him like cats.

I have implied, I think, that this Dr Andrew Andrews came from a good home, and so he did. They had a big house in rural Hampshire and a social position to match. By ordinary standards they were comfortably off, but put beside their exalted tastes and expenses, they were pretty near destitute. It was therefore hugely encouraging to his parents that, during his student years Andrew

Andrews had become pally with Veronica, the only child of rich, elderly neighbours. They rode together and played tennis and bridge together and both joined the Young Conservatives. They were regarded as a pair by their Hampshire set and were always invited together to dances, balls and parties. Eventually he gave in to his mother's promptings and at a party to celebrate his graduation, he popped the question to the lovely Veronica and was accepted.

Veronica was a naïve girl; poorly educated about men. She knew that young men were supposed to 'sow wild oats', but she never really thought about what that meant, nor for a moment imagined how diligently and enthusiastically her best friend and fiancé was dedicating himself to this oat-sowing activity. She never so much as thought of another man, and she naturally assumed Andrew was equally well focussed.

While a student, Andrew came home most weekends and he enjoyed a decent amount of holiday. It all stopped when he was posted to St Ethelburga's, miles away, and most weekends he was either on duty or claimed to be too tired to make the long journey south. At first he had phoned Veronica or written, but even that communication had dried up after a few weeks.

Her gentle, trusting heart went out to him. 'The poor dear's working so hard! He must be so lonely and must miss me as I miss him.'

She consulted her diary, found that she was free the coming weekend, and wrote to Andrew saying she would be coming to stay. The news, as you can imagine, did not provoke unalloyed pleasure in his cheating heart. He phoned and tried to forestall the trip, but she would not think of denying him the pleasure of her company. In blind panic, Andrew swapped his duties around with colleagues so that he could take her out of the hospital during the day. He was meticulous in his planning: he booked tables at restaurants, borrowed a car, and planned excursions to local beauty spots and places of interest.

The weekend arrived and so did Veronica. He met her at the station and whisked her off for a late lunch. More time was consumed in a long drive to a cathedral city where they ambled around and shopped like lovers will. Then there was a lingering

7

candle-lit supper before returning, late and tired, by a circuitous route to St Ethelburga's.

'I'll take you up to the mess. That's where I hang out most of the time. Meet some of the chaps!'

'But I would so love to see the wards – to see where you work.'

'The wards? Surely not! Not a safe place for a nice girl like you. All kinds of rough people and germs.' The real reason of course was that due to his unswerving commitment to amorous liaisons, there was scarcely a ward in the hospital where one could guarantee there was not a nurse he had seduced.

'But you go to those places, darling. I think I should learn to share with you. It would bring us closer together.'

'That I very much doubt,' he replied, leading her up the narrow stairs to the doctors' mess.

The mess was a dismal, smoke-filled place in those days. The three incumbents at that late hour – Jeffreys, Dunford, and Mukerjee – were civil enough, though their shock at witnessing their colleague's semi-marital status was plain to see. But they were all pretty well gone on the establishment's cheap beer so they were poor company, and Andrew, after the minimum interval required for politeness, steered his fiancée out and up the stairs to his quarters.

It was the first time they had spent a whole night together, and any trifling suspicions Veronica had been entertaining in her none too incisive mind were soon banished by the ardour and tenderness of his love. He had become a much better lover during the period of his absence, and naturally she put this down to the effects of deprivation rather than to regular practice.

They woke late and continued to enjoy each other's company until it was well past breakfast time. 'Never mind, Veronica. I know somewhere. Dress up! I've built up quite an appetite!'

'I'm not surprised, darling!' She looked at him adoringly.

So they were soon out of the place and motoring to a small hotel where the food was excellent. They enjoyed their breakfast and, feeling lazy after their disturbed night, they retired to the lounge and the Sunday papers. They decided to stay for lunch and late in the afternoon, driven by a middle-class obsession with fresh air, they went for a bracing walk down quiet country lanes.

8

Supper was at another country hotel, and it was late before they returned to the hospital. On this occasion Veronica was quite content to be taken straight upstairs to his room without a trip to the mess.

'I have an early start in the morning, darling, but you'll be able to sleep in. I can get off at around ten to take you to the station.'

'I really don't want to go, darling. I'd love to stay here with you forever and ever.'

'I would love that too, darling, but it won't be long now and we'll be able to be with each other always.'

'Oh! That does sound wonderful, darling!'

And this, their second night together, was no less magical than the first. Andrew's enthusiasm for her was undiminished, but when she woke from a blissful sleep he was no longer at her side. She gazed around at his spartan environment, happier than she could remember, then she rolled over, buried her face in the pillow that still bore his scent and dropped back into a dreaming slumber.

Mrs Welsh was a little late that morning. She liked to bring a cup of tea first thing to her poor, overworked doctors. She knocked gently on the door. There was no reply, so gingerly she opened it. The sight that met her eyes – of a girl in Dr Andrews' bed – was not one that surprised or embarrassed her in the least. She had often enough brought two cups to that particular room. Neither did it surprise her that it was a new girl, judging from wavy auburn hair spilling over the pillow and counterpane.

'Morning, dear!'

Veronica stirred and rolled over. 'Good morning,' she blinked, unfocused at the stranger.

'Hey! You're a new one! Haven't seen you here before, have I? I can't keep track!'

'What do you mean?' Veronica's mouth fell open.

Mrs Welsh had the slightest intuition she might not have said quite the right thing. 'Just brought you a nice cup of tea, dear, and then you'd better be getting back to the Nurses' Home before Matron catches you! Would you like a biscuit?'

9

Dick's Dick

'When you've a moment Lucy,' said Sister Morgan. 'It's Richard Crow. He's become incontinent of urine over the past few days and he has a large scrotal swelling, I guess it's a hydrocele, but I'd be grateful if you could have a look at him. He's quite distressed, though it's never easy with him to know what's getting at him.'

Richard had originally been admitted with chest pain and had been on the coronary care ward for a couple of days before they had decided it was a false alarm. He was sent to a medical ward to recuperate and had now been on the same ward for weeks. The problem was that he was, to put it simply, mad and physically frail. He had been in and out of mental institutions all his life, but latterly had become lost to the system: homeless, sleeping rough, or sometimes staying in hostels if they would have him. A lifetime of smoking had given him bronchitis and breathlessness. For him to be discharged from the hospital, social services would have to find him decent, safe accommodation in a care home, or perhaps sheltered housing. It wasn't easy. Until the problem could be resolved he was 'blocking' a bed in an acute medical ward.

The psychiatrists had been to see him on the ward and had suggested treatment, but it hadn't helped much and he was too physically ill to go to their ward for proper assessment and management. Lucy had done her best for his mental condition, though that was little enough. The other patients shunned him and many of the nurses were little better. He was a sad man in his own world of hallucination and delusion at the far end of the ward.

Richard was standing in his accustomed place between his bed and the wall, bowed forwards, looking at the lino, arms flexed, and shaking. He was a gaunt man of average height, with wispy grey hair and several days of stubble. Lucy pulled the curtains across, which was all she could do to respect his privacy, but cloth did little to stop sound.

'Sister tells me you've a problem with your waterworks, Richard.'

'Yes Doctor,' he grimaced.

'How come?'

'I can't find my dick Doctor!'

'How do you mean?'

'I can't find it. It's gone!'

'How do you mean you can't find it?' She could not help a slight chiding, mocking tone in her voice. She knew about knight's moves in thought; of thought insertion and other features of the disordered thinking of schizophrenics, but she did not remember anything about them mislaying their private parts.

'I just can't! It's gone!'

'I think I had better try to find it for you, Richard. You'd better lie up on the bed.'

'Okay Doc. Thank you Doc.'

The quest for Dick's dick – at least it was something different. She undid the cord of his pyjamas. There was a strong smell of stale urine. She exposed the area.

'Well, well, Richard! You've got quite something down here!'

'Yes Doc.'

'Not the usual thing a girl finds around these parts!'

'No Doc.'

'Well, well, well! I can see your problem.' It was a startling sight: his genitalia had been replaced by a pink swelling the size of a large grapefruit. He was right: his penis had disappeared. 'Do you mind if I have a little feel around there? Tell me if it hurts.' The swelling was like a balloon. One prod and even a surgical non-starter like herself could tell it was not a solid mass, but filled with fluid and quite tense. She got out her pencil torch and pressed the light against the swelling. It glowed as the light shone through the clear fluid that filled it. This was quite a common problem in old men: liquid accumulated in a sac around the testicle.

'You've got a couple of great big hydroceles. No wonder you can't find your penis! It's submerged!'

Richard did not respond. She looked at his face. He was staring at the ceiling; his jaws were moving from side to side.

She pulled up the pyjama bottoms and straightened up. He would undoubtedly need an operation, but first off she needed to arrange an urgent ultrasound to make sure there wasn't an underlying cancer. She wanted to aspirate the fluid, but she needed to make sure there was no tumour first. If there was cancer she risked spreading it to the scrotum with the needle.

'Richard, you've got a lot of liquid around your testicles. That's what the swelling is.'

'Can you take it away, Doc?'

'Not right now, Richard. You need an ultrasound examination first. If the test is okay I can suck off some fluid, but until then we will have to put a little tube into your bladder so that you don't wet yourself any more.

Then she hastily filled in a request for the urologist to come and assess him.

'It's the Catholics, Doc!'

'What is?'

'They've done this to me. It's because my mum never had me baptised!'

'Don't worry about it. We'll fix it, but you'll need a little operation to stop the liquid coming back.'

He stared at her, shocked. 'No Doc! No operation! They will kill me!'

'Of course they won't! If you want your dick back you'll have to have it done.'

'No Doc. Sorry Doc. No surgery!'

Two days later, as the ultrasound was fine, she aspirated most of the liquid, but she couldn't remove it all.

'Richard, you're certainly going to need an operation.'

More in hope than anticipation, she had collected a consent form from Sister's Office and had brought it to him, but he remained adamant in refusing surgery.

The next day the fluid was reaccumulating. The urologist phoned her from the operating theatre. 'If it's coming back that quickly he'll certainly need surgery.'

'He refuses. He won't sign the consent form.'

'You need to persuade him, Lucy.'

'He's deluded.'

'Maybe the psyches can help. They could section him.'

The next day the psychiatrists hadn't come. For the fifth time Lucy took the consent form and traipsed down the ward. Richard was slumped over his bedside table.

'My dick still hurts, Doc. I don't like the tube.'

'I'm not surprised. I've talked to Mr Mullins. He's the expert – the surgeon. He says you have to have the operation. There's no alternative.'

Dick looked up at her, angrily. 'No! I've already said I don't want it! I keep telling you!' he shouted. 'The Pope won't let me have it! My mother didn't have me baptised!'

'It's the only way to get your dick back, Richard.'

'It won't work! The tubes . . .' suddenly, he snatched the form from her hand. 'What's this?'

'It's the consent form for the operation, Richard. You sign it there. Here's a Biro.'

He snatched the pen from her hand and scrawled his name where she had indicated. 'I hope you're satisfied! Leave me alone! I'm not going to be cut, however often you ask me.'

She stared at him in disbelief.

'You have to tear it up,' said the Staff Nurse, 'it's not a proper consent.'

'I know it's not, but he does need the operation. He'll get infected if this goes on much longer. I'm not really sure the poor fellow can consent to anything properly anyway. He's hearing voices all the time, and he's quite deluded.'

'Maybe you should increase his haloperidol.'

'I'm reluctant. He already has side effects. His tardive dyskinesia is quite bad.'

'So you have to get the psyches in again.'

'I'm waiting for them.'

The Staff Nurse shrugged her shoulders.

'I'm going to talk to Mullins.'

Mr Mullins had just come out of theatre. He was feeling tired and tetchy. 'Sorry Lucy, I don't know about him saying "no". You say he signed the consent form.'

'Yes, but . . .'

13

'If he's signed the consent form and you properly witnessed it, what are you worrying about?'

'I suppose I'm worried that he didn't know what he was signing, or why.'

'You physicians just love to complicate things, don't you? Haven't you got enough to worry about? As I understand the situation, you have recommended an operation, and explained it clearly and in detail to the patient. He is not demented, and therefore it is reasonable to think he understood what you told him. He signed the form of his own free will. I wholeheartedly agree that he needs surgery, and am willing to perform the needful procedure. Moreover, you have rightly pointed out that if we do not operate promptly he may develop complications.'

'I'm still not happy, Sir.'

'My dear young woman, you don't have to be happy. Who's happy? How can we be happy in this sad place? I'm going to do the operation, and you've told me the background, and I have understood it. You've done your job. Leave it for me to worry about the subtle ethical issues involved. I guarantee your patient will thank you when he is better.'

So it was that the dickless Dick Crow was taken to theatre, knowing that the Catholics had finally come in person to get him and that it was pointless to resist. 'As the lamb to the slaughter is dumb . . .'

After the operation, which proceeded without complication, he was nursed on a bright surgical ward that he imagined to be an Augustinian Priory. Days later, after they had taken the catheter out of his bladder, he had dared to feel down there where it had been so sore.

'I've got a dick!' he exclaimed. Patients within earshot, not realising the background, found the announcement as amusing as it was redundant. But the man in the next bed was hard of hearing. He assumed he had heard wrong, but was sure that congratulations were in order.

'That's splendid news!'

And, indeed it was.

The Valentine Card Massacre

It was the thirteenth of February and I had cooked supper for my flatmate. Angie was starting a week of nights, and the gesture was intended as a send-off. It was only spaghetti Bolognese, but it was better than she would get in the canteen, and I'd bought a cheap bottle of Beaujolais.

'What a way to spend Valentine's Day! At everyone's beck and call on Female Medical.'

I nodded. Nursing certainly mucked up your social life.

'I suppose you'll be out partying – enjoying the high life, dancing the night away.'

She was being ironic, knowing my lifestyle was fuelled more by Ovaltine than Champagne.

'What about that doctor you like?'

'Who's that?' I knew full well who she was talking about, but I wasn't going to encourage her. I had admitted, just once, after a few glasses, that I had thought he was okay. Nothing more. 'Anyway, what about him?'

'Have you sent him a Valentine?'

''Course not!'

'Why not? A bit of fun.'

'More your idea of fun than mine! God! If he found out I wouldn't dare show my face on the ward again.'

'You always take things too seriously, Cheryl. Lighten up!' She got up from the table and went through to her bedroom and returned with a pink envelope that she slapped down on the table. 'There you are! You can send this.'

'Don't be silly! Anyway, it's too late now.'

'No it's not. I can take it in and leave it on his results clip. He'll see it first thing in the morning.'

'No! I don't know him well enough! I don't want to stir anything up.'

'But he won't know it's you, stupid!'

15

'What's the point then, apart from further inflating his already overblown ego?'

'It'll make him guess. He'll wonder who's making a pass at him. You'd be on the shortlist, for sure, and he might ask you out. You won't have committed yourself either way.'

'I'm not sure.'

I drew the card from the envelope. It was innocuous enough. 'Hey! Good looking! Be my Valentine!' – over a photograph of James Dean.

'He looks nothing like that.'

Of course he doesn't, but this will make him think he does. I think he's pretty vain.'

'So what do I want to do that for?'

'Do it for a laugh.'

The Beaujolais was beginning to get to my head. I took another sip. 'Oh very well!' I opened the card. The message inside was: 'I've got the hots for you!' I threw it down on the table. 'I'm not sending that!'

'What's wrong? You have got the hots for him.'

'I'm not hot. Tepid at the most; nothing more. I strongly suspect the man's a prat.'

'Look! This ain't supposed to be a precise definition of your precious feelings. You've got the hots for him, but not too much. You're not about to melt. Fine! Natural enough when you think of an arrogant git like that. Tepid is about right. It's all he deserves.'

'Okay! Okay! Enough!' I took the card and printed, in blue ink:

'HAVE A NICE DAY, JAMES!'

xxx

'At least he won't be able to guess much from the handwriting.' I tucked the flap into the envelope and handed it to Angie.

She smiled broadly and then giggled. 'I've just had an idea!'

'What?'

'Oh, nothing much Cheryl, just an idea for a bit of Valentine fun. We all need fun, don't we Cheryl?'

On Valentine's night I got off duty at nine. My shift had been particularly busy and trying, and I had no time to consider the card or its possible repercussions. Fortunately it was a medical study afternoon and James Jarvis had therefore not been on the ward. I got back to the flat, but Angie had already left. I kicked off my shoes and collapsed in front of the TV. There was half a bottle of white wine left over in the fridge, so I drank a glass and ruminated sadly on being tired, washed up and alone on a night when most women of my age were having fun.

I couldn't settle to the TV so I opted for an early night with a romantic novel, and had a shower. I had just put on my nightie and dressing gown when there was a ring at the door.

'Who is it?'

'Me! James.'

'Who?'

'James Jarvis!'

'Oh!' I was flabbergasted. I didn't even realise he knew where I lived. 'What do you want, James?'

'Hey! It's Valentine's night, remember? I thought I was invited.'

My mind was in a whirl. What invitation? I laid my hand on the latch. It was tempting, but I knew I shouldn't open the door.

'I've got the hots for you too, Cheryl!'

'Oh, really? Since when?'

'For a long while Cheryl! I just didn't know you were interested.'

'I'm not sure I am. It's been a long day. Will you take me out for a drink?'

'Okay! Whatever!'

'Wait there while I get dressed.'

'Why do I have to wait out here?'

Of course he should wait out there! I thought. *I hardly know him.* But then I thought, *Well he is a colleague. I've seen him around the place for months. He seems okay.* 'All right, you can come in but behave yourself.'

'Scout's honour!'

I opened the door. He came in, smiling. I was used to seeing him in his long white coat – a symbol of medical authority – but now he was wearing a light jacket over a navy jumper and grey trousers, he looked pretty average. I suppose he was a bit of a pretty boy, with his dark hair and girly eyelashes, but he was a very poor woman's idea of James Dean. He shut the door.

'Wow! You're looking good!'

I was dressed only in a cotton dressing gown over my nightie. Not exactly the ideal garb in which to entertain a randy virtual stranger. I ignored his comment.

'You sit down over there while I get dressed.'

For a moment he didn't move, but stood staring at me, smiling.

'Sit down!' I insisted. 'And you can have a glass of wine while you wait.'

He sat down on the sofa and I found a glass in the kitchen and poured him a little of the cold white wine. There was already a smell of alcohol on his breath. As I laid the glass on the coffee table he laid his hand on mine and looked up at me.

'Don't be long.' He leered at me.

'Piss off!' I pulled my hand away.

I made for my bedroom, and shut the door behind me. Unfortunately there was no key in the lock. I opened the little wardrobe that housed my meagre selection of clothes. I reflected that even if I had wanted to impress him I had nothing remotely suitable. My clothes were frumpy and out of fashion. I decided it would just have to be jeans and a jumper. I felt vulnerable taking off the few clothes I was wearing, with him on the other side of the unlocked door. I gathered up my underwear, a shirt, jumper and jeans and put them on the corner of my bed next to the door. I stood with my back close to the door and began to undress. I could hear him moving around and going into the kitchen.

'Have you got any more wine?' he shouted.

'No!' I heard him open the fridge.

'Hurry up!'

As rapidly as I could I tore off my dressing gown and nightie and pulled on my clothes. With a stout pair of jeans properly buttoned and zipped up, I felt a little more secure. I brushed my hair and rejoined him.

He had found a half bottle of cheap brandy that we used for cooking.

'You took your time,' he slurred. He indicated that I should sit next to him on the sofa.

'No, I want to go out.'

'What do you want to go out for?'

'Because it's Valentine's night and everyone's out having fun. I want to join them. I want you to take me somewhere.'

'Like where?'

'Well I don't know, Romeo. That's for you to work out.'

'I don't know anywhere. Everywhere worth going to was booked up months ago.'

'Anyway, we're going out.'

'I don't want to go out,' he said petulantly. He was looking decidedly worse for wear.

'Okay, I'll help you up.' I put out my hand for him to grab hold of. He had no intention of getting up. He took my hand and dragged me down onto the sofa and immediately his hands were all over me.

'Let go!' I managed to briefly free myself and I jumped up. 'Now you just get out of my flat this instant, James Jarvis!' I shouted, backing off.

Worse for wear or not, he leapt up from the sofa and came after me. I couldn't escape. He trapped me in the corner by the small dining table. He grabbed me and pulled me towards him in a bear hug. I smelled the alcohol on his breath. I had my hands against his chest and was trying to push him away, but he was too strong. He was trying to kiss me.

'Get off, you arsehole!'

I brought my knee up sharply to his groin. He cried out, but rather than letting me go he became wilder. He was tearing at my clothes. I was screaming. My hands were still pinned against his chest.

It was the only thing I could do. It was the only part of his anatomy I could get to. I brought my hands up and grabbed his throat. My thumbs were pressing into his windpipe. I was panicking. I pressed harder and harder, he was tearing at my hands to release him. He was making awful gasping sounds then he was silent and his struggling weakened.

It seemed only a couple of seconds before he collapsed onto the floor and I was lying on top of him, my hands still clasped to his throat. His face was purple. His eyes were bulging. I let go. He did not move.

There were voices and people banging on the door.

They took me to the police station, and much later, when the terror and shaking had subsided, and when a lady doctor had examined me, they cautioned me and asked me what had happened. They were very sympathetic and kind. I told them everything I could remember. I knew that I should have waited for a solicitor, but I didn't have anything to hide. He was trying to rape me. I didn't mean to kill him. I just wanted to defend myself. Then an officer brought out a folder in which there was a pink envelope and an open Valentine card.

'Do you recognise this, Cheryl?'

I nodded.

'We found it in his pocket. Would you like to comment on the inscription?'

I turned the folder over. There were my printed words

'HAVE A NICE DAY JAMES'

xxx

but under them, in the same colour ink was printed:

'I REALLY WANT YOU JAMES!! TONIGHT 9.30 MY PLACE, CHERYL'

XXX!!

Tb or not Tb?

The Senior Physician, having dealt with his correspondence and flirted with his pretty secretary, had toddled down to the Friends of St Luke's tea counter for a cupper. It was off the main corredor, and a useful meeting place. Dressing-gowned patients, some of them trailing drip stands would rub shoulders with white coated doctors. Pleasantries would be exchanged, while clinicians would discuss business. He had just received an update on Mrs Johnson's renal dialysis, when he became aware of some respectful throat clearing behind him.

'Excuse me Sir.' It was his registrar, Dr Jefferson. His thin face, long nose and serious expression gave him airs of learning and aristocracy. He spoke quietly with nicely rounded vowels. He would have made an excellent butler. 'There is a crisis on A2, Sir.' This was one of the male medical wards.

'Don't tell me,' said the Senior Physician. 'Jimmy Cross is playing up again, or is it that bloody drug addict?'

'No Sir, it isn't one of the patients. It's Staff Nurse Patel.'

'What are you talking about, man? She's just about the best nurse we have! What have you been doing to her?' Over the months that Jefferson had worked for him he had developed a dislike for the man.

An awkward smile flashed across the registrar's serious face. 'Nothing Sir. We've just found out she's got open tuberculosis. Dr McFie says it's quite definite on the chest film and he suggests she may be the primary source of our two cases on the ward. Dr Jacques says they will have to deport her back to India.'

'What?'

'Yes Sir. She should never have been allowed into the country, but apparently a lot of blacks manage to dodge the health checks.'

'Perhaps they conduct them in a darkened room.'

'Sir?'

The Senior Physician stared at the floor. 'I can only think that you are talking absolute rot, Jefferson.'

Registrar adopted a condescending air. The Boss was out of touch - he knew more about race horses than patients, and he admitted as much, but this was over the top. 'I have seen the X-ray, Sir. She has a cavitated lesion at the apex of the right lung, Sir. It is characteristic of tuberculosis. I'm sure you will agree with the diagnosis when you see the film.'

Staff Nurse Patel had been with them for about a year. She was a great asset to the ward, and he had thought that she would make an excellent ward sister. She was also a stunner.

'She has a cough?'

'Er, well, no, Sir, she doesn't actually.'

'Open Tb without a cough eh? How do you and your Medical Officer of Health friend propose that the poor girl spread it to her patients?'

'It is unclear, Sir, but we cannot ignore the possibility, or the risk, Sir.'

'This all smells strongly of bullshit, Jefferson. Is she losing weight?'

'Actually no Sir, but I guess it's an early lesion.'

'You're swimming against the stream, man. Does she have night sweats?

'No Sir, actually her temperature is normal.'

'How's her appetite?'

'Actually normal Sir.'

'Have you examined her?'

'I didn't like to – she saw the Occupational Health doctor, who said she was normal on examination.'

'I would have thought you would jump at the opportunity for a thorough examination of her chest.'

'I think you ought to see her films, Sir.'

'Maybe, but first I would like to know why a completely symptomless member of staff had a chest x-ray in the first place.'

'Sir, I had a hunch that this might be the case. I discussed it with Occupational Health when we found we had two new cases of Tb on the ward. An Indian person on the ward would be an obvious vector.'

'But you already said she had no cough. Without a cough you can't spread the disease.'

'I figured, Sir, that she might be lying on that point, and I still believe that.'

'What you have done, Jefferson sounds a lot more like victimisation and prejudice than medical prudence.'

'You can say that Sir, but her x-ray film shows I was correct.'

Jefferson led the way down the corridor and through the swing doors into the Radiology Department. A woman in a trim white uniform was arranging X-ray films on a table.

'Do you know where Dr McFie is?' asked Jefferson.

'He's doing a barium meal.' She pointed to a wide closed door above which a red light glowed. A notice warned of radiation danger.

'It is urgent, Barbara,' said the Senior Physician. 'Could you ask him if he could spare a couple of moments?'

She knocked on the door and then opened it and spoke into the dark interior.

'He'll be out in a moment.'

'Meanwhile Barbara, can you find us a film please?' Jefferson gave the details.

A minute later they were standing before a bank of bright X-ray screens in a small darkened side room. 'Here they are, Sir. She's had a PA and a right lateral. She banged the films onto the screens.'

'You can see here, Sir ...'

'Not so fast, Jefferson. Let's make sure the details are correct.' He took both films down from the screens and peered closely at the indistinct writing in the top left corner. 'Nirmala Patel' – films taken two days ago. Right! Nice to make sure we're dealing with the correct customer.'

'Yes Sir. The problem is this opacity at the right apex. He jabbed a finger at the top of the right lung.

'Do you think me blind as well as stupid?'

'No Sir.'

'Just stupid then – that's a relief.'

23

'Dr McFie says the opacity is definitely cavitated, so she's almost certainly open - and highly infectious.'

'I don't believe a word of it!'

'But the opacity is definite enough, and it has a soft, acute look about it.'

'She's about the wellest-looking girl I've seen. She positively radiates robust womanly health, Jefferson.'

Dr McFie bustled in, a grey haired, lean elderly man with a slight Scottish accent. He smiled with surprising affability for a professional who had just been interrupted while performing a skillful procedure.

'Thank you for coming along, Tom. This must be our nurse lassie.' He focussed on the film. 'Yes, that's right. Right apical lung opacity with a small cavity here.' He pointed to the spot. 'I can't make it out on the side view, but that doesn't surprise me. It might be a good idea to confirm it with some tomographic cuts.'

The overlying shadows of the collarbone and first rib often hampered interpretation of shadows at the top of the lungs, but despite that there could be no doubting that there was an abnormal shadow in that area. Tuberculosis was the first diagnosis one would suspect. In an Indian, even more so. Tuberculosis was three hundred times more common in Indians in Britain than in the white population.

'I've already done the form, Sir,' said Dr Jefferson.

'Well cancel it!' said the Senior Physician. 'I don't want the girl irradiated for nothing.'

'I don't follow your thinking, Tom,' said the Radiologist deferentially. We could lose valuable time if we don't clinch the diagnosis, and there are important public health considerations.'

'Dr Jefferson here has already made a diagnosis, and has got the drains doctors involved.'

'The drains doctors?' asked McFie.

'You know, the public health chaps, and they want to send the poor woman straight back to the Sub-Continent on the next plane. We will be losing one of our best nurses, and we can't afford that, and I won't allow it!'

'But surely Tom, you can't just ignore it. She could spread it to others. I understand this may have occurred already.'

'If you want my honest opinion, I do not believe for one moment that this young woman has any infectious disease to spread to anyone! Excuse me, Angus, but I believe there is a mistake and I intend to get to the bottom of it.'

'The shadow is real enough, Tom.'

'I'm not even sure of that.'

Staff Nurse Patel sat on her bed and wiped her red, swollen eyes. She had to finish packing, for they would come to collect her any moment. She had to be ready.

She was resigned to her fate now. She had been shocked and then disbelieving, but as the reality of her situation came home to her she was frightened and angry. She feared for her family and how they could cope without her money.

She had worked her heart out at this hospital. She had treated her patients as if they were her own flesh and blood, but now that she was in need, requiring care and treatment, she was being rejected, thrown out as quickly as they could. They would not give her treatment. She had to return to India and sort this out for herself, but they knew that good treatment would be hard to come by there. They didn't care whether she or her family could afford it. They didn't care that she might die. They had used her and discarded her. It was so unfair!

There was nothing she could do. This was the law that Dr Jacques had explained to her. He had said he was sorry but there was nothing he could do. Dr Jefferson had said the same but she didn't trust him. This was all his fault. To her it seemed cruel and ungrateful.

She felt a deep sadness. She had been happy here even though she was so far from her family. She had enjoyed her work, had learnt a lot and she had made many friends. They said she would soon be promoted to Ward Sister. She didn't want to leave.

The Senior Physician hurried back to his room and told his secretary to drop everything and find Nurse Patel urgently.

'I don't care if you have to drag her off the plane at Heathrow.'

25

But such a last minute rescue was not required. The nurse was located in her room, packing. She stepped, rather sheepishly, into the Senior Physician's office, dressed in a sari. The sparkle had gone from her eyes. She had been crying.

'Good heavens – you do look different!'

Her brow furrowed.

'Your sari – I have only seen you in your staff nurse's uniform.'

'Oh yes, of course, Sir. I don't think I'll be needing that in the future.' Tears again welled up in her eyes. 'I have to leave tomorrow.'

'That's terrible! Who says so?'

'I think it's Dr Jacques.'

'Ah, the drains doctor – the Medical Officer of Health.'

'He says it's the law. I pose a risk to public health, he says.'

'Personally I doubt it's the law, and I very much doubt you are a risk to anyone.'

'But Dr Jefferson says there is no doubt about the diagnosis. He has talked to Dr McFie. He says I might have given it to Mr O'Connell and Mr Clark.'

'That's baloney, and I'm sure Jefferson knows it. Do you get on well with the good Dr Jefferson?'

'I think he is a very good doctor.'

'That's not quite what I asked you. He seems very keen to get rid of you.'

'I think he feels that he is only doing his duty, Sir.'

'He seems to be jumping to conclusions in his anxiety to be rid of you.'

She looked blankly ahead.

'So, Staff Nurse, tell me – is he really keen to get rid of you?'

'No, I do not think so, Sir.'

'You've never fallen out with him, or anything like that?'

'It wasn't anything important, Sir.'

'What was it about?'

'I don't like to say, Sir. It was private.'

The Senior Physician smiled. 'That's rather what I guessed.'

She looked at the floor.

'So the amorous Dr Jefferson asks you out, but you refuse him.'

'He had no right, Sir! He has a fiancée of his own, and I am also spoken for. He kept asking me. He wanted me to go to his flat. He didn't want to be seen in public with me! And I wasn't rude or disrespectful to him. I just told him 'no thank you', and said I had a fiancée and therefore I couldn't. In the end he stopped asking me and began to be off-hand and rude to me. Then all this trouble blew up.'

The Senior Physician smiled. 'Even I have noticed that his manner towards you has changed over the last little while.'

'But Sir, this is not relevant I think. I have contracted Tb and I therefore have to return to India, but it does not seem very fair to me.'

'Nor to me, but we are jumping ahead too far.' The beginnings of an idea was forming in his mind. 'You look different today.'

She looked down at the sari and smiled. 'So you said Doctor. It's not much like my nursing uniform.'

'No, I don't mean that. There's something else.'

'I've not eaten much since I heard, and I've been crying a lot. I'm so worried about my family. They are proud of me and they depend a great deal on the money I send them. This is a disaster for my family as well as for myself.'

'I understand. But no, it's not that.'

He looked her up and down, and she looked down, embarrassed. Then he realised what it was, and that sparked another train of thought. He had been in India during the war, and a long forgotten fact came back to him.

'I have an idea, nurse.'

She smiled at him dubiously. 'Can I know what it is?'

'It's just a hunch. If you don't mind, we'll do a little experiment.'

She looked alarmed. 'What sort of experiment, Sir?'

'Nothing difficult or dangerous. But first, tell me something about your health.'

'I am very well Sir. Dr Jefferson tells me I have Tb, but it does not seem like that to me. I have nursed many people with Tb, and they all lose weight, have a fever and cough. Some cough up blood. They wake up at night sweating. They have no appetite and are very tired.'

'And you have none of these symptoms?'

'None Sir. I am never ill.'

'But you could have caught it from one of the patients on the ward. There is always a risk. When I was a junior doctor Tb was a significant occupational hazard for the caring professions, particularly nurses.'

'I have had the BCG vaccination Sir.'

'I wish it gave one hundred percent protection, but it doesn't.'

'So I could have caught it?'

'I'm afraid so.'

'Do you think that's what's happened, Sir?

'No, as a matter of fact I don't.'

'So, can you help me?'

'I sincerely hope so. Shall we go?'

'Where to, Sir?'

'Oh, to the Radiology Department, of course. That's where our little experiment is to take place.'

'Is it really necessary, Sir?'

'Oh, absolutely!'

They walked together down the corridor. 'You have a large family in India?'

'Well, by Indian standards it is not huge. I have two brothers and a sister. They are all younger than me. One brother is at university and the others are at school.'

'So you are the responsible sister who goes to the West to make good and earn money.'

'Well yes Sir, I suppose so. My parents had to save and go without to pay for my education, and for my fare here. I am just repaying the family to allow my siblings to have the same opportunities.'

'They must be very proud of you.'

She smiled as he pushed open the door to the radiology department. They found Dr McFie seated facing a bank of films. A secretary was sitting with him, taking notes.

'Angus, you will remember Staff Nurse Patel. I have brought her down for another chest film.'

'What do you have in mind, Tom? The appearances are not likely to have changed in forty-eight hours.'

'I'm not so sure, Angus. The diagnosis is of crucial importance to Nurse Patel and her whole family. I want to check.'

'Very well, Tom, you're the boss. I'll ask one of the girls to take it.'

'Now, Nurse Patel I want you to have it taken just as you are. Don't change anything. Just as you are.' Dr McFie took her away and the Senior Physician paced anxiously up and down the reception area. It was a long shot but he hoped to goodness that he was right. McFie returned, smiling but clearly puzzled by the Senior Physician's behaviour.

'You're being cryptic,Tom.'

'I'm hoping to get her off the hook while not making a fool of myself.'

'She's a nice lassie.'

'An excellent nurse who we can ill afford to lose, and she does her bit to brighten up our lives.'

'I can imagine.'

A moment later she returned. McFie got up and offered her a chair.

'The film will take just a couple of minutes to develop. I am quite intrigued!'

She smiled. 'Me too.'

They heard a woman's footsteps. The Senior Physician found his heart pounding. He hoped desperately he was right, and did not know what he would do if he was proved wrong. He had played the inscrutable detective, and had challenged the judgement of his colleagues, all on a hunch. Medical wisdom said they were right. An acute upper lobe lung lesion in an Indian was tuberculosis. That diagnosis was way up there at the top of the list – so far up that there was effectively nothing else to consider. He could argue that she had caught it here, and should be treated here, but he had no guarantee of success. She would not be able to afford proper drug treatment in India, even if it were available where she lived.

Dr McFie smiled, pulled the film from its temporary folder and slapped it onto the screen. 'Goodness me! Look at that!'

'What is it? Has it got worse or something?' said the nurse.

The Senior Physician had already seen it.

29

'It's clear as a whistle, missy! There's nothing there!'

The Senior Physician breathed a deep sigh of relief and wiped the sweat from his brow. 'That was a close one, Staff Nurse!'

'I am very relieved, Doctor, but I do not understand. Do I have Tb or not?'

'Definitely not! Not now, and not then.'

'You have me at a loss, Tom,' said the Radiologist.

'I didn't want to say anything before, Angus, but I just had a hunch. Nurse Patel, would you mind letting your hair down for Dr McFie?'

She looked puzzled, but unpinned her plaits and they fell down over her shoulders. She looked down, embarrassed.

'I still don't see I'm afraid, Tom.'

'Well, look at this plait on her right. It sits behind her shoulder and has a slight curl in it towards the end.'

'But surely you're not suggesting that we are seeing it on the X-ray film?'

'That is my contention, Angus, and I think Nurse Patel will confirm that the original film was taken with her hair down like that.'

'Yes Sir, I remember it was. I remember because when I had a film taken in India before I came they insisted I pin my hair up.'

'Good heavens!'

'I was out East in the war, Angus, and there was something at the back of my mind about this. Caucasian hair is usually much thinner than the Asian stuff, which is solid enough to stop a few X-rays. Incidentally, I guess the fact that the so-called lesion was lying behind the thorax explained why it didn't show up on the side view.'

The relief was overwhelming. Nurse Patel dearly wanted to embrace the Senior Physician, but her deference stopped her. She looked at the floor and said a prayer of thanks.

'Well, thank heavens for that!' said the Senior Physician. 'I am very relieved.'

She looked up at him. 'I am so grateful to you, Sir!' To her surprise she saw that there were tears in the Senior Physician's old eyes.

The Chocolate Fountain

The Chairman looked sourly at his Chief Chemist. 'So, Alan, you're saying that it's not much of a drug.'

'It has very few advantages, if any, over the competition.'

'So you've wasted £500 million?'

'Don't be ridiculous!' The Chief Chemist was a stocky man with a large head and thinning grey hair. His tie was loose and his sleeves were rolled up. His attitude to his Chairman was one of tolerance only.

'It looks that way to me. We've spent at least that sum, and what have we got for it? A me-too drug, that's all.' The Chairman was a big man in his sixties. He sported a large brown moustache, matching toupee and a red bow tie. His background was in finance. His interest was in finance.

'Many companies have made a fortune out of me-too drugs, Brian. The Phase II trials show it works well. It is certainly not inferior to the competition.'

'Not good enough! You're too late. Others are already established in the market. We must abandon it or find some advantage, even if it's unproven. Perhaps one of our clinical friends could do a trial.'

'Maybe, if you want to risk that route. We could add a touch of dodgy statistics here, and a bit of data selection there. If it comes out in our favour we publish, if it doesn't we don't. Or maybe you would like a small study to show it's effectively the same as the opposition but cheaper - you know, the sort of study that is so feeble it couldn't show a difference between chalk and cheese.'

'We've done it often enough before.'

'Yes, Chairman we have, and so have our competitors, but the world is becoming a smarter place and a more sceptical place. Herxheimer and his band of do-gooders have rubbished our claims, so no one believes what we say It'll be on your head. You'll likely be found out and no one will touch the drug with a barge pole.'

'What then?'

'Talk to Marketing. They'll tell you to sell it cheap. It's a decent argument – "as good as the opposition, but cheaper.'

'Yes, yes, of course.'

'And spend a bit of money on good advertising. Why not get Zappy-zap involved?'

'Throwing more good money after bad.'

'Actually, Brian, I think we could do better, but it will cost a little. Perhaps we could do something about the mode of delivery.'

'Like what?'

'To get it into the system more quickly.'

'What? You want the punters to main-line the stuff.'

'Not quite, snort it more likely. What I mean is that we could deliver it as an aerosol. That way it will get straight into the blood supply, and hey presto! Blast-off in a few minutes!'

'Like one of those things they use for asthma.'

'Exactly.'

'How much would that cost?'

'Not a lot. We could get someone else to put it in an aerosol. There are a few specialised companies that make inhalers, but we would have to prepare the drug in a fine powder form or a concentrated liquid form that would go through the nozzle.'

'How long would it take?'

'A year.'

'Do it in six months.'

Nine months later the plans were in place for the Grand Launch of the Sidereal Pharmaceutical Corporation's latest product. Development had gone better than expected. Rapidly conducted clinical trials had shown a small, but statistically significant shortening of the time it took to be effective. Approval had been granted by the Drugs Agency with little delay. The Chairman had gone from gloomy pessimism to tepid optimism and was now, after trying the product for himself, was becoming wildly enthusiastic. To launch the drug he therefore insisted they would spare no expense. The Zappy Zap Advertising agency were involved, and they had planned a launch ceremony to be big and brash, impressive and memorable, if not necessarily in the best taste. Invitations had been sent not just to the press and the usual medical and pharmacological luminaries, but had been thrown wide to society movers and shakers, assorted celebs, two minor royals and a clutch of opinion makers. The Chairman was so confident he insisted their rivals in big pharma should also come. He loved to gloat.

It was going to be the launch of the decade!

A glittering company has gathered in the sparkling ballroom of the Pamper-U-Good International Hotel. Word has spread that this will be something special, so everybody is here and already celebration is in the air. Excited chatter is punctuated by the popping of champagne corks. Pretty girls, minimally encumbered by clothing are circulating with trays of glasses of bubbly, others with exquisite canapés.

A fanfare alerts the chattering crowd that something is about to happen. All eyes turn to the stage from where the trumpet call is coming. It is shrouded in mist on which multi coloured spotlights are playing. As the music reaches a climax, a man in a dark suit emerges from the mist.

'Ladies and Gentleman, Sidereal is proud to launch its latest and greatest product - a product that the world has waited for too long. None of us like to wait, and for some things waiting takes away the wanting. This is why we have turned to the aerosol as the ideal means of delivery.'

The mist having now dispersed, images of multicoloured floating aerosol droplets filled the screen. 'Drug delivery is all about surface area for exchange. Think of the surface area of the particles of an aerosol, and think of the surface area of where it is going to.' Now the image changed to that of a pair of lungs. The camera zoomed into the trachea and down the repeated bifurcations of the respiratory tract to the alveolar sacs. 'The surface area for exchange is vast, the membranes to be crossed are thin and the blood supply is rich.' A drug reaches the bloodstream in a fraction of a second, the rest of the body within a minute. Not too long to wait. But what is the rush?'

The screen now shows pastel, soft focus images of a man and woman, their bodies entwined. Nothing can be clearly seen, but their movements are passionate and urgent. But slowly we sense that their passion is subsiding until they separate and are lying side by side. The camera pans to her face that displays concern, frustration and perhaps the beginnings of anger, while his face shows shame and disappointment.

'Erectile dysfunction is a common enough problem, experienced by just about every couple at some time in their life, but for some it is a frequent or constant problem when it puts a strain on the relationship or destroys it. It denies a couple the intimacy, pleasure and bonding that they so desire and thus causes frustration, guilt and loss of self esteem. Indeed, the English term 'loss of potency' expresses what many feel. Erectile dysfunction strikes and the very heart of us.'

'Of course there are treatments. We have come a long way but not far enough. Not far enough that is until today. Today the Sidereal Corporation brings to the world the next giant leap towards the ultimate solution. TachyTurgo comprises a great new drug in a great new delivery system. TachyTurgo works within minutes and is easy and pleasant to use. TachyTurgo has no serious side effects and TachyTurgo is cheaper than the other, old fashioned drugs in its class. TachyTurgo is truly the drug of the future, now.'

This was a cue for four slender models dressed in black cylindrical outfits in the shape of the TachyTurgo inhaler to appear from either side of the stage and to strut about while a screen above proclaims in big letters:

'TACHY TURGO - A STIFFY IN A JIFFY!'

Then we see the man reach for his black inhaler, take a puff and lie back in contentment. Seconds later the couple are back at it in soft focussed rhythmic ardour.

'Today is not the occasion for a detailed description of this product. As much information as you could require is available at the door. Please help yourself, and for now, enjoy yourselves!'

The screen fades and spotlights illuminate a dais at the centre of the room covered by a silk awning. The awning is slowly lifted. Beneath it are three leggy girls in bikinis – two blondes are standing while the brunette is seated on the floor, cross legged. Now the blondes decorously bend over something that is dark and amorphous. They gingerly touch it. The audience moves closer to get a better view, pressing close against the low rails ranged round the edge of the dais. The blondes begin to caress it, but it remains as it was - a crumpled mass of dark material. The girls are becoming frustrated. They give up and stand pouting with their hands on their hips. Now the brunette stands up and brandishes an oversized inhaler, making sure all can see the insignia 'TachyTurgo'. She aims it at the crumpled brown material. A dense mist swirls around but as it clears we see that things are beginning to happen. The beast is stirring. Now the girls regain their enthusiasm and get really stuck in, massaging and caressing. There is a deep throbbing pedal note. The brown thing is swelling and growing. It is cylindrical, lengthening and rising, and now in the audience pennies are beginning to drop. They begin clapping, whistling, cheering and laughing while the blondes continue their massaging and caressing. Soon it is knee high, then waist high, head high. Now their arms are round it and they are kissing it, embracing it. The deep throbbing note becomes louder and louder and then is pierced by a high brass note. It is the opening sequence of *'Also Sprach Zarathustra'*. Slowly and triumphantly the music rises in glorious crescendo as the ten foot taut black phallus reaches its full extension, towering over them in erect glory. As the music finally reaches its triumphant climax so from its heaven-facing meatus the giant phallus ejaculates a fountain of gooey white liquid that flows mellifluously down the shaft. The chocolate fountain is in operation! There is uproar.

The Chairman smiles and looks down from the lectern with great satisfaction. Indifference was what he dreaded, but of all the emotions on display indifference was not one of them. The place is a riot. A minor royal is jumping up and down in excitement, a prominent disc jockey is standing with arms raised in triumph. The younger executives are over the moon, laughing and shouting their approval. Tachyturgo executives are rubbing their hands in glee. Equally pleasing is the look of disgust on the face of a well-known lady columnist, and the embarrassment shown by many of the women. Even more pleasing is the envy and anger that so clearly showed on the faces of their rivals. Zappy Zap had excelled themselves in the bad taste he had expected of them. It will make a great story, particularly if they can get a picture.

The press were scribbling notes and photographers were pressing forward to get a picture. The giant penis towered in triumph over all. This is what TachyTurgo will do for you!

'In the worst possible taste,' said Julian Fitzroy-Gore, Chairman of Global Drug Inc., wondering why his lot seemed incapable of such publicity catching stunts.

'It's disgusting! Quite disgusting!' said Emerald Ramsbottom, the Marketing Executive of Right-on Pharma whose own remedy for this problem, 'Hard-on', was currently the market leader. 'Come here!' she pulled her young male assistant towards her. 'Smithers! Deal with it!' she shouted at him over the uproar.

'How do you mean?'

'Do you want me to spell it out for all to hear?'

'But…'

'But nothing! If you value your job, and you fancy a bonus at the end of the year, you'll deal with it! Go!'

The crowd was densely gathered round the turgid member that quivered and squired chocolate, while its semi-naked acolytes collected the ejaculate with spoons, pouring it over wild strawberries in exquisite small porcelain bowls which they were handing to those within reach.

Smithers, with his natural diffidence, eased and pushed his way to the front.

'Excuse me! Excuse me! Sorry!'

And it was only when he got to the front, and a girl was trying to hand him a bowl of strawberries that he realised he had no idea what he was going to do. The giant swaying, spewing member towered over him. It wasn't good for his self esteem. The girls were bending, flaunting and strutting. Viscous rivulets of white chocolate were running over the black rubbery material. Onlookers were touching and prodding it, laughing and shouting. Girls were leaning forward and kissing it in mock adulation.

He looked around for a socket and plug, but its power supply was hidden. There seemed no way to injure the beast, and anyway, they would see him, they would see the name of his company, so clearly shown on his name badge. It would be all over the papers, and his company's good name would be tarnished. They would be inviting retaliation. No bonus lay that way. So at least he realised that he had to remove his name tag. He fiddled with it, and when he had it in his hand he at once saw what to do.

The Chairman was again speaking from the stage, shouting over the hubbub. 'Ladies and Gentlemen. There is no treatment to match TachyTurgo! With TachyTurgo erectile dysfunction is a thing of the past!'

All eyes were turned to the stage. This was the only chance he would get.
'You can be sure with TachyTurgo!'
He took the badge, bent back the pin.
'TachyTurgo, the drug of the future!'
He took a deep breath, summoning up his courage.
'TachyTurgo will never let you down!'
He thrust the pin into the firm shaft of the giant rubber penis.

BANG!

Like a balloon it burst with a loud report. Shards of chocolate-coated rubber membrane exploded outwards and collided with

37

close bystanders, who took the brunt of it in their fat faces, their expensive lapels, twinsets, frocks and waistcoats. The blondes were coated from head to toe in chocolate goo and fragments of brown rubber. Shards of rubber and globs of chocolate described parabolic trajectories to impact with walls, ceiling, light fittings and guests. The helmet, separating from the shaft, shot upwards with such force it struck the ceiling and adhered to it by virtue of its sticky coating. The chocolate pumping mechanism, now freed from the need to propel the stuff ten feet upwards through a narrow tube, dramatically, if briefly, created a true fountain of chocolate that sprayed vigorously in all directions.

For one second the ballroom was silent before everyone erupted in exclamations of shock, disgust and anger. No one had escaped unscathed. Every expensive suit and outfit showed evidence of the explosion. Those who had been closest were barely recognisable.

The Chairman looked on in consternation. Suddenly everyone was glaring at him and shouting. Celebrities and royals alike were waving fists and gesticulating angrily. He began to fear for his safety. He raised a hand for silence and smiled bleakly.

'Ladies and Gentlemen, the Sidereal Corporation...'
At this moment the giant penile helmet unglued itself from the ceiling above him and dropped like a stone onto his head, a huge, sticky brown phallic sombrero. Cameras clicked and flashed and suddenly there was once again a measure of joy in the ballroom. The various executives from rival gangs of Big Pharma began to laugh. They laughed until it hurt then laughed a good bit more.

But TachyTurgo was well and truly launched!

How Could I Have Done That?

Hong Kong flu

In mid 1968 the UK health authorities were fearing a flu pandemic. An epidemic of a new strain of the influenza virus (Influenza A/H3N2) had emerged in SE Asia at the beginning of the year and had infected tens of thousands of people. This was 'Hong Kong flu'. It was predicted to spread to the rest of the world, and it was reckoned that it would reach Europe at the end of the year. Transcontinental travel was much less common than today so viruses moved around the world at a more sedate pace than at present. Arriving in the middle of the winter, the virus was likely to cause tens of thousands of deaths, particularly of the old and frail.

I was a pre-registration house officer and had a two year old daughter. In September she developed a persistent cough. Her GP grandfather was worried about whooping cough (pertussis) so I swabbed her throat and sent it off to the Microbiology lab in the hospital where I was working.

About a week later, my friend in Microbiology phoned.

'Doug, you remember that throat swab from your daughter that you kindly sent down, query pertussis?'

'Yes.'

'Well, you will be pleased to hear that it's not our old friend Bordetella pertussis, but guess what!'

'Anthrax?'

'No you silly sod. We've grown a virus! You remember those little things Doug?'

'Get on with it, I'm a busy man.'

'Well, you'll never guess anyway. We've gone and grown H3N2. It's the dreaded Hong Kong flu virus, no less.'

'Blimey! It didn't seem to do her much harm. Anyway she's better now.'

'Got any clue how she caught it?'

'None.'

'Any contact with the mysterious Orient?'

'Not that I am aware of. We live in Barns.'

'That's not very far east I suppose. Has she travelled recently?

'Only to her play group. She's two.'

'Well look, Doug, I'll have to report this, and I guess the authorities will want to talk to you, and maybe they'll want to do some investigations.'

In fact all that happened was that I was contacted by a lady virologist from Mill Hill who sent me off swabbing my daughters contacts - her family and the little friends at her play group. All were negative, so we never found out how my daughter caught it. It was a complete mystery. It was the first detection of the virus in Europe, months ahead of schedule.

The country was far from prepared in terms of vaccines and there was a degree of well controlled consternation in public health circles. But it wasn't reported on the news though it did spark a leader in the British Medical Journal.

This lack of apparent concern and action was surprising considering that the previous Asian Flu (A/ H2N2) pandemic in 1956-8 had killed maybe 2 million people worldwide, and now we can compare this laissez-faire attitude to what happened when in 2009 the first UK cases of Mexican Swine Flu (A/H1N1/09) were reported. Then I remember TV images of reporters camped outside a Scottish hospital and people tramping around in white protective clothing, as if they were dealing with Ebola! The government spent millions on antiviral agents of dubious efficacy. It was big news, terrible things might happen! The stock market faltered. But in 1968 my daughter's denouement was effectively ignored. The Stock Market did not plummet; we were not besieged by the press; men in bodysuits and breathing apparatus did not invade my daughter's play group.

Of course Covid-19 has been another thing altogether.

In fact, Hong Kong flu did not peak in the UK until the winter of 1970. Worldwide, approximately one million people died.

Weeks later, my friend in Microbiology phoned me again.

'Doug, you know what?'

'No.'

'I've just heard on the grapevine that your daughter's virus was acquired by a pharmaceutical company and they are using it to develop their flu vaccine.'

'Really!'

'There might be something in it for you, Doug. You ought to write to them, as they might wish to express their indebtedness to you with a small honorarium.'

'I'm not sure I ought to. This is just hear-say.'

'Go on Doug! What harm can it do?'

'I don't want to. It's demeaning.'

'Please yourself.'

But poverty is poverty and I eventually allowed myself to be persuaded. To this day I still wince when I think about it. Was I really that desperate? Clearly yes. The Medical Director replied that things must have reached a pretty low ebb for me to have resorted to flogging my daughter's microbes! He was clearly correct, and moreover the miserable fellow didn't see fit to lift my financial burden, even to the extent of a book token!

There is no justice!

The Most Important Person

Asthma and Fiction

I was in the laboratory when the phone rang.

'Hello Douglas, it's Roger!'

'Hi!'

'Douglas, I was thinking of coming down to see how you are getting on, but I've just spoken to Jack's secretary and she tells me the great man is away. As you know, I usually stay with him when I come down. Next week he's back, but then I go away and I don't want to leave it that long. I think I'll come down anyway if that's alright with you.'

'Fine, and why don't you come and stay with us?'

'Well, if that's not too much trouble - you'd better ask your wife.'

'I'm sure she'll be okay.'

Roger Altounyan was a remarkable man in several ways. His grandfather, an American trained Arminian doctor, established the Altounyan Hospital in Aleppo, Syria. Roger's father, Ernest, born and educated in England, spent school holidays with a friend at Coniston in the English Lake District and eventually married Dora, the friend's sister. Roger was born in 1922 in Syria but was educated at a public school in England. At the beginning of the Second World War he enlisted in the RAF and trained as a fighter pilot. He later retrained as a bomber pilot, and was so skilled that he became an instructor.

At the end of the war he studied Medicine, and while a medical student, developed asthma. On qualifying he followed his father and grandfather to the family hospital in Syria. In 1955 however, political changes there meant foreigners had to leave. In England he joined a small pharmaceutical company, Bengers, as a research scientist. His work on two projects led nowhere, and then he began work on a plant, khellin, that was used in the Middle East as a folk remedy for asthma. He decided that the guinea pig model of asthma that his laboratory used was unreliable and began a long practice of using his own wheezy bronchi as a testbed for compounds made from khellin. He found that some could block allergic reactions in his bronchi. Hundreds of compounds were synthesised and tested on Roger until, after many setbacks, and after the company had instructed Roger to stop, they hit on sodium cromoglycate ('Intal'). In order to see whether the drug was clinically useful they persuaded Jack Howell, who later became my boss, to perform a placebo controlled trial on a handful of asthmatics. The trial confirmed a significant beneficial effect, and Intal became a useful drug worldwide in the treatment of allergic asthma.

Fisons, who had taken over Bengers were trying to find more effective analogues of Intal, but testing new compounds for efficacy was difficult, because there was still no suitable laboratory method, or animal model. Roger had developed a challenge test using non-asthmatic volunteers, and it was this that I was using to test a range of compounds. Roger's purpose in coming to visit was to review my progress.

We spent the afternoon looking over my data and then I took him home. My girls, seven and five were very excited about the 'most important person' who was visiting. Roger was a charming guest and a wonderful 'uncle'. He was a very open, modest, friendly man, rather gnome-like, short with prominent ears. His accent betrayed his upper-crust background. He was somewhat breathless moving about, and despite his asthma he smoked a pipe.

He played with the kids and helped put them to bed. Afterwards we were chatting when my sister, Julie and her husband John, called in. Our conversation somehow led around to the subject of sailing, and Roger said that he would still sometimes sail on Coniston Water where he had a house.

'Ah!' says John, 'just like "Swallows and Amazons".' John loved these adventure stories by Arthur Ransome[1], and often referred to them.

---

[1] Arthur Ransome (1884-1967) was an author and journalist. During the First World War he was a foreign correspondent in Russia. In 1917 he became acquainted with Lenin and Trotsky and eventually married the latter's secretary. It is thought that he

'Yes,' replies Roger, 'It is actually the "Amazon" that I use. We don't have the "Swallow" any more.'

'Sorry? How do you mean?' asked John.

Roger smiled. 'The dinghy is the actual "Amazon" of the story books. Me and my sisters used to play in it when we were children, though then it was called the "Mavis".'

'But they are fictional stories... Arthur Ransome...'

'Yes, Arthur Ransome. He was a friend of my parents and he was at Coniston in the summer of 1929. I don't remember him very well. It was he that bought the two dinghies, the "Swallow" and the "Mavis", and he and my father taught us to sail. It was our adventures that gave him the inspiration for the books.'

John stared at him, wide-eyed. 'So you're the "Roger" of the stories, Roger Walker.'

'I'm afraid so.'

For John this was a bit like meeting Luke Skywalker, or perhaps Harry Potter!

'Yes, he used our names, and I think also our characters, which annoyed my parents. I was the ship's boy - I was only seven when the stories started.'

'That's amazing! I was brought up on those books, I think I've read them all.'

Roger died in 1987 at the age of 65 as a result of his respiratory condition that had doubtless been aggravated by the countless bronchial challenges that he had inflicted on himself in his search for a better asthma treatment. Intal, the drug he was instrumental in discovering is still used to treat asthma, though it has been eclipsed by the use of inhaled topical steroids, which are more effective. It is still widely used as a nasal spray, or eye drops in the treatment of seasonal hay fever.

---

may have been a double agent. "Swallows and Amazons" was published in 1930 and was followed by eleven other books based in Cumbria, the Norfolk Broads, China and Scotland. Sailing was a lifelong passion. "Swallows and Amazons" has been variously adapted for TV, film, radio and theatre.

Such a Closely Guarded Secret

Carbon Monoxide Poisoning

I was on-call for Accident and Emergency when a gentleman was brought in, deeply unconscious. He had been found by a friend, lying with his head in a gas oven, with the gas on. In those days domestic supplies were of town gas, which contained carbon monoxide (CO), unlike the natural gas we use today, which doesn't. That he was suffering from severe CO poisoning was confirmed by finding more than 50% of his haemoglobin occupied by CO.

Haemoglobin is an oxygen transporting molecule. When blood passes through the lungs each haemoglobin molecule can bind four oxygen molecules. All or some of these are released when the blood passes through the tissues, like the brain or muscles. Haemoglobin binds oxygen easily, but it binds CO more than 200 times more easily. So any CO in the lungs will be hoovered up, binding very firmly to haemoglobin. The presence of one CO molecule on a haemoglobin molecule alters its handling of oxygen on its 3 other binding sites. The oxygen now binds more firmly, to the extent that haemoglobin may not give up its oxygen when it passes through the tissues. The tissues thus become starved of oxygen, and the organ that is affected most is the brain, followed by the heart. The patient was unconscious because his brain was starved of oxygen.

We started conventional treatment with high concentrations of inhaled oxygen and set up an infusion of mannitol to prevent swelling of the brain, but as he was so severe I thought we needed to treat him with hyperbaric oxygen (pure oxygen at more than atmospheric pressure) in order to speed the elimination of the CO and to reduce the oxygen starvation of his tissues. The problem was that I did not know where a hyperbaric oxygen facility was to be found. I therefore phoned the Poison Unit - a central body in London that was a repository of knowledge and advice on acute poisonings of all kinds. They did not, however, know about hyperbaric oxygen, so I was obliged, more or less at random, to phone hospitals around London. It took me about 3 hours, following a variety of wild goose chases, to locate the unit at the Westminster Hospital. Half way through this search the patient suffered a cardiac arrest (due to his heart being starved of oxygen) from which we surprisingly managed to resuscitate him.

I accompanied him on the hairraising ambulance ride through the busy streets to Westminster Hospital, and saw him put in a chamber at 2.3 atmospheres of pure oxygen. After 2 hours in this he was fully conscious.

Sadly his subsequent clinical course was difficult and protracted. He had suffered significant patchy brain damage and needed a great deal of retraining to get back to acceptable functioning. This is typical of severe CO poisoning, and the cardiac arrest could not have helped either. Whether the hyperbaric oxygen treatment helped is unclear, but I note that, 40 years on, hyperbaric oxygen is still a recommended part of the treatment of severe CO poisoning.

When my boss heard of this saga he insisted I write an account of my endeavours and submit it as a letter to the medical journal, the Lancet. It ended, provocatively with *'It is unfortunate that the availability of hyperbaric oxygen in London is such a closely guarded secret.'*

This was picked up by the Evening Standard, where I shared an inside page with Jackie Onassis.

Doctor battles with secrecy to save patient

I was a hero! Clearly I had ruffled a few feathers. There was a flurry of letters to the Lancet following mine from a variety of interested parties. Hyperbaric oxygen didn't have many clinical uses and I got phoned by someone whose unit was under threat of closure, asking whether I could do anything to help. I pointed out that I was hardly out of my clinical nappies!

A Tale of Two Physicians

Psychocardiology and Ethics

In 1997 Peter Nixon was in disgrace for unethical medical practice. Four years earlier, Maurice Pappworth, an unflinching campaigner for better medical ethics was finally, at the age of 83, elected to the fellowship of the Royal College of Physicians (RCP).

Peter Nixon, a long time fellow of the RCP had been practising unconventional and frequently dangerous medicine for many years. He met his nemesis when he attempted to sue Channel 4, who had accused him of quackery, for libel and lost. He was forced to stop practising medicine. He was a colleague and I find his story particularly unbelievable and sad.

He initially practised cardiology in Leeds where he made an important advance in his subject and was in many ways at the forefront of his specialty. He moved to London but over the following few years his personal and professional life became increasingly difficult. He felt under considerable stress. He was smoking too much to calm his frayed nerves. He began to experience chest pain which he thought could be angina (pain from the heart due to a blocked coronary artery). This was very worrying and he decided he needed his coronary arteries to be looked at. Nowadays coronary angiography (visualisation of the coronary arteries by injecting a radio-opaque dye into them via a catheter inserted through an artery) is routine. Then, in the 60's it was in its infancy, being developed in centres in the USA. So Peter Nixon decided to go to the Bellevue Hospital, New York to be investigated by the great Andre Cournand, the Nobel Laureate pioneer of this technique.

Crossing the Atlantic by sea he had time to think. He suspected there was actually nothing wrong with his heart. His problem was stress and he resolved to sort himself out. He decided not to go to New York, but rather to relax by walking in the Appalachian Hills, which he did. He stopped smoking and sorted his life out. His 'angina' disappeared.

This was a life changing experience, and he felt that what applied to him must apply to others. Stress, often mediated by hyperventilation, became for him the central cause of cardiac problems often to the exclusion of competing mechanisms.

Of course, Peter Nixon was fully aware of the physical pathology of coronary heart disease and heart failure, but he was convinced that symptoms were frequently aggravated by emotional and/or physical stress. The combination of physical pathology (e.g. damaged heart muscle, diseased heart valves, blocked coronary arteries) and stress overwhelmed the system. He talked about the 'human function curve' which related an individual's stress to his or her response. When someone is stressed they respond by upping their game and dealing with it. More stress evokes more effort and performance, but there comes a point where the stress is overwhelming. It actually reduces performance. Even more stress and performance declines further. His idea was that a period of complete rest, asleep would break into this vicious circle and bring the patient back to a point where they could once again respond positively to stress. He therefore admitted patients with heart failure or angina to hospital and put them to sleep for a week or more using sedative drugs in large doses.

I am unclear whether any patients actually benefited from this. For sure, this treatment had real dangers - prolonged bed rest causes wasting of muscles, demineralisation of bones, and blood clots may form in the leg veins (deep vein thrombosis) and may cause fatal pulmonary embolism. A patient that I had looked after was precipitated into respiratory failure by this treatment and spent a week recovering in Intensive Care.

Stress and associated anxiety is often associated with hyperventilation - breathing faster and more deeply than metabolism demands. This eliminates more carbon dioxide than is usual, increases the alkalinity of the blood, reduces the blood supply to the brain, and alters neuro-muscular function. Uncommonly it causes spasm of the coronary arteries and therefore can cause angina (Prinzmetal angina) but chest pain may be experienced without coronary spasm. So an anxious or stressed person who hyperventilates may present to the doctor with a variety of physical symptoms including dizziness, collapse, breathlessness, numbness, tingling sensations, muscle spasms and chest pain. Peter Nixon was not alone in believing hyperventilation to be an important source of symptoms that is often overlooked. In fact he claimed that hyperventilation was *the* explanation for a variety of symptoms in a wide variety of diseases from AIDS, chronic fatigue syndrome, premenstrual tension and Gulf War Syndrome.

So his convictions about 'psychocardiology' were based on his own experience of stress induced chest pain. It is natural for us to generalise from the particular to the general, and from ourselves to others, but anecdotes are not a sound basis for medical practice.

I was a member of the Academic Department of Medicine in his hospital and as such I viewed him as a maverik. On occasions he presented his ideas at our departmental meetings, and the usual response from the audience was scepticism. 'Where is your evidence?' was the question people asked. 'Where is your control group?' Perhaps due to this chiding he eventually got some funds to employ a research fellow, and tested his ideas on stress and hyperventilation. He published the results of several studies which appeared to vindicate his views.

In 1994 after he had retired from NHS practice, the investigative journalist Duncan Campbell secretly filmed Nixon during a private consultation with an AIDS sufferer, Ian Hughes. He performed a rather odd and unscientific exercise test, on the basis of which he claimed the patient's fatigue was caused by stress and hyperventilation. He advised sedatives and recommended two weeks of sleep. The interview was broadcast by Channel 4 as part of a program entitled 'Preying on Hope' which focussed on several Harley Street practitioners offering unproven remedies to desperate AIDS patients for large fees. They accused Nixon of 'quackery'.

49

This seemed rather unfair - his ideas were not so very strange and in fact were seemingly supported by his research. He therefore felt confident enough to sue Channel 4 for libel. He claimed damages of £2 million. But at the trial in the High Court in 1997 Channel 4's lawyers showed there were major inconsistencies and errors in his published research papers that were the scientific bases of his opinions and practice. There was the suggestion of fraud, particularly as the 'errors' altered the data to give support to his thesis. He admitted that these amounted to 'more than an honest slip of the pen'. It was also pointed out that both in his National Health and private work he had performed what amounted to experiments on patients that could have caused harm, without obtaining their informed consent and without ethical permission. At this point he withdrew his libel action on the grounds that he was no longer mentally fit to give evidence. The trial cost him more than £750,000 and the Medical Defence Union, who defended him, £2 million. He was also instructed to cease medical practice or the trial documents would be sent to the General Medical Council who would have the power to strike him off the medical register.

Peter Nixon was a believer, a man of deep convictions that he maintained despite the scepticism of many of those around him. I don't know whether he deserved to be labelled a charlatan or a quack. I think the advice and treatment he gave was sincere and what he thought was best. He had many ideas about his subject that were sensible and ahead of his time. But fraud, or carelessness in medical publication is a serious matter. Thousands will have read his papers and been misled. Others will have quoted him and caused further misinformation. The Sunday Times, for instance, reported that Dr Nixon had found a 100% effective treatment for chronic fatigue syndrome! Misinformation can have serious consequences. The fraudulent claim by Andrew Wakefield and colleagues that the MMR vaccine could precipitate autism in young children has led to a drastic decrease in the vaccine take up and a return of measles outbreaks and deaths.

Medicine has progressively become a scientific, evidence based discipline. It was only partly like that when Peter Nixon trained and worked. The subject was evolving from centuries of ignorance and superstition when virtually nothing was known and when the physician's authority was one of his few therapeutic tools. Even when science began to make inroads into the practice of medicine, the system continued to encourage senior doctors to behave like gods and to think of themselves as omniscient. They were far better educated and of a higher social status than most of their patients and their nursing colleagues. Their junior doctors might have known enough to challenge some of their notions but generally did not dare antagonise the god who had the power to make or break their career. Peter Nixon never really adapted to the new realities of medicine and his approach was basically authoritarian. He didn't really engage with the opinions of others, or with the scientific method. It seemed he had not even read all the papers that bore his name.

Nixon retired from NHS practice in 1991. He had been practicing his unconventional, unethical and dangerous medicine for about 25 years and no one stopped him. To be clear, the way he practiced medicine was well known in the hospital but to my knowledge neither his fellow consultants (including myself) nor the hospital authorities, including their ethics committee stopped him. Maybe we couldn't have stopped him without a huge fight, and doubtless there were many who would have supported him. It was easier to let him get on with it.

Nowadays there are clear guidelines on how to treat most clinical conditions - the NICE Guidelines in the UK, and a physician departing from these on the basis of a personal belief would quickly be open to censure. Unconventional treatment might be the subject of a clinical trial, but only with permission from an ethics committee, and only with the informed consent of the patient. Because in Nixon's time guidelines on therapy were unofficial, consultants had more leeway and independence. Still, he was out on a limb. It is not as if these issues were new.

Before Nixon began working as a consultant, Dr Maurice Pappworth had been investigating and discovering numerous incidents of unethical and dangerous practices of the medical profession. He found it difficult to publicise his work, but in 1967 he managed to publish 'The Human Guinea Pig' in which he itemised many examples of doctors performing what were basically experiments without consent, or ethical clearance. Patients usually thought the procedure was part of their treatment and they were not told otherwise. Although perhaps contributing to medical science, Pappworth felt that career advancement was a bigger incentive for the doctors involved.

Rather than embrace Pappworth's criticisms, the Royal College of Physicians (RCP) snubbed him and whinged about him. When I was training at around that time Pappworth was viewed in my academic medical department as a misguided irritant. Admittedly it's many years ago, but I find it incredible that attitudes among senior medical men (they were mostly men) were so out of line with modern thinking.

They said that because of his campaign against the medical establishment Maurice Pappworth would never be elected to the Fellowship of the RCP, but in this they were wrong. In 1993, Maurice Pappworth was elected to the Fellowship. This was 57 years after he passed the Membership Examination (the usual interval between Membership success and Fellowship of the College was around 15 years). He was 83. At the ceremony, he received a standing ovation from the Fellows of the now ethically minded RCP.

Better late than never, I suppose.

The Laryngeal Swab

This is basically about the late Abe Guz, who was, at stages in my career, my teacher, my boss and my colleague. He was an amazing character. I owe him a lot. All of us who knew him well learnt a lot, and have many stories to tell. These arose from his extensive knowledge, his passionate nature, his explosive temper, his absent mindedness and his determination to press on regardless. He was an extremely knowledgeable physician but his approach to his subject was unconventional. Above all he was a clinical scientist of distinction who made many advances in his area of expertise.

As a medical student I spent the first several months in the Academic Unit of Medicine. Abe became aware of me because during the initial lectures and tutorials I was the only one of our group to be able to remember any physiology. As a result he involved me in some of his experimental work. His laboratory was a sea of equipment. There were amplifiers, oscilloscopes, chart recorders, and wires like jungle creepers hung down from the ceiling. On one side was a large box, a body plethysmograph in which a subject would be seated in order to measure their lung volumes and airway resistance. (The box had to be airtight and this homemade version was sealed with clips from the outside. On one occasion Abe had his assistant in the box when he got called away. He quite forgot that there was someone still in the box and left the hospital. After some hours this poor fellow, beating on the side of the box and shouting was rescued by a passing Professor).

I spent 3 months as his pre-registration House Officer - that is I was the dogsbody on his clinical outfit, responsible for the knitty-gritty care of his ward patients. I enjoyed working for him, although he shouted and threatened a lot:

'Okay Burke, first we will locate this X-ray report and then I wlll fire my House Officer!'

Burke was his aristocratic Pakistani registrar.

It was just a bluff. He was play-acting. I never really felt threatened. He could be equally overwhelmingly complimentary. When challenged he expected you to fight back. He expected his team to be scientists as well as doctors.

'Halford, science is the only thing that can help us!'

Above all he wanted us to be clear logical thinkers. He appreciated me because I had an academic bent and had a BSc in Physiology.

During my time on his team one of his elderly acquaintances was admitted for investigation. She was a formidable Jewish matriarch. We will call her Mrs Cohen. She was not feeling well and had lost some weight. There were some dubious shadows on her chest X-ray film and she had a dry cough.

We saw her on the ward round. She was unconvinced there was much wrong with her and was not inclined to be cooperative. Abe decided she might have tuberculosis.

'Tell me Halford, how do we find the organism if the patient is not coughing up any sputum?'

'A laryngeal swab?'

'Quite right! Did you know that Burke?'

'Of course!'

'Okay then Halford, we'll do a laryngeal swab. You'd better get one.'

'I don't think we have them on the ward. I've never had cause to use one.'

'Christ! You're no bloody good for anyone. Come!'

He stormed off down the ward, me a yard or two behind, down the stairs and along the whole length of the hospital corridor - maybe 200 yards and then another 50 yards to microbiology. We walked in silence while I wondered about this great laryngeal swab mystery. *Did we need a secret code or did you need to be a consultant to get one? Were they only available to Jewish people?*

We arrived at Microbiology Reception. A girl was seated at the desk looking bored.

'Laryngeal swab,' says Abe.

'Just one?'

'Two.'

She disappeared while he paced up and down, sighing.

'Christ, how long can she take?'

In a couple of minutes she re-appeared with two longish things in sterile paper bags. He took them and without further words we retraced our steps back to the ward.

Now I had been initiated into one of the mysteries of medical practice. I was part of an inner circle!

We took up positions on either side of Mrs Cohen's bed. I took the swab from the bag. The swab itself was inside a glass tube about 10 inches long, slightly angled at the business end.

'You know what to do?'

'I think so.'

The idea was that you insert the glass tube into the mouth so that the angled end goes over the back of the tongue where it will be positioned above the larynx. The swab is then protruded and with any luck will make contact with that structure. (The larynx is not visible from the mouth without a mirror).

'Right Mrs Cohen I want you to open your mouth,' says Abe quite gently.

Mrs Cohen turns her head away, mouth firmly shut.

'Now please Mrs Cohen this is terribly important, please, I beg of you!'

She clenched her jaws.

'Now look Mrs Cohen! This will never do! I beg of you now!'

No response.

'Right Sister, get the mouth openers!'

She bustled off. I had no idea what he was referring to or what Tower of London style equipment store she had. With a surprisingly short delay she returned grasping the implement. Abe snatched it from her, but there was an immediate problem - it was necessary to get the prongs of the implement between the patient's teeth, and the mouth remained firmly shut and teeth clenched. But, fortunately for Abe, at this moment Mrs Cohen lost the plot and lost her cool. She opened her mouth to protest or insult, but before she could say a word Abe, with a deftness I didn't know he possessed, had the prongs between her teeth and had opened them so that she was now unable to shut her mouth.

'Right Halford! Get on with it.'

I advanced with my long swab only to discover that Mrs Cohen had yet another line of defence. She pressed her tongue to the roof of her mouth and there was no way past it.

'Mrs Cohen, please, I beg of you! You have to let us do this. It won't take a moment. We're not going to hurt you. It is very very important.'

Mrs Cohen was not inclined to oblige. She was now making loud gurgling noises

'Right Sister! Get the tongue holders!'

Again she rushed off while I again marvelled Abe's knowledge of the instruments of torture.

Once more she returned promptly and handed them to Abe who grasped the offending organ with these tongs and yanked. The back of her throat was now fully revealed and through it Mrs Cohen was hollering. I cannot imagine what the other patients in the ward were thinking was going on behind the drawn screens.

Now I advanced and positioned the glass cover well down over the back of her tongue before protruding the swab another couple of inches. Suddenly the noise stopped and she began to cough violently and hoarsely.

'Brilliant Halford! You must be in the larynx, right between the vocal cords!'

So we had our swab and if there were tubercle bacilli around we should have caught one or two of them. We left the scowling Mrs Cohen to lick her wounds and walked back the length of the ward, the patients regarding us with fear and respect.

'That woman,' said Abe, 'she came from nowhere. Her first son, a professor of Physics at Harvard, second son a barrister, a QC, her daughter a concert pianist, another daughter a novelist. You know, Halford, this is the Jewish meritocracy that will sweep away your filthy aristocracy and your inbred royals!'

'The aristocracy has nothing to do with me. I'm a poor grammar school boy.'

His comments, however, had bothered me. They put me in a quandary. You see, the following week I was due to attend the University of London degree convocation at the Albert Hall, where we were to formally receive our degrees in the presence of the late Queen Elizabeth the Queen Mother. If Abe found out, I would be due for a modicum of mockery. I had arranged for someone to cover me, but felt I ought to clear my absence with himself. As a compromise I went to see his secretary.

'Oh, there's no problem, Douglas, he's away himself that day.'
'Please don't tell him where I'm going.'

So, the following week I was all togged up in my robes, seated in the vast Albert Hall. It was good to meet up again with those I qualified with. After passing our Finals we had separated to the four corners of the medical world to start our house jobs in whichever hospitals would have us. The hall was slowly filling with proud, adoring parents and gowned students displaying a variety of coloured sashes depending on their faculty. In the front row of the stalls, right under the stage were three figures in rather florid red and purple robes of the Doctorate of Medicine degree. The man in the centre, whose bald patch betrayed that he was older than most of us, kept moving around, looking about and gesticulating. Then he turned and looked in my direction and I saw that it was none other than Abe Guz himself!

Eventually the academic luminaries, representatives in the multi-coloured robes and funny hats of the various graduating faculties entered and took their positions on the stage with much theatrical cap doffing and bowing. They resembled a light opera company about to embark on the Mikado, or some such. Then the Queen Mum came in, all smiles and graciousness and we were soon underway. Abe was one of the first up:
'Abraham Guz, Doctorate in the Faculty of Medicine.'

Abe made his way across the stage looking like a poor man's Cardinal Wolsey. He knelt on a little stool to be 'hooded' by her Majesty.

Oh, oh, if only I had a camera! He was actually kneeling to the Royalty he so despised! To the 'filthy aristocracy'!

After the ceremony I ran into him with his parents.

'You're a bloody sycophant!' I said.

'It's just for the parents!' he countered in a harsh whisper. I was amazed that Abe, who was of average height, had absolutely minute parents. They were refugees from Eastern Europe.

Going back to the laryngeal swab incident it is remarkable how far we have come on from those bad old days (1968). Such abuse of a patient would be totally unacceptable today and would not be tolerated. It was of course pretty outrageous at that time, but I don't think that Abe was in danger of reprimand or dismissal by the hospital, let alone the GMC. I'm not clear if patients had much in the way of stated rights in those days.

The story also reflects the fear of tuberculosis which was more prevalent in those days. Patients and health care workers sometimes caught Tb in hospital. Treatment, which was unpleasant, still took about eighteen months. The question of whether the patient had Tb or not was an important one.

Another thought is that it is rarely a good idea to play the doctor with relatives or friends.

'A prophet is not without honour except...'

We went to see Mrs Cohen a few days later. She was better. She poked her tongue out at Abe. It sported a round ulcer at the spot that had been held by the tongs.

'Nothing to do with me!' said Abe.

She looked at me.

'You're just as bad!' There was no irony. I figured that I wasn't going to be invited to the synagogue Christmas party any time soon!

After I passed my qualifying exams to become a physician I became Abe's research fellow. He had seen a paper in the American journal, 'Science' that described a method for measuring interstitial fluid pressure - that is, the pressure of the thin layers of fluid that surround our cells. Since dehydration is common in disease but often difficult to detect, it seemed it might be clinically useful to get a handle on this. By now his lab was even more of an equipment jungle than it had been years before. One assistant was building a giant amplifier from scratch. His other assistant was silently chain smoking as she poured over reams of data at the far end, and his secretary in a little island of clerical sanity tapped away at her typewriter.

'We have to find room for your project, Douglas,' he said.

But there was no room. He paced up and down and then had an inspiration. There was a glass-topped trolley, I assume 'borrowed' from the wards. The top shelf was already covered with junk but the lower shelf, about 40cm off the floor, was unaccountably clear.

'Right!' said Abe, 'we will reserve this space.' He found a sheet of paper and wrote in big letters 'TISSUE PRESSURE PROJECT' and placed it on the shelf.

I would have to do my research on my knees!

The End of the Road

Barry Green (not his real name) and I were junior hospital doctors together. We were friends and shared a sense of humour and a desire to do medical research.

Barry married a beautiful Iranian woman of the Baha'i faith. After the Islamic Revolution the longstanding persecution of the Baha'is in Iran intensified, and hundreds were executed.[2] Barry and his wife emigrated to the US and managed to rescue many of her relatives, bringing them to safety in America. We used to meet at conferences and I visited him at his home.

Barry wrote to me from America and asked me to see his elderly father who still lived on the outskirts of London..

'He's lost confidence in his health and isn't getting out enough. I don't actually think there's anything seriously wrong with him. I would appreciate it if you could check him over, and reassure him, assuming everything's okay.'

So I saw Barry's father in my outpatient clinic. He was in his upper seventies, but spritely and fit. As Barry predicted, I found little wrong with him and all my tests were normal. I reassured him accordingly. I told Barry the good news.

Months later I received a second letter from Barry.

'Thanks very much for seeing my dad and checking his health. He was very buoyed up by your reassurances to the extent that

---

[2] I had an Iranian research fellow who worked with me. He was a very devout Muslim to the extent of having a prayer mat in the lab. One day he told me that Iran respects and tolerates all religions.
'What about the Baha'i? You persecute them.'
'Ah, but Baha'i is not a religion!'
Actually, I think more to the point, the Iranian authorities view it as a Muslim heresy.

he went off with a friend driving up to Scotland. He had a great time. Unfortunately on the way back he had a heart attack and died.'

Whoops!

Be Prepared!

For several years I had happy and productive dealings with the local Asthma Association, and its enthusiastic organisers, The Association was a patients' group. That is, it was a forum for patients, their carers and their relatives to learn more about their condition and to share their experiences. I had been invited to speak at their meetings on several occasions. The first time I prepared a talk about the condition that I thought would be useful for a lay audience, but I had hardly started when someone raised their hand with a question. The question in fact bore little relationship to what I was talking about, but I was obliged to answer it for all that. This question was followed by another and another, so I never managed to deliver my well honed dissertation. It didn't matter, I guess the customers got what they wanted.

On the second occasion I again was prepared to lecture them, but the same happened, so on my third invitation I arrived without a prepared talk, expecting another question and answer session. This proved embarrassing for two reasons. Firstly there were no questions and secondly, sitting in the front row was the doyen of British Respiratory Medicine, Professor Sir Charles Fletcher. He was, I believe, a friend or relative of one of the organisers. He had, by this time, retired from the Royal Postgraduate Medical School at Hammersmith Hospital. Fortunately the distinguished guest fell asleep, which was actually the best thing he could have done.

Charles Fletcher had a very distinguished career in respiratory medicine and epidemiology, despite being an insulin dependent diabetic from when he was a young man. His most notable work concerned smoking and lung disease. It was long known that smokers develop a productive cough - chronic bronchitis. The more important effect was more subtle - a progressive narrowing of the airways, causing shortness of breath on exertion. His epidemiological studies showed that airway function deteriorates twice as fast with age in cigarette smokers than nonsmokers, but that the rate of decline becomes normal with abstention from smoking. He worked ceaselessly to promote non-smoking even to the extent of haranguing doctors that they had a moral duty not to smoke, so as to give a good example to their patients. His wider fame came from two notable firsts. As a doctor at the Radcliffe Infirmary in Oxford in 1941 he worked with Chain and Florey - the men who isolated and purified penicillin. He was the first doctor in the world to administer penicillin to a patient. In 1958 he became the first 'television doctor', presenting the first BBC series of *'Your Life in their Hands'* about surgical practice. I guess he got the job because he was a distinguished looking man and an excellent communicator. His Eton, Oxbridge background gave him the patrician air that people in those days expected a doctor to have. In fact he really was part of the medical aristocracy. His father, Sir Walter Fletcher was the first secretary of the Medical Research Council.

Of Guts and Breasts

When I became a clinical medical student I was allocated for two months to the 'Tanner-Greening' surgical firm. The word 'firm' was used for the team of two or more consultants and their retinues that formed a clinical teaching unit. Norman Tanner was a famous gastroenterological surgeon and his colleague, Peter Greening a well-respected breast surgeon. They both had large Harley Street practices.

In those times gastric and duodenal ulcers were very common and a great burden to both patients and the health service. Arguments raged over whether they were caused by too much stomach acid, too much stress, spicy food, too many cigarettes or the wrong type of personality. Surgical wards were full of patients with peptic ulcer disease. Patients' lives were threatened when ulcers bled profusely, or when they caused the stomach or duodenum to rupture. Many suffered a lifetime of pain and dietary restriction. Gastric acid was clearly important, but there were no effective drugs to reduce its production, so surgery was often resorted to. Gastric acid production is stimulated by the vagus nerves, so cutting the branches supplying the stomach reduces the acidity of its secretions. But identifying and cutting all these branches wasn't simple. Tanner was an exceptionally skillful surgeon, and had it to a tee. He, his assistant and the theatre nurse worked in choreographed harmony, like a well-oiled machine and so the operation was very quick and smooth.

One hot summer day I was assisting Mr Tanner when I came over faint and thought I was going to pass out. I made my excuses and went to lie down, sweating profusely. Later I recovered and went back into the operating theatre. At the end of the case I apologised to Mr Tanner.

'Oh, you had to leave, did you?' he smiled. 'I have to leave myself after the next one.'

What he meant was that he was going to his private practice in Harley Street while his assistant would finish the operating list. It was common practice in those days.

As a junior doctor a few years later I was assisting another surgeon at a peripheral hospital also doing a selective vagotomy. He was a very experienced and competent man, but after about ninety minutes he looked up at the clock and ruefully said: 'I guess Norman Tanner would have done two of these by now.' He wasn't far wrong. Tanner was an ace.

Since then the world of peptic ulcer disease has been transformed for the better. In 1976 the first effective drug to reduce stomach acid, Cimetidine, became available. In 1985 it was shown, by a trainee surgeon in Australia, that a bacterium, Helicobacter pylori, had a crucial role in causing ulcers. Eradication of this infection with antibiotics was usually curative. Hospital wards are no longer filled with patients with ulcer disease; lives are far less often marred by pain and indigestion. We now have safe drugs that can virtually eliminate gastric acid secretion, and we have simple cheap tests for the presence of Helicobacter pylori in the stomach.

--o-O-o--

But breast cancer, Peter Greening's field of expertise has proved more resistant to transformation, though much progress has been made. Peter Greening was a true gentleman. As was appropriate for a breast surgeon he was a lady's man. He was a short, dapper gent with silver hair and a twinkle in his eye. He had a way of greeting and speaking to his patients as if they were old friends - even when it was the first time of meeting. He would have made a great game show host or maybe a politician! As a young man I was hugely impressed. It was enormously reassuring to the customers, who were in the main terrified ladies with a lump in the breast.

Radical mastectomy for breast cancer, the removal of the whole breast plus lymph nodes from the axilla (arm pit) was more widely practiced then than today. It was of course a hugely disfiguring and dreaded operation. One afternoon I was in the operating theatre assisting Mr Greening. The lady had a breast lump about an inch in diameter and because it had all the features

65

of a malignant tumour - a cancer, she was listed for a radical mastectomy.

The procedure was first to make a small incision to expose the tumour and to obtain a small biopsy specimen, to check the diagnosis before commencing the mastectomy. In the time available it was not possible to properly prepare and stain the tissue for microscopic examination. Instead the pathologist froze the tissue, prior to cutting thin slices and examining them under the microscope. It wasn't perfect but it was better than nothing, and only took about 20 minutes. So, on this occasion the pathologist was in the operating theatre, waiting. He hurried off, taking the specimen back to his laboratory, while we stood around twiddling our thumbs.

The tumour that had been exposed was pale cream in colour and looked like a star. More to the point it looked just like a cancerous tumour. It appeared to be invading into the surrounding breast tissue.

At the head end of the patient was the hospital's senior anaesthetist, Dr Ashworth, an exceedingly experienced man who had worked with Peter Greening for more years than either would like to admit. As we waited, and as ten minutes turned into twenty, the anaesthetist became impatient. The longer the duration of the anaesthetic, the more likely are complications.

'Come on Peter. You know what it is. It can't be anything else - 100:1.'

Peter Greening just smiled.

Twenty minutes turned into half an hour. Dr Ashworth tried again.

'Peter, it's 1000:1, just look at the thing!'

'We have to wait, I'm afraid, whatever the odds,' said Peter Greening with his usual good humour. 'We cannot proceed until we know for sure.'

At 35 minutes the phone rang outside the theatre. A moment later a staff nurse pushed open the door.

'Mr Greening, there's a message from Pathology. She read out from a slip of paper, giving the name and hospital number.

'The biopsy shows fat necrosis. There is no sign of malignancy in the sections.'

'What did I tell you?' said the anaesthetist.

Can you imagine how happy and relieved that woman must have been when she woke from the anaesthetic, still double breasted, and no longer under a death sentence?

Fat necrosis in the breast occurs after trauma. A patch of fat degenerates and the area heals by scarring, producing a solid star shaped hard mass that can easily be taken for a malignant tumour. I guess Peter Greening had seen a few cases before.

Learning on the Job

In my day, training on the performance of most routine clinical procedures was not given in medical school. You learnt how to do things on the ward as a student and after you qualified. You learnt from your colleagues and you in turn taught others. We were busy, so it was usually 'see one; do one; teach one.' No joke. You observe a procedure - say a lumbar puncture, later you do one yourself, after which you teach someone else to do it. Obviously this is fraught with problems. You may be taught an incorrect technique and pass it on to others.

Sadly on other occasions you find yourself expected to do something that you have never observed. This can really lead to trouble as this anecdote illustrates.

It was during my pre-registration surgical house job, and I was assisting the registrar with the operating theatre list which was long and not going terribly well. The next case on the list was surgically simple and the registrar, who clearly had more faith in me than was warranted, told me to go and do it. Of course, at that stage in my career I was only supposed to operate, if at all, under strict supervision. He was in the next theatre and I could get him if there was a problem.

But it was only a circumcision on a little boy so it was not a big deal. In fact the deal was very small indeed, and I was keen not to overdo the trimming. When I had finished I neatly sewed up the wound in the little member with four little stitches. So far, so good, or so I thought.

Now, there is a simple common rule when sewing in surgery. It is usual when sewing internally - say sewing up the internal layers of an abdominal wound to use catgut. These stitches slowly dissolve and thus do not act as a 'foreign body' that might cause chronic irritation. If sewing up a skin wound we use silk, and these stitches are removed once the wound is healed, after several days.

So, naturally I sewed up the little willy with very fine silk sutures.

The little boy had come round from the anaesthetic by the time the registrar came to observe my handywork. He was not pleased.

'Well, you've put them in so you can take them out. Make him an appointment for next week.'

You see, I should have used catgut in this instant, to avoid the necessity of removing the stitches. No one had told me.

The following week, as is easy to imagine I had one hell of a job, with a disapproving father looking on, while trying to help the nurse to hold on to the squirming screaming child, trying to catch hold and snip the tiny sutures without doing the boy a permanent injury with the scissors. I am breaking out in a sweat just thinking about it!

So, you learn from your mistakes and those of others, at least most of us try to.

The Brighton Walk

For several years in the sixties the Guinness brewery sponsored an annual London to Brighton Walk. It was a low key competition between the ten London medical schools and their teaching hospitals to see which could get the highest percentage of their staff and students to complete the walk. Crazy really! It started in the evening at the Tower of London, crossed Tower Bridge and followed the A23, 54 miles to Brighton. Each year around 2000 people attempted it and most got there. It wasn't a race, but a few weirdos, including myself, raced - a double marathon. For many, it was basically a pub crawl.

Looking back from this risk averse age, it is remarkable that it was ever thought to be a good idea to encourage 2000 people, many of them inebriated, to walk, run and stumble down a busy arterial road all through the night. Much of the way there were no pavements or street lights. I think in the end someone got killed and the walk was abandoned.

I was mad enough to complete it three times. On my last attempt I trained and was able to run most of the way, taking about 9 hours and coming 4th. At college I was in the cross-country running team, in which despite training and much effort I could never beat my friend, Dave. That was over about three and a half miles. He was a good runner while I was mediocre. However, I had high hopes that over the much longer distance things might turn out differently.

So, on this my third run, a group of us set off running at quite a pace and we kept it up until we got to Croydon, about 15 miles. I then conked out due to lack of glucose. I knew this was so because it had happened to me a few times before, and I had a supply of glucose tablets with me. I took one after another and gradually my strength returned and soon I was running again, but Dave was out of sight. It was getting dark and I pressed on. It wasn't until I was on the bypass around Gatwick airport that I spotted my friend ahead. Gradually, gradually I reeled him in.

He was far from delighted to see me in such good form. Taciturn at the best of times, he hardly uttered a word as for the first time in our running careers I overtook him and left him far behind. I continued through the night, overtaking a couple of other runners. Dawn was approaching, and the dawn chorus of song birds was well under way when I reached a refreshment station at the foot of the South Downs. I had a hasty drink of orange and took a Mars bar, for by now I had run out of glucose tablets.

The long uphill slopes of the Downs proved quite a challenge to a fellow who had already covered about 40 miles. I slowed down and then suddenly came over strange, I tripped and found myself head down on the side of a ditch in the wet dewy grass. I must have laid there for several minutes. I unwrapped the Mars bar and began to eat. I felt my strength returning, but I was still lying prone when I heard footsteps. I turned my head. It was Dave!

'Morning,' he grunted, but without concerning himself with my collapsed state he 'passed by on the other side'.

Now this had become truly personal! I finished the Mars bar and set off stiff and aching, half running, half stumbling after him. It took me half an hour to overhaul him again. I was pleased to note how slowly and painfully he was progressing. On the south side of the Downs I felt I was nearly there, but the road seemed interminable. Even after, with joy I came to a sign proclaiming I was entering Brighton, the suburbs dragged on and on until, at last I had made it to the finishing line. I had beaten Dave!

Ominously, near the finishing there was a huge black, superannuated funeral hearse parked. I sat down on its running board. Inside was a couch on which the lad who had come first was lying. There were two seats occupied by No 2 and No 3. It gradually became clear that of the four of us crazy lads, I, the slowest, was in the worst condition. I tried to take fluids but started vomiting. In turn we changed positions in the funeral vehicle until it was me laid out on the couch, intermittently vomiting out of the window.

I needed medical attention, so they took me to the Royal Sussex County Hospital. I seem to remember that I travelled in the hearse, but that surely is too surreal to believe! I must have been pretty far gone because I was admitted and stayed in the ward for about 12 hours while they rehydrated me under the supervision of a fierce staff nurse named Moriaty.

Patients

The Bird's Nest

It's not much further - just a few yards. I stop again to recover my breath. My chest is heaving, but I'm nearly at the top. I'm going to make it. When I was a kid I would often come up here to play and explore, but I doubt I even noticed the slope then. Now I'm struggling. I never thought I would see this place again.

Ever since Dr Starling pronounced sentence four months ago I've been in the hands of women. They have appointed themselves nurses, cancer experts and gaolers. What is it that lets them believe they know what's good for me? I mean, Joan, she's my wife, has never studied health or the human body, let alone lung cancer, but that doesn't stop her being dogmatic and dictatorial. She reckons she knows better than Sue, the health visitor, who, I guess, has studied these things. Of course, Joan uses a team of advisers. There's Mrs Smithers who she meets in the paper shop, and Amy who comes round to gawp at me and criticise, and Mrs Balderstone, whose sister was an auxiliary nurse in the Infirmary some time before the discovery of penicillin. So I'm under a regime of rest, royal jelly, raw eggs, detox, vitamins, laxatives and acupuncture. And since Amy is a Catholic, there's talk of a trip to Lourdes.

Of course, I won't get away with this little outing. She has spies everywhere. There is bound to be trouble.

I'm at the top now, but God, my breathing is terrible. I'm gasping so much I can't think of anything else. Stupid bugger! I stop and slowly it subsides. I'm relieved and a little proud that I've made it. I've only got about half a working lung and I'm completely out of condition.

I came here on a sudden whim, and out of frustration at being cooped up indoors for so long. Joan and the team went off on a day trip to Town. Their excuse was to visit a health food emporium for 'research'. Of course, they won't stop there. They'll do more shopping, have a light lunch and linger until their return can be delayed no longer. It's all just diversionary activity. I don't think any of them care whether I die sooner or later. Joan finds it hard to be at home with me now, and she grasps any excuse to go out. It's not surprising I suppose. We grew apart years ago. We've nothing but poverty to keep us together. She'll be relieved when it's all over. So will I, I suppose.

'Now Jim, you've got to rest,' she orders as she puts on her coat. She can't get out of the house quick enough. The Team each pitch in with their penny-worth of advice. 'Have a little soup if you're hungry. Watch a bit of television, but nothing too exciting.'

They're killing me faster than the bloody cancer! I often feel like I'm dead already. I can't even have a fag.

But now I'm up here, free and irresponsible, even if I'm not feeling too perky. At least I'm feeling alive and alert. It's the first time in months that I've felt this way. I've only been out of the house to go to the hospital, and even then Madam insists on a wheelchair. I've hardly put one foot in front of the other for the past six months, so it's not surprising that I'm knackered.

I'm standing here, bent over like an old fellow, gasping on the crest of a hill, that's not much of a hill, looking down on row upon row of grotty Victorian villas - dirty red brick with slate roofs. They were substandard and depressing when I was bright and new from my creator. Now they're going to outlive me! A bit further off is the spire of St John's where Joan and I were married. She was four months pregnant with our son, but it didn't really show much. To the right, half a mile away there's the big empty shed and smokeless brick chimney that was once Benson's, where I wasted most of my adult life. It's been closed for years, and good-riddance to it.

I'm a bit dizzy, so I sit down on the grass. It's a warmish morning – not bad for May, but the grass is still wet with dew. Never mind, it's unlikely to kill me. There are black spots swimming across my vision, so I lie back, and the grass tickles my ears. I shut my eyes; I feel okay; I'm at peace; I'm free.

I must have dropped off or perhaps I passed out, because when I open my eyes someone is gazing at me from close to. I didn't hear him coming. I thought I had the place to myself.

'You okay Mister?' He's only a kid, maybe eight or nine. 'You look a bit pale, like.'

'Do I? I think I'm okay. Not been out much recently.'

I sit up. For a moment everything swims about me. It's warmer now. The boy is in a T-shirt and jeans, and his fair hair is all over the place. I vaguely recognise him.

'I used to come up here when I was your age. There used to be a ruined mill over there.'

'I've been bird's nesting.'

It wasn't so much of a statement, but it certainly hit me. I hadn't even thought of bird's nesting for decades, and now the memories came flooding back. We used to explore far and wide down hedgerows, into the distant unfamiliar spring countryside. There were fields bright with buttercups, fields whose edges we skirted for fear of wild long-horned cattle, and there were silent pine woods. Different nests and different eggs. I amassed quite a collection. I had a flat box with little compartments, each egg nestling in cotton wool, each with a little label – 'Blackbird' 'Hedge Sparrow' 'Starling' 'Mistle thrush' 'Hedge warbler' 'Robin'. I wonder what's happened to it. Now most of the hedgerows are gone.

I thought modern kids just played computer games.

'Found anything?'

'Not much. There's a blackbird's nest over there.' He pointed. His expression suggested he had been looking for something more exotic.

I suddenly had an urgent desire to see it. 'Could you show it to me?' He looked dubious – perhaps he was remembering what his mother had told him about strange old men. Maybe there was no nest.

'It's not far.' He set off without looking back, putting a distance between us. I struggled to my feet and followed, but my breathing was quickly bad again. I had a bout of coughing, and there was bright red blood on my handkerchief. He was heading for a clump of trees and bushes that I well remembered, though now the place was far more overgrown. He reached it and looked back at me, waited a few seconds and then went on. I was struggling.

He was standing on the other side of the bushes, by a sprawling elderberry and a large holly. I was still twenty yards off.

'It's in the holly.' He pointed and backed away. I guess I was an alarming sight.

'Where?'

'Up there!' he pointed again. I came up to him. 'You've got blood on your face, Mister.' He ran off.

I wheezed as I watched him go, remembering when I was that age – adventurous, and scared; shy and awkward. Then I addressed myself to the tree. I parted the pliant branches of the elderberry and stepped between them so that I could look up into the holly. The nest was at least twelve feet up, a soup bowl of knitted grass and straw in a fork of the branches, and from it the bird's black tail stuck up at an angle, snake-like and sinister.

I had to get up there. I had to feel what it was like again to touch nature and to experience her mysteries and the thrill of discovery. I would never get another chance. Like a kid I sized up the handholds and footholds. It looked doable, but my chest was still heaving. I waited and waited.

All these years I have been fighting nature – doing what I ought, and not what I wanted, living in a synthetic environment, eating synthetic food. Even now I'm not allowed to die the way I would want. But at least this was real.

I put my right foot into a fork, low down on the trunk. My arms were weak, but strong enough to haul my wasted frame up a couple of feet. I waited, studying the smooth greenish bark of the tree, until my breathing stabilised. I got my left foot onto a branch and pulled myself higher. One more gasping step brought my head just below the nest. I reached up to it. With its strident alarm call the bird exploded from the nest. I felt the draught from its wings on my face and almost lost my grip. I was winded again, and black spots swarmed again across my vision. The world swayed alarmingly. I held on and waited.

Cautiously I raised my hand to the nest. I touched its rough edges and felt the smooth dry mud lining. There were four warm eggs. How I remembered that moment of a find; of warm wild eggs in the secret inside of a nest! With great care I took one out and held it in the palm of my trembling hand. Three quarters of an inch long, greenish-blue with brown spots concentrated round the blunt end. I marvelled that nature took so much care to decorate something so ephemeral. I put it back, and for a long time hung there in the holly, savouring the moment, and looking out through the branches to the fields beyond.

I don't know how I got down. I was again lying on the grass, luxuriating in the warmth of the sun. The breathlessness had gone, and at last I felt well. The boy came back, bright eyed with a ruby glow to his cheeks. He wasn't frightened of me now. We were mates and there were more nests up near the mill. My mum would be expecting me home for lunch, but there would still be time if we were quick.

'Fat, Hairy and Mad'

Doris came to my clinic having previously seen one of my colleagues. She was 65 years old and a mild asthmatic whose respiratory condition had been aggravated by a lifetime of cigarette smoking. She had a history of unspecified mental illness. My colleague had taken a medical history, and at the beginning of his account of his physical findings he given a thumbnail sketch of her:

'Fat, hairy and mad'!

It can be useful to give a brief description in this way - 'a tall, anxious man with staring eyes'; 'a talkative woman who was unable to give a clear account of her symptoms'; 'a pleasant man who looked emaciated'. But it is tempting to try to be funny or rude. 'Thick and thin'; 'Dirty and disreputable'. My colleague's comments clearly came into the latter class. Nowadays, in the modern NHS, doctors are a lot more circumspect, if only because patients now have that right to see their own clinical notes.

I made some adjustments to her treatment and asked her to come again in a few months' time, and on this second visit to my clinic she brought me a little present - a diary.

'Doctor, I wanted to bring you this because it's my fortieth wedding anniversary and I'm so amazed that Jim, my husband, has stuck with me all these years! Sometimes I give him such a hard time, but he always forgives me. I can't believe we are still together!'

Congratulations! But surely it's me that should be giving you a present to commemorate the occasion?'

'No, doctor, I just wanted to do something because I feel so lucky.'

I can tell you, I was quite moved.

Some months later she came again, but this time the consultation could not have been more different. She rushed in, and was in a high state of anxiety and excitement.

'Doctor, doctor, I'm pregnant! I think I might be going into labour!'

Her barrel-like abdomen made the suggestion plausible, but her age, of course, ruled it out. What does a good doctor do when faced with such craziness? There's no answer to that. I put her on the couch and examined her abdomen, but reckoned it was reasonable to forgo listening for a foetal heart beat!.

Then I called the psychiatrists.

Three days later I went down to the Psychiatric Ward to see Doris. It was not my first visit to that ward, but no less confusing. In the type of ward I usually inhabited you could tell at a glance who was a patient (the ones in pyjamas or nightie; usually in bed) who was a nurse (in uniform) who was a doctor (wearing a white coat) and who was a visitor (none of the above). In Psychiatry, the dress code, which might be described as 'scruffy casual', applies equally to patients, nurses, psychologists, assorted therapists, psychiatrists and visitors. There are no pyjamas, uniforms or white coats. The patients look only slightly more unhinged than their carers, so the distinction is even more fraught. I decided not to try, and as no one seemed in the slightest interested in what I was doing there, I just wandered around, glad to be wearing a white coat, until I found Doris in a sitting room, chatting. Seeing me she jumped up and greeted me as an old friend.

'Doctor, I'm so embarrassed! How could I have thought that? It was so stupid!'

'No, no!' I smiled. 'No problem at all.'

I pointed to two chairs at the opposite side of the room. We sat down facing each other.

'I'm awfully sorry! I can't think what got into me.'

'No need to apologise, Doris. Actually it was quite exciting! I thought I was going to have to be a midwife!'

'No, don't tease me doctor. I really did believe I was pregnant, though. The feeling had been coming on for a few days.

At first I knew it was silly and I tried to put it out of my mind. Then I heard a voice - a woman's voice that sounded like my old Aunt May, and she kept telling me I was a dirty slut and it served me right that I was in the family way. Then I began to believe it. Aunt May was a smart lady, though she wasn't very kind.'

'But anyway, you are better now, Doris.'

'Yes.' She smiled broadly. 'Isn't it amazing! I was very confused when I came in here but I think they gave me an injection and it all went away.'

'I'm sure they did. It's just as well that I was on the ball and didn't send you to the Labour Ward.'

'You're right Doctor, I would still be crazy.'

I smiled.' And now you are quite well - your asthma's okay?'

'Fine, thank you doctor.'

I stood up to go. 'I don't suppose they'll need to keep you here much longer. I'll ask them to arrange an appointment to see me in a few week's time.'

'Please wait a moment, doctor. I know you're busy, but I'm worried about my husband.'

I sat down again.

'You see, I told him he was going to be a father again.'

'And what did he make of that?'

'He seemed quite pleased. He said "That's nice" and smiled at me, but I think he may not have heard me right. He's very deaf and old now.'

'He's older than you?'

'Oh yes Doctor, much older.' She paused as if enjoying a happy recollection. 'You know Doctor, he was a very naughty boy. When we were thinking of getting married he didn't look his age and he told me a fib. He said he was thirty-one when he was really forty-two. I think he felt he had to because I was only twenty five.'

'Oh dear, and what happened when you found out? You must have been very cross at being deceived.'

'No, not at all Doctor!' Again she paused and smiled to herself. 'I thought it was quite lovely! Just to think, he wanted to marry me so much he was willing to lie to get me!'

'I suppose that's one way to look at it.'

'And he's been such a lovely husband to me! Always kind and respectful and helpful. He's a real gentleman - he would always hold the door open for me when I put the bins out.'

I tried to keep a straight face.'You're a lucky lady to have such a devoted husband, and I'm sure he'll understand how you were mistaken about the baby. After all, he knows you pretty well after all these years.'

She nodded. 'I think he'll be okay. I hope so.'

'By the way, Doris, before you came in, weren't you taking medication from the psychiatrists to keep you on the mental straight and narrow - to stop you hearing voices?'

'Yes, I'm sorry Doctor. I was supposed to take them every day. I used to tell the CPN I was taking them, but I don't like them. I don't feel right on them, and they make me put on weight, and they stop me wanting sex.'

'You're still having sex?' I was thinking more of her antique husband.

'Yes Doctor, how else could I be pregnant?'

It was a reasonable question even if it wasn't one I had considered. 'Your Jim sounds to be a remarkable fellow for his age.'

She smiled. 'We make love whenever he can manage it, which isn't so often now. ' She giggled nervously. 'You see, I thought I was like Sarah, in the Bible if you know who I mean.'

'No, I'm sorry.'

'She was Abraham's wife - my mother told me about her because she had me when she was getting on a bit. Sarah had not managed to have children, but God told her she was going to be the mother of a whole nation. She laughed because she reckoned she was past it, but she wasn't. So it just goes to show that anything can happen.'

'I see what you mean.' I stood up again. 'Maybe we should send you home with some contraceptive pills, Doris!'

'Do you think so? I really do believe in miracles, Doctor.'

'I think we can take the risk, don't you? Have they told you when you are going home?'

'No, but I've told them that I'm not sticking around much longer. I'll take my own discharge. They didn't put me on a section when I came in because I cooperated with treatment, so I

82

can go when I want. I must get home and make sure Jim's alright. I'm worried about him.' She looked up at me. 'You know Doctor, he's had such a rough time with me over the years, but he's still stuck by me! I reckon I'm a fortunate woman!'

'I suspect he's been pretty lucky too!'

Daisy Loses Touch

Daisy rolls over, opens her eyes and gazes, unfocused around the bedroom. She has slept here for fifty years, but she no longer knows it. She cannot recognise the wardrobe or the straight-back chair or her pile of discarded clothes. She doesn't know where she is. She sits up, frightened. She is emaciated. Her eyes are sunken into their sockets, her cheeks hollow. Her grey hair is matted with grease.

'Mummy!' she calls, but Mummy doesn't come.

For the past year it has been the same every morning, but familiarity with the situation cannot breed contempt or reassurance, for she cannot remember from one day to the next.

'Mummy!' she begins to cry. 'Daisy's lost!'

After a couple of minutes she stops, wipes her eyes on the filthy bed sheet and looks again at her room. This time she notices, propped up on the chest of drawers by her bed, a dusty gilt-framed black and white photo of a soldier. His face is familiar. Her breathing comes more easily. She remembers she has a husband.

'Where are you, Sam?'

He isn't beside her in bed where he ought to be. This is not surprising as he has been dead for the past five years.

'He's gone out to fetch the paper.'

She decides to get up because her bladder is full and her stomach is crying out in hunger. Slowly she gets her legs over the side of the bed and sits there. Now, somehow the room is beginning to make some sense. She remembers the chest of drawers - a wedding present from his mother, and the wardrobe that had frowned down on her when she was in labour. It is as if she hasn't seen the room for years. On the wall there is a black-framed picture of a young woman in a diaphanous robe, dancing. She never liked it. She will tell Sam to take it down.

She wants to wait until Sam comes back because she is frightened of what might be on the other side of the door. She cannot remember, but Sam will know; he will take her.

'Come on Sam! Where are you lad? Mother needs you!'

She can wait no longer. Her bladder is bursting. She gets unsteadily to her feet and pushes open the door onto the dim, narrow and quite unfamiliar landing. Somehow her instincts tell her which of the three mysterious doors is the toilet. She sits and waits, but still her husband doesn't return. She needs a cup of tea and something to eat. Barefoot in her soiled nightie she walks unsteadily down stairs, holding tightly to the banister and moving crab-like to lessen the pain in her knees and hips. In the squalid cold kitchen she fills the kettle, lights the gas and searches for her cigarettes, but she cannot find them, so she sits down on a stool and leans against the white tiled wall.

The kettle boils. She gets up and finds the tea caddy in its proper place, but it is empty. Confused and bothered she rummages for the umpteenth time through her empty cupboards. There is no tea, no coffee and nothing to eat. Despairing she flops back onto the stool and wails.

'Where the hell are you, Sam? Sam! Sam! Sam!'

Then among her jumbled thoughts she thinks of the milkman.

'Perhaps he's come!' She has no idea of the time.

She shuffles to the front door, and with difficulty opens it. It opens straight onto the pavement. The wind propels a shiny crisp packet down the road, and it blows cold on her legs. The brightness dazzles her. She cannot see any milk bottles, but she is desperate and steps out to take a better look around. The pavement is icy. She looks without recognition at the row of terraced houses opposite. She is beginning to panic. She doesn't know where she is. Then she sees two full milk bottles on the pavement a few doors down.

'Silly sod's left them at the wrong door!'

With more purpose she shuffles along and picks one up. There is a gust of wind and a door behind her slams shut. She turns. All the way down the street the front doors are shut and she doesn't know which one is hers. She is panicking again.

'Sam!' she shouts. 'Where the bloody hell have you got to?'

A neighbour opposite peers through her net curtains. She knows Daisy, but doesn't like her. She knows she should help, but she doesn't want to get involved.

Daisy is shivering.

'Christ! I'll have to go round to Margaret's.'

She doesn't know the way to her daughter's, but that doesn't prevent her setting off down the terrifying unknown street past shiny parked cars and an abandoned supermarket trolley. She is unsteady on her feet, and uses the fronts of the houses for support. At the corner some boys on the opposite side laugh at her. They scare her, but it isn't her nature to show it.

'I'll get my Sam on you! You see if I don't. He'll give you a hiding you won't forget!'

'Shut up!

'Stupid old cow!'

She rounds the corner. A woman with a sallow complexion and a pinched expression is coming towards her pushing a buggy.

'Are you okay Love?' A rancid, ammoniacal smell reaches her nostrils.

'Do I look okay?'

'I was only asking.' She pushes past and quickens her step.

Daisy looks despairingly at the row of front doors receding from her down the street. None is even vaguely familiar. She is shivering uncontrollably and dizzy. She holds onto a lamppost. She has forgotten what she is looking for; she doesn't know where she is or how she got there. She has forgotten who she is. She drops the milk. It shatters at her feet. Slowly, holding tight to the lamppost she slips to the ground and shuts her eyes.

When she comes round, hours later she is on a hard couch in a bright place. On all sides there are floral patterned curtains. She is under thick blankets but still shivering. Fear of the unknown sweeps over her. Although she doesn't remember, she had been in places like this before, and subconscious terrors are surfacing. She tries to get up. There is a plastic tube sticking out of her arm. She grabs it and pulls it out. It hurts and she is bleeding. She screams. Staccato footsteps are approaching. She wants to escape, but there are cot sides on the trolley. She levers herself up, grabs hold of the right hand side, hauls herself over and slides ungracefully over, and lands on her head on the hard, unforgiving floor.

--o-O-o--

They sit in easy chairs either side of the low coffee table in his office. Dr Starling opens the file on his knees.

'First let me say, Mr Biggs, how sorry we are for what happened to your mother-in-law. Mistakes happen, I'm afraid even in the best run institutions...'

'It's easy for you to say that, Doc, but she was family – my wife's mother. She's devastated.' Mr Biggs is a short, stocky man wearing a navy jumper and tracksuit bottoms.

'I can well understand, Mr Biggs. It's a tragedy, and it's never nice to think that your loved one's life was shortened by an avoidable accident.'

'She's very upset. She's too upset to come today.'

'I'm not surprised, but please tell her, when she is feeling better, that if she wants to see me, she is at liberty to phone at any time, and I will see her without delay.'

'The thing is, Doc, my mother-in-law was very precious to both of us. We doted on her. You've got to compensate us for our grievous loss. You admit that it was your fault.'

'I agree with you, Mr Briggs. You may be due some compensation from the hospital in due course, but you'll understand that it's not my decision, and it's a little complicated.'

'How come? As far as I can see she fell on her head when the nurses weren't watching her.'

'Yes, I believe that's what happened, but we'll have to get a report from the nurses. And there are other factors that have to be taken into account before blame can be apportioned and compensation agreed.'

'How d'yer mean?'

'We have to work out how much it was our negligence that caused her death and how much it was due to the negligence of others and how much due to factors beyond anyone's control.'

'That's not fair! You're just quibbling. It's the hospital's fault. You should have kept a closer eye on her.'

'I do not deny that the hospital is to blame, but we have other information that may be relevant.'

'Like what?'

'Mr Biggs, your mother-in-law was hypothermic when she arrived at the hospital. That is, she was so cold that her body temperature was well below normal. She had been found semi-conscious and very confused lying in the street, just in her nightclothes on a very cold morning. The pathologist tells us that she hadn't eaten for many days, and blood tests showed she was vitamin deficient, and severely dehydrated. She had head lice, bruises and pressure sores. X-rays showed she had several healing fractures, suggestive either of falls or domestic violence.'

'You're lying! My wife looked after her real good. Nothing was too much trouble.'

'Are you sure, Mr Biggs? Were you yourself involved in her care?'

'Well no but…'

'The full details will come out at the inquest.'

'What inquest?' Biggs seemed to go a little pale.

'Any accidental or unexplained death has to be reported to the Coroner. Certainly a death associated with possible neglect and possible domestic violence must be reported. He will want to fully investigate the circumstances of the death, and you and Mrs Biggs will have your opportunity to give evidence.'

'She wasn't neglected, whatever you say.'

'After she was admitted here, the neighbours smelled burning and called the fire brigade. Your mother-in-law had left the gas on when she went out. Fortunately no damage was done. The fire brigade involved the police as the house was empty and they had to break in. The police informed us there was no food in the house and the electricity had been cut off due to non-payment of bills. The place was apparently filthy and they got Social Services in to get the place fumigated due to the public health risk.'

'You've got the wrong place.'

'I don't think so. Your mother-in-law had a pension, of course, and we understand it had been regularly claimed, but there was no money in the house.'

'I don't believe you!'

'Mr Biggs, you don't have to. I am just telling you what I have been told, but I do trust these sources of information. The police and the coroner will sort the matter out, and no doubt will want to interview you and your wife.'

Mr Biggs stood up abruptly, pushing his chair over.

'Fuck you!'

He stormed out.

A lifetime of professional work had taught him neither to be judgemental nor to be surprised. This was a common enough story, and he had seen this type of thing many times. Caring for the elderly demented was horribly difficult and unrewarding. Even in hospital demented patients were often neglected.

He was getting on a bit himself. His memory was not what it used to be, and often enough he could not for the life of him remember what he had been doing the day before.

He wondered how his own near and dear would care for him when he became incapable. He realised he could not afford to be very complacent.

Dr Starling sighed and put the notes back into the drawer.

Assistance from a Very Fast Neurologist

Chronic Vegetative State

The patient was a young woman called Eva. She had developed a severe attack of asthma but there had been a delay in the ambulance getting to her house. She had gone unconscious before the ambulance arrived, and despite being hand ventilated with oxygen on the way to hospital she remained unconscious. In Accident and Emergency she was fully resuscitated so that she was breathing without apparent difficulty, but she remained unconscious. Her blood pressure and circulation were fine so there was no indication to send her to Intensive Care. She was therefore sent to a general medical ward under my care.

I went to see her and found her to be deeply unconscious. I assumed she had suffered brain damage due to a lack of oxygen before the ambulance came. Her husband, a man in his early thirties, was in a terrible state of both anxiety and anger. He told me she had been bad but didn't want him to call the ambulance. Then her inhaler ran out and she got worse. So he had called the ambulance but it had taken half an hour to arrive and by which time she was unresponsive and not breathing. He had given her mouth to mouth but it made no difference.

'Why didn't they come sooner? She would have been alright. She's had attacks before and she was always okay.'

I commiserated and said we would do all we could.

'Why doesn't she wake up, doctor?'

'Her brain has been deprived of oxygen. The brain is very sensitive to that. All we can really do is wait and see.'

'You mean she might not recover?'

'No, I'm afraid we cannot be sure. It all depends how severe the damage is.'

'But she's still breathing.'

'Yes, that means the lower part of her brain that controls breathing is okay.'

'Oh God!'

'I'll get one of our neurologists to come down and advise us whether there should be anything else we should be doing to encourage recovery.'

As I predicted, there was little active treatment that would help. It was just a case of good nursing care to prevent complications of unconsciousness, like bedsores or pneumonia from developing while she was given the time to recover. We began to give her liquid intravenously and the next day a nasogastric tube was inserted so that she could be fed. Her bladder was catheterised. Every hour her mouth and throat were suctioned to prevent secretions getting into her lungs. She was fitted with pressure stockings to prevent deep vein thrombosis in her legs. Physiotherapists came twice daily to thump her chest.

Despite all this care she remained deeply unconscious. There was no appreciable recovery, and as day followed day any hope of recovery faded, and the complaints of her husband increased. He had endless real or imagined issues - mainly about the nursing care - she was not being turned often enough and the skin of her buttocks was breaking. Nothing was being done often enough or well enough. He was constantly fighting with Sister Wells. He spent hours sitting with his wife, talking to her and stroking her.

'Doc, I'm sure she can hear me. She moves her eyes and nods. I think she's like that Stephen Hawking bloke.'

'Angus, our examinations suggest that cannot be. The damage to her brain is very severe.'

In a sense it did not matter what he thought or we thought. We were doing what we reckoned was best for her regardless of what we feared about her prognosis. But matters became more and more difficult. He continued to fight with the nurses and accuse them of all kinds of neglect. He was proving a very disruptive influence on the ward.

Then she developed a fever. A chest or urinary infection were most likely. We sent off the appropriate specimens to the laboratory. It was now two weeks from her admission and the

91

hopes of recovery had long faded. So the question arose as to whether we should start antibiotic treatment.

'Angus, she's got a temperature. We're trying to find the cause. We could start antibiotics if you think it would be the right thing to do.'

'Of course. You must make her better, Doc.'

So we did. Every few days we examined her neurologically, specifically to see whether she had higher, cortical function, and each time the tests were negative. We performed a CT scan of her brain, which wasn't particularly helpful, and an EEG which was compatible with very severe damage to the cerebral cortex. We managed to persuade one of the hospital's neurologists to examine her again. He pronounced she was in a persistent vegetative state, implying severe brain damage with only a remote possibility of recovery.

We discussed all this with Angus, but he remained unconvinced. He felt sure she was still responding to him, and he continued to accuse the nurses of neglect. I think he reckoned we were all conspiring against him and his wife.

We were in a complete bind. He was making life on the ward intolerable for the nurses, though it was difficult to blame him. The nurses had many other patients to look after. He would not or could not accept our view about the hopelessness of the situation. I think he felt guilty that he had delayed before calling the ambulance and for what had happened to her.

The Head of Department called me to his office.

'Douglas, I've noticed there's a problem on the ward with one of your patients. Sister feels like resigning.'

'She's not a quitter, Abe.' I explained the background. 'The poor man just can't or won't believe his wife is effectively brain dead, despite all our tests and opinions. He has had a second opinion but I think he needs a third, one from outside this hospital. I was wondering about asking someone from the Neurological Hospital in Queen Square, but I'm not sure of the procedure.'

'Right,' said Abe. 'How about someone really famous? Maybe that'll impress him. We'll get Sir Roger Bannister, if he will agree. The Department will pay.'

I should explain that this was the same Roger Bannister who was the first man in the world to run a mile in under 4 minutes. He achieved this feat in 1954 when he was a medical student in Oxford. This was a very famous triumph for boys of my generation. At my school on the wall outside the gym were a series of lap by lap black and white photographs of Bannister with his pacemakers Christopher Chataway and Chris Brasher performing the feat.

At the time the joke was that when he qualified as a doctor Bannister was so fast that he got to the patient before she had time to fall ill!

He became a distinguished neurologist working at our neighbouring hospital, St Mary's and also at Queen Square.

So we contacted the great man. He was willing to help and so the following Saturday morning I met him at the hospital entrance and conducted him up to the ward. I summarised the case and watched while he examined her. It is a joy to watch a real expert examining a system. We are all trained to examine the nervous system, but the real skill is knowing what is normal or abnormal, and this only comes with thousands of such examinations.

Sir Roger concluded that our patient was in a 'persistent vegetative state'. There were no signs of brain cortical activity. Since she had shown no improvement for several weeks the prognosis was grim. The chances of any recovery were effectively nil. He provided a report a few days later and we went over this with Angus.

The strategy worked. Angus calmed down, though he continued to criticise the nursing care, and he gradually withdrew from the ward. Eventually Eva developed a chest infection and died.

Cases like this, of sudden demise, or where there is uncertainty about the cause of death are always referred to the Coroner who is obliged to investigate. In this case, because Angus had been so critical of the ambulance service and of the nursing staff there was a formal inquest at which the ambulance service, nursing staff and myself gave evidence. Death was by misadventure and happily there were no criticisms of her management.

Severe unstable asthma is a dangerous condition. People regularly die in asthma attacks. Milder attacks are common and usually resolve without hospital treatment, but it is difficult to judge severity. The intensity of the patient's distress or the loudness of their wheezing are unreliable guides to severity. The best indicator of severity and risk is a 'blowing test' - the peak flow rate. Nowadays most severe asthmatics will have a peak flow meter at home and know how to use it and interpret the results. Patients often deteriorate at night when their judgement and that of their carers may not be at its best. Either way, it is common for asthmatics to get this wrong, and delay too long before seeking emergency medical help.

There is one aspect of this story I find particularly distressing to recall and consider. You see, Angus may have been right that Eva had some level of consciousness. It is now thought that maybe 10% of patients who are apparently in a chronic vegetative state may have some degree of covert consciousness at times. This new understanding comes from our ability to visualise brain activity with isotopic techniques, MRI and EEGs. Damage due to lack of oxygen is patchy, so that some parts of the brain may still be working. When the brain is performing a task, metabolic activity and blood supply increase in the active areas and these changes can be detected by scanning. Some apparently unconscious patients show responses to spoken instructions when studied in this way. So the 'brain dead' may be living. It is appalling to think of Eva in a dreaming, nightmarish limbo. Aware, but unable to respond, terrified but unable to ask for help. In pain, but unable to tell anyone. Maybe Angus's company, his expressions of love and his conversation were a great comfort to her.

It is also worrying that although the prognosis of someone in a chronic vegetative state is appallingly bad, the occasional patient eventually wakes up, spontaneously or with the help of drugs.

These findings just add to the ethical dilemmas that such patients pose for their loved ones and professionals caring for them.

In the Blue

I was a general physician specialising in Respiratory Medicine. As an academic I taught about the respiratory system and did medical and physiological research into the system. I ought to have been pretty competent in this area. I knew how oxygen gets through the lungs into the bloodstream, and I could have given you an authoritative lecture on how this may go wrong in lung disease.

So I should have immediately known what to do when my daughter went blue.

It was years ago when I was a postdoctoral fellow at the University of California, San Francisco. One winter we drove up into the Sierra Nevada mountains for a few days cross-country skiing. We stayed in a friend's cabin in a pretty isolated spot near Lake Tahoe. While we were there, my daughter, who was seven years old developed a mild chest infection and was a little wheezy. Asthma runs in the family.

Despite this she had been out in the snow all day, but in the evening she became rather breathless and did not feel well. I examined her and found her chest was wheezy and her tongue had a bluish tinge. The colour of the tongue indicates the colour of arterial blood, and a blue colour (cyanosis) suggests a significant lack of oxygen transfer into the blood. You wouldn't expect to see this in an otherwise healthy young person with a mild chest infection, though at altitude (we were at about 5000 feet) cyanosis will be seen in a milder illness. Still it was worrying.

My wife began to panic. We didn't know what to do. It had been snowing for hours and we were in the middle of nowhere. This was the era before mobile phones and there was no phone in the cabin. In the end we decided to try to contact a paediatrician. So I got dressed and tramped down to the road. There was a resort half a mile away and I guessed there would be a phone there. The road was covered in hard-packed snow. The temperature was well below zero and it was still snowing hard. It was about 11pm. I found a phone and a phone book.

There were several paediatricians in the town of Truckee, twenty miles away. I thought: 'Who is going to come out on a night like this?' or 'How are we going to get there in this weather?' I also thought about the expense, for as a postdoc fellow I was effectively a student again and we were on a very tight budget.

Suddenly it came to me. I realised what I should have done in the first place. I put the book down and marched back to the cabin.

'Is a paediatrician coming?' my wife asked.

'We don't need one.' I said, attempting to evoke an air of masculine medical infallibility.

'But...'

My daughter was lying on a bunk bed still poorly and blue. Her breathing was troubling her. I picked her up and laid her, head down, over my knees. I then did some chest physiotherapy - that is, I thumped the back of her chest a few times. Immediately she coughed, and out came a small lump of jelly. We sat her back on the side of the bed and I asked her to poke out her tongue. I had performed a miracle! The tongue was nice and pink. She felt better. She was better!

Asthmatics tend to produce gelatinous bronchial secretions that can obstruct bronchi, and this had presumably happened in my daughter's case. It could have been a main bronchus supplying a whole lung that was blocked or a smaller bronchus. Either way some part of her lung was not receiving air when she breathed in. Blood supplying that part of the lung would therefore not receive oxygen as it passed through, and would retain the low oxygen content of venous blood. This would mix with the blood coming from the normally oxygenated parts of the lung and lower the overall oxygen saturation. Depending on the severity and extent of the obstruction the arterial blood will lack its normal bright red colour and will appear bluish.

When I trained in medicine it was generally assumed that if you understood the basic anatomy, physiology and biochemistry of the body, and you knew what went wrong in disease, you would be a competent practitioner, able to work from first principles. We now better understand that this is not necessarily true. One is not always able to apply knowledge promptly and effectively. Modern medical education now teaches and tests competencies much more thoroughly and objectively than was the case in my day.

--o-O-o--

Years later as a consultant and Senior Lecturer at a London teaching hospital I was sometimes obliged to drive out into the leafy suburbs and teach students on medical attachment in peripheral hospitals. So on one occasion I found myself standing with a group of rather posh young men at the foot of the bed of an unconscious male patient. I cannot recollect what was wrong with him, but one thing was obvious. He was strikingly blue.

'So gentlemen what do you notice about this patient?' I started.

Silence for several seconds.

What is obvious to the trained eye is not necessarily apparent to the beginner.

The patient was just covered by a sheet. His feet protruded from its bottom.

'No ideas?'

'Er he has six toes on his left foot,' said one fellow.

Indeed he had.

'Anything else? Anything of greater medical significance? ...No?'

So I had to point out the cyanosis and they observed the patient's tongue and compared its bluish tinge to their own pinkish tongues. The shade of pink, or mauve, or purple of the tongue is usually a good guide to the colour of arterial blood and that reflects its level of oxygenation. In health, blood in our arteries is crimson red. By contrast, blood taken from a vein in the arm has a distinctly bluish tinge because oxygen has been removed by the tissues through which it has flowed. Because the tongue has a high blood flow relative to its metabolic demands it's colour is a pale version of that of arterial blood. Doctors have for years relied on their skill in recognising bluish colouring of the tongue to diagnose a lack of oxygenation. Nowadays we have simple, portable finger oximeters and give reliable and accurate information about the patient's oxygenation.

I was concerned about the patient. You only see this degree of cyanosis when there is something seriously wrong with the process of oxygenating the blood. Lack of oxygen is not good for you. The heart and the brain particularly require an adequate supply of oxygen. For all I knew the patient was unconscious due to oxygen lack. So, though the management of the patient had nothing to do with me, I went and found a nurse.

'He should be on oxygen?'

'Yes, Doctor but there is no oxygen today.' (!)

Actually I seem to recall (this was 30 years ago) that she said they didn't have oxygen on Wednesdays, but such an idea is so outrageous for an NHS hospital that I will assume I misheard or it was a misunderstanding. Any unavailability of oxygen in a hospital is, of course, scandalous, and was then.

Paracetamol Overdose

A nineteen year old girl was brought into the Medical Admissions Ward. Twenty eight hours previously she had broken up with her boyfriend, and in her distress had taken an overdose. Her parents were out, and she had scoured the house for tablets, but only found paracetamol, which her mother took for migraine. She found about thirty-five and swallowed them. She had expected some dramatic effect, but in fact as she lay on her bed waiting for her fate, she merely felt a little nauseated. After an hour, feeling a little better, she went downstairs and consumed a sizable glass of gin. Then she returned to her room and fell asleep.

She woke in the morning with nothing worse than a hangover. She stayed in bed until lunchtime when she got up but ate little, her appetite not being good. As the afternoon wore on, she began to feel odd, and she developed a tummy ache. Her mum gave her some antacid, which didn't help. It became clear to the mother that she was becoming quite unwell, and in the end the daughter confessed about the overdose. Her mother was concerned and phoned the GP who told her to take her daughter to the A&E immediately. The daughter was reluctant, and at first refused to go. She wasn't that ill. Her mother was insistent and drove her daughter to the hospital two miles away.

I saw her on my ward round first thing the next morning, by which time she was feeling better, and did not look at all unwell. Her mother and father were at her bedside. She was a pleasant, intelligent, attractive fashion student.

Every 24 hour period the Admission Ward would typically take in two or three young people who had taken an overdose of pills. Usually these were not serious suicide attempts, but more of a gesture, or a cry for help. They rarely did themselves any harm because most commonly prescribed medicines are reasonably safe in overdose. But not paracetamol.

I examined her and found that she was exquisitely tender over her liver. The team that had admitted her overnight had found a significant level of paracetamol in her blood and her liver enzymes in her blood were sky high, indicating severe liver damage due to paracetamol. They had given an intravenous infusion of acetylcysteine to protect the liver despite the fact that it is not usually effective when given after such a long delay from ingestion of the paracetamol.

This was an awful situation and made all the more poignant by the fact that she looked so well, and seemingly had her life ahead of her. Her parents appeared concerned but not overly worried. She wanted to go home. But her situation was actually desperate. She was facing acute liver failure with all its attendant risks. Precisely how severe the liver failure would be was unpredictable, but it was likely to be severe and potentially fatal. She had certainly taken enough paracetamol to kill herself. Some patients are rescued by liver transplantation, should a donor organ become available.

While the team phoned the Liver Unit in the Teaching Hospital 40 miles away I had the awful duty of taking the parents aside into a side room to explain that their daughter's life was in peril, and explaining why. They were, of course, horrified.

The Liver Unit agreed with our assessment and agreed to take her. She was nursed on Intensive Care.

Four days later we heard that before they could perform a transplant she lapsed into coma and died of acute cerebral oedema (swelling of the brain with fluid) secondary to severe liver failure.

Such a needless waste of a life!

Being a Patient

Let it All Hang Out

About 20 years ago I decided to have a vasectomy, having by then done my bit for world population growth. I agreed to have the operation under local anaesthetic.

So, a few weeks later I found myself lying wide awake on the operating table with the surgeon doing his thing in my nether regions while a pretty nurse at the top end was engaging me in trivial conversation.

'Have you been on your holidays yet?'
'Er yes, we managed to get away in June.'
'Where did you go?'
'Tenerife.'
'Oh, I love Tenerife.'

But at the same time I was aware of other voices, quite a few of them actually. People seemed to be coming and going and passing the time of day. It was as if I was being operated on in the hospital corridor, or in the canteen! There I was with my bits hanging out for any passer-by to see. I thought the hospital mobile library came through at one point, and also at least a couple of tea trolleys! I half expected the surgeon to take a break and have a cup of tea and a chat. At least there was no derisory laughter.

It's not strictly relevant, but this informality and genital exposure reminded me of happy times long ago as a medical student at Kingsbury Maternity Hospital. To complete this Obstetrics attachment I had to assist in 20 deliveries. It was common for women in labour to have an episiotomy (a cut at the vaginal opening in a harmless direction to prevent a tear in a dangerous direction when the baby's head emerges) during labour. After the delivery it was the medical student's job to sew up the cut. It was usually in the early hours of the morning. The midwives would be chatting and joking as they clattered around clearing the place up. I, barely out of my teens, would be there at the mother's abused tail end, trying to stitch the correct tissue layers to each other while chatting away to the woman who was usually euphorically happy with her new baby. No one was embarrassed; it was all very strangely normal. I used to joke about how I should do the sewing, bearing in mind her and her husband's marital pleasure.

'How tight shall I make it, dear? Shall we make you a virgin again?'

We had, after all, been taught by a particularly crude obstetrics registrar that *'sex with a multiparous woman* (one who has had several babies that is) *is like waving a rolled umbrella in the underground.'*

So I sewed away and made sure that this was not the case for sex in London NW9.

Of course, times have moved on and we've become more professional. Nowadays episiotomies are sewn up by someone who knows what he or she is doing, and I guess the conversation is also a lot less crude.

-o-O-o-

A Slow Ambulance but a Fast Surgeon

Years later I was playing in the consultants vs the rest cricket match. I was in the outfield sprinting after the ball when I felt something bash me on my right calf. It felt as if a cricket ball had hit me, but as I fell forwards, and before I hit the ground, I realized what had happened. It was a classic description of the sensation one has when an Achilles tendon (the tendon that joins the calf muscles to the heel) ruptures. I rolled onto my back and looked at my foot. I tried to move the ankle. Nothing doing. I said something unrepeatable.

Soon my fellow medical cricketers gathered around and began giving me advice and medical opinions. A professor gave the opinion that it was only a partial break (I think the Achilles tendon actually breaks completely or not at all, but it wasn't his special area).

'Are you in BUPA?' the posh Senior Surgeon asked me.

I phoned my wife to tell her what had happened.

I don't remember being in pain, but I came over faint. I looked grey and was sweating profusely. I think they thought I was having a heart attack so they called an ambulance. It was a little while coming, as we were far from town, but eventually it came and I was bundled in and we set off. I was accompanied by a medical colleague. The ambulance got to the end of the lane and promptly conked out.

'Sorry about this Sir!' called the driver. 'There's something wrong with it. It keeps on doing this, but if we sit here for a few minutes it'll be fine!'

It was surreal!

'Shouldn't you get it fixed?'

This was an ambulance service recommended by Exit International! The rest of the cricketers had followed the ambulance down the lane in their cars, and were queued behind us. I guess they thought it was me that had conked out!

Eventually we got underway again and without any further delays arrived at the A&E Department of the hospital that I worked in. In a few minutes a colleague, one of our orthopaedic surgeons arrived. This being Sunday evening I guess he must have been warned that I was on my way and had come in from home. He examined me and confirmed the diagnosis.

'You have a choice, Douglas. Either we operate now, sew it up and put you in plaster, non-weight bearing for 6 weeks, or we forego the operation and put you in plaster, with your ankle extended and knee flexed for about 12 weeks. It's up to you.'

'Which approach do you recommend?'

He outlined the pros and cons of each.

'So you don't prefer either?'

'They have different advantages and disadvantages.' He smiled.

I looked at my medical colleague. 'What do you think?'

'I don't know, Prof. Being in plaster for 3 months doesn't sound like much fun.'

'But I don't want an operation if it can be avoided.'

'No, that's true.'

'But I do want to get on with things, to get better as soon as possible.'

He nodded. 'I think that's how I would feel.'

I lay back on the couch and mulled over the options, then I looked at the surgeon.

'I'll go for it. I'll have the op.'

He smiled again. 'That, Douglas, is the correct decision!'

Oh, the mysteries of doctor-patient communication! Why couldn't he have said so in the first place? I suppose it's all about ownership of the decision. If he recommended a particular course of action and things went pear-shaped I might blame him for dodgy or arbitrary advice.

So it all went well and I am very grateful for the prompt attention and the skill of the surgeon. I was off work for about three weeks but I could get around pretty well on shoulder crutches. My worst moment came when they removed the plaster, and sent me off with a NHS bent wood walking stick. I went from being a youngish fellow who had suffered a sporting accident to a shuffling old bloke with all those associations of immobility, incontinence and tartan rugs. I hung the stick up on a window frame in the corridor and continued without it!

It is common, as I subsequently discovered, for people who should be using a walking stick for stability, not to use one for precisely the reasons I felt. I can think of few things more likely to make you feel like a geriatric person than an NHS walking stick! After this experience I advise people to use an aluminium elbow crutches. They more give the impression you've just had a skiing accident in the Alps.

-o-O-o-

Shut up and Trust the Surgeon

Being a patient when you are medically qualified, and a bit of a know-all, can be problematic, as the next tale illustrates.

I'm going to tell you about my hernia. Not too shocking, but I grant you, a little indelicate for the vicarage tea party. I developed it on the second day of my retirement. We were moving abroad for 3 years and were renting our house, so the place had to be cleared. I was heaving boxes of books etc and the strain pushed out the hernia.

Now I need to explain that groin hernias come in various types. I thought mine was what's called a *direct* inguinal hernia, and when I saw my GP about it he agreed. The danger of a hernia is if it strangulates. This occurs if the contents of the hernia - eg a length of small intestine, gets twisted and it loses its blood supply. The contents die and go rotten and this is a surgical emergency. The point here is that direct hernias don't commonly strangulate. So I did nothing about it. Being a coward and a virtuoso procrastinator I decided to live with it.

I had it for a few years and then began to develop another on the other side, so I sought a surgical opinion. To my surprise he said it was in fact an *indirect* hernia - the potentially dangerous type. In my book, an indirect hernia didn't look like this. I got the Anatomy Prize at medical school and reckoned I knew a bit about the anatomy of this region.

'Surely not,' I had the temerity to say. 'Isn't it too far medial (near the midline)?'

'No, I don't think so.'

'Wouldn't it go down into my scrotum?' (The indirect hernia goes down the path that the descending testicle took during embryonic life.)

'Not necessarily.'

I suspect I did not look convinced. He could have taken offence, but didn't. He was a very pleasant and affable Irishman.

Months later I had the operation. After the op I was lying in bed in a drugged stupor when I heard footsteps and the curtains being pulled back.

'Well Mr Halford, the operation went very well...' The surgeon's voice came from the end of the bed. The Irish accent was unmistakable.

Then I heard footsteps coming closer. I felt his warm breath on my cheek. I opened my eyes. He was bent over me and he whispered loudly very close to my ear.

'...and it was indirect!'

-o-O-o-

A Surgical Miracle

At about the same time I had a cataract operation. This means having your old cloudy lenses removed and plastic replacements inserted. It has become a routine procedure, but that should not detract from the marvel of the operation.

I was impressed how old it made me feel to have to ask my children what a road sign said or to have to use a hand lens to read small print. A bit like the walking stick!

My other visual problem was lifelong and I had worn specs since the age of five. I have an astigmatism in both eyes. This means that the curvature of the cornea (the outer transparent front of the eye that is responsible for the greatest part of the bending of light as it enters the eye) is not equal in all plains. This means that if I looked at a cross drawn on a piece of paper I could bring either the horizontal stroke or the vertical stroke into focus but not both at the same time. This fault of the cornea can be corrected by using a replacement lens that has the opposite irregularity of curvature - a so-called toric lens.

So, after attending for assessment and examination I went for the operation. They do one eye at a time separated by several weeks. It is done under local anaesthetic. The eye is numbed using anaesthetic drops, and by a local anaesthetic injection to the back of the eye done with a wicked looking long curved needle. The odd thing is that one is not really aware of anything being done to the eye. There is no pain and no vision. You hear strange noises from the suction machine and you feel pressure on the side of your head. It is over in a few minutes.

The eye is covered by a patch which they advise should be kept on for 3 hours. When I took it off I had terrible double vision because, I guess the external ocular muscles that move the eye were still paralysed. I could see okay with one eye, and having nothing else to do, I went out on my bike with my wife. This was off-road cycling I hasten to add. After 6 or 7 miles we stopped at a picnic place. I took off the patch and with my newly serviced eye looked at a group of scots pine trees that had the impressionistic quality of a Cezanne painting. The surgeon had warned me that I would be slightly short sighted.

'I'm short sighted,' said my wife, 'try my specs.'

For years my eyes had been in 'soft focus', but now suddenly all was gloriously sharp. No more impressionist landscapes! And having had the other eye similarly treated I now have far better eyesight than I can remember. It is a modern miracle, nothing less!

There was one disadvantage. I got out of the shower and looked at myself in the mirror opposite.

'Who's that old bloke staring at me?'
Soft focus was much kinder!

-o-O-o-

A Psychiatric Miracle

For about six years of my life I suffered from depression. It was not severe, but very unpleasant. It runs in my family. There is a huge stigma around mental illness that impedes its recognition and treatment. Up to the time I got depressed I had advised scores of patients about the condition and told them that it is an illness, and not something to be ashamed of. When it came to myself I was not so enlightened!

When this first happened to me I was deeply ashamed. Initially I didn't even tell my wife. I went to Boots and bought some St John's Wort (Hypericum) tablets. These have been shown to have some efficacy. Later, when it was worse I persuaded my wife to give me a private prescription for an antidepressant. I didn't want depression on my medical record. Eventually I plucked up the courage to see my GP.

Throughout my life, from childhood I have had periods when I felt low and sad. Most people are like this. The bouts occurred because of a setback, failure, embarrassment or loss. The misery lasted a few weeks and then gradually faded. I guess this is quite natural in a sensitive person. The thing that happened during the three years before I retired, and the three years after I retired was that I would get bouts of misery out of the blue with no inciting cause. Often the bout began suddenly, when I was enjoying myself. This is typical of what used to be called 'endogenous depression' and is now called Major Depressive Disorder.

When I studied depression at medical school I learned that the endogenous type of depression was characterised by a morning-evening variation of mood. The sadness, anxiety and lack of interest were worse in the morning and gradually eased as the day wore on ('morning depression'). Actually it's pretty uncommon, but it was exactly what I experienced. A psychiatrist friend was delighted by my description. I would feel miserable from when I woke until the middle of the afternoon, when I would feel 'shafts of happiness' seemingly coming from above. By 6 pm I had often forgotten that I had a problem.

My wife (a psychiatrist) predicted, reassuringly, that I was slipping into a melancholy old age. Happily, her prediction was wrong. My depression has gone. I haven't had it for 16 years.

Initially I got prompt relief from antidepressants, but gradually they became less effective, even at higher dosage. I was living in Kuala Lumpur and one morning, having driven the kids to school, I felt very frustrated, and instead of going indoors I went for a walk. A few days later I discovered Bukit Kiara (Kiara Hill), an old rubber plantation where each morning hundreds of energetic Malaysians go to exercise. I joined them, initially walking fast and then running down the hills, and eventually running up and down the hills. I got very fit, and my depression lifted. It took about three weeks. It has never returned! The mechanism of my cure is mysterious. In addition to the exercise, I made many friends on the hill and that social contact was probably beneficial. Or perhaps I got better for some other reason that had nothing to do with my change in life-style. Who knows?

I still jog several times a week.

As you may have observed, now I will tell anyone who is willing to listen or read about my depression. It's something that happens, like measles or haemorrhoids. Nothing to be ashamed of.

Telling the Patient

*I have good news and bad news for you: you are not a
hypochondriac*

In the past patients were often not told their diagnosis

It was a case presentation. The young doctor described a
patient who had been diagnosed with lung cancer. The patient's
symptoms and the physical findings on examination were
outlined. The chest X-ray films were put up on a light box and
the audience got out of their seats for a closer look. There was an
obvious mass arising from the upper part of the root of the left
lung. It looked like cancer. The diagnosis was confirmed by
obtaining a piece of the tumour through a bronchoscope. The CT
scan showed there were enlarged lymph nodes in the
mediastinum (the tissue between the lungs) and there was a
probable secondary deposit in the liver.

It was concluded that the tumour was inoperable and that the
patient would be offered palliative radiotherapy, and probably
chemotherapy. It was a straightforward and pretty typical case.
There were a few questions about the management, then a
visiting American student from the back row piped up:

'What has the patient been told about the diagnosis?'

'Err, I believe the Prof had a word with him.'

The Professor sounded a little testy. 'I told him he needed
serious X-ray treatment.'

'You didn't tell him he's got cancer?' asked the student.

'No, I told him he's got something serious but that I was going
to make him better.'

There was a slight gasp from the meeting. People shifted in
their chairs.

Attitudes to informing the patient of his or her problems and prognosis had moved on a long way, but clearly the Professor's practise hadn't travelled with them. The old school had been very reluctant to tell people bad news for fear that the patient could not handle the information, and patients were often reluctant to ask, maybe out of fear or maybe because they bizarrely did not think it was their business! Even if they asked what was wrong with them they in all probability would not be given a straight or truthful answer.

'But you can't make him better!' said the student, going much further with this than the homegrown variety would have dared.

'Look!' said the Professor. 'I just don't like telling people they are going to die, so I tell them they are going to get better. They are happier that way.'

'But you have lied to the patient.'

'Doctors have done that from time immemorial, for the patient's own good!'

I have always tried to give my patients the truth, albeit perhaps slightly an optimistic, rose tinted version of the truth. Of course, most have already guessed what the situation is and take the news seemingly with equanimity. Most people rapidly come to terms with their likely fate. It is important that people know what the likely outcome will be. If they only have a limited time left they have every right to know that so that they may spend what is left to them how they will. They may have something important to do.

--o-O-o--

In the past, you were not even told what medication you were taking:

In the fifties and sixties my mother was on tablets for severe high blood pressure. Her pills came in little containers marked 'The Tablets'. No name and no leaflet listing side effects to look out for. This was the norm in those days. 'The doctor knows best' was the attitude, and most people believed that. On one occasion her tablets came in their original container with a sticky label over the name. I peeled it back to reveal she was taking a drug called reserpine. I felt I had cheated the system and that Dr Norman would not be pleased if he knew.

Crazy!

Practice has changed radically. Now we positively encourage patients to know the names of the drugs they are taking and their possible side effects. There is no attempt to hide anything, and indeed it would be unethical to do so. There is a vast amount of information, gargon free, on the internet.

If you are facing an operation or procedure you will be told the likely outcomes and risks, and you will be asked to formally sign that you give your informed consent. You can ask to see your medical records and have a copy of hospital letters to be sent to you.

--o-O-o--

But although the doctor is straight and honest, the patient doesn't necessarily absorb the information that has been given.

I went to collect a friend from hospital where she was having an endoscopy to help understand her stomach problems. I was directed to the recovery area where half a dozen semi-comatose patients were sitting in a circle of easy chairs. They were all still under the influence of the strong sedative required for endoscopy. One of them was my friend.

'You will have to wait until the surgeon has seen her,' the nurse said.

So I waited until the surgeon came out dressed in blue theatre garb. He stood in the centre of the sleeping circle of his victims and addressed my friend for all to hear.

'Well, Ms Porter....'

She opened her eyes and looked at him with an unfocused gaze.

'...everything went well. The stomach looked normal but it did contain a little bile which may be causing a little inflammation and discomfort.'

We were driving back and I asked her, 'What did you think of what the surgeon said?'
'Did he say something?'
'Yes, he told you the results.'
'I don't remember him at all. What did he say?'
I told her.

Medical training over the last thirty years has seen a much greater emphasis on communication skills. These were never tested in my day, but now they are, and standards have improved, even amongst surgeons.

--o-O-o--

You can give information quite correctly but still you don't get through. Bad news may be met with denial.

A woman in her late thirties was admitted under my care. She had pain in her back and abdomen and had previously been in a surgical ward where no cause for the pain was found. We performed a CT scan of her back and abdomen and found that she had a large tumour in her retroperitoneal region (behind the guts, in front of the spine, in the same plain as the kidney). It looked to be malignant. To confirm this a biopsy would be necessary and to do that we would need her informed permission. So I went and explained what the CT scan showed and that we feared it might be a malignant tumour.

She hardly batted an eyelid.

'Well, thank you doctor. I hope I won't have to stay in hospital too long, we are planning a holiday.'

I was far from clear that I had got through to her so I decided to talk to her husband. The next day I managed to catch him as he was leaving. He was a pleasant and polite man with a rather boyish manner. I took him through to the patients' sitting room which was fortunately empty, and sat him down.

114

'I assume your wife has told you what I told her.'

'She said she might need a biopsy.'

'Is that all?'

'Yes, doctor, that's about it.'

'Well, that's not all I told her.' And I explained about the malignant-looking tumour and its significance. I explained that the prognosis depended very much on what the biopsy shows.

'Well, thank you for telling me, doctor, but if you will excuse me I have to get away now as I have to run the scouts' meeting this evening.'

Like his wife he showed no emotion and asked no questions. He was not curious about what treatment might involve or what hope his wife had of recovery.

The next day she took her own discharge before we could arrange for the biopsy to be taken. I wrote to her GP to explain what we had found, but I heard nothing further about her for several years.

Each week the hospital ran a 'Grand Round'. This was a meeting in a lecture theatre of the medical school at which interesting cases would be presented and discussed. Where possible the patient would be brought in at some stage so that he or she could explain their symptoms, their reactions to the disease and its treatment, and the progress they had made. The audience would usually ask questions.

On this occasion I arrived late and found that the presentation was about a woman with a retroperitoneal sarcoma (a malignant tumour, a type of cancer, arising from muscle, scar tissue, fat or connective tissue). She had gone through a long saga of treatment from surgical removal, radiotherapy and chemotherapy and the team hoped she was cured, though only time would tell. Lo and behold, when they brought her in it was the self same woman who had been in my ward years before. The audience asked her various questions and these led on to her initial symptoms and how she presented to her doctors.

'Yes,' she said, 'can you imagine? When I was first admitted a doctor came to me and told me I'd got cancer!'

Stunning!

When not to go Along with the Patient's Wishes

Medical management necessarily involves negotiation. The doctor assesses the patient and may recommend investigations and treatment. Both of these may involve unpleasantness and risk. Most patients are content to allow the doctor to decide what is needed, but still need to be involved in the decision. However, the patient may have a radically different view from the doctor. It is often possible to come to a plan with which both parties are happy, but it may not. The doctor must respect the patient's views, but equally must not go along with a policy that is dangerous or inappropriate. Sometimes the doctor and patient need to part company. This is quite subtle. On occasions I have got it wrong, as this case illustrates.

The patient, a man in his 50's, had presented to his GP with a cough, and a chest X-ray had shown what we in the trade refer to as 'bilateral hilar lymphadenopathy'. That is, there was a symmetrical swelling of the lymph glands at the root of the lung on both sides. The appearances were very suggestive of acute pulmonary sarcoidosis, a condition of unknown cause that often resolves spontaneously. The X-ray appearances and presentation, however, were not entirely typical so I suggested a number of investigations. These included bronchoscopy, a technique in which a flexible scope is inserted through the nose, through the larynx and into the bronchial tree under local anaesthetic. It is not exactly a fun experience - it can make you cough pretty severely, but it is safe and allows tiny tissue samples to be taken which may confirm or refute the diagnosis.

He wasn't happy about bronchoscopy and biopsy. 'Don't cut me, Doug!' I pointed out that the 'cut' was minute and that he wouldn't feel it, but despite my reassurances about safety he wouldn't have it.

I considered what else could be causing these shadows on the X-ray. Lung cancer usually first appears at or close to the root of the lung, but you don't expect to see it on both sides, symmetrically as in this case, but lymphoma, a primary malignancy of lymphoid tissue could do this, and this was a concern at the back of my mind.

It wasn't standard practice to perform bronchoscopy on all cases of acute sarcoid, and I decided to temporize, hoping to confirm the diagnosis from blood tests and his clinical course. I organised a Kveim test, where a sterilised extract from the spleen from a patient with known sarcoidosis is injected beneath the skin. Typically in sarcoidosis there is a reaction to this that can be identified by a small biopsy 4-6 weeks later. (The Kveim test is now obsolete).

When I saw him the following month matters were no clearer and the X-ray shadows were no better. The result of the Kveim test was not yet available. I explained that I was unsure of the sarcoidosis diagnosis and that bronchoscopy was necessary to confirm or refute it. He was still adamant that he didn't want it. At this point I was becoming uncomfortable, but I decided to wait for the Kveim result.

To my surprise and relief the Kveim test was positive, but still when I saw him again I was unhappy with the appearance of his chest X-ray. If anything, the opacities were bigger. The Kveim test did not prove the diagnosis of sarcoidosis, but it did make it more likely. I asked him again about bronchoscopy and again he refused. 'Don't cut me, Doug!' Against my better judgement I therefore temporized for a further month. I probably should have told him that either he had the investigation or I would not be able to see him further. He should consider seeing someone else.

Anyway, a month later the shadows at the roots of his lungs were definitely bigger, and he seemed less well. He still refused to be bronchoscoped and I was becoming convinced that he did not have sarcoidosis, but rather something more sinister. I therefore reluctantly discharged him from my clinic because I was becoming associated with a course of management which I knew was wrong. He was not pleased. I informed his GP.

A few weeks later I received a phone call from a colleague at a neighbouring hospital. He was one of the country's premier authorities on pulmonary sarcoidosis. My patient had been referred to him by his GP, and somehow he had persuaded the patient to undergo bronchoscopy. As I feared, the biopsy showed Hodgkin's lymphoma. I learnt that a small proportion of patients with this diagnosis had a positive Kveim test.

I don't know what happened to him. Fortunately, even then the majority of patients with Hodgkin's lymphoma were curable.

Months later I received a solicitor's letter accusing me of negligence in my management of his case. I gave it short shrift and heard no more.

Dr Starling's Casebook

Miserable Mrs Joy

Dr Starling had seen her on several occasions over the previous couple of months. She was 63 years of age and always attended with her husband. She was always very quiet and uncommunicative. Her husband did most of the talking. She had been referred by her general practitioner because of persistent abdominal pain. Dr Starling had examined her every time she came. He had ordered a barium meal which was normal, as was an ultrasound examination and a CT scan. There was no evidence of kidney disease. The pain was constant. The only associated features were that she had lost weight and seemed very miserable. She, however, said she was only miserable because of the pain and otherwise she was okay. Her husband thought she might be depressed, but she categorically denied this.

Dr Starling could think of no further relevant investigations but he reckoned her mental state could not be ignored.

'I think, Mrs Joy, that we should bring you into hospital for a few days of observation.' He made a note that the psychiatrists should see her and assess.

A couple of weeks later she was admitted. She said she felt much the same, and the initial assessment was as unrevealing as previously. Each day she lay in bed staring at the ceiling. The Senior Lecturer in Psychiatry, Dr Rubin came to see her, but he was not convinced that she had a depressive illness. It was possible but he wasn't sure. The same applied when he returned two days later. Then after she had been in the ward for 5 days Dr Starling met Dr Rubin in the hospital corridor. The latter was smiling.

'You know your patient, Mrs Joy,' said the psychiatrist, 'She has decided she is, after all, depressed.'

'Oh, and what do you think?'

'Well, if she thinks she is depressed, she probably is.'

'So much for psychiatric science!'

'Yes, ours is not a precise discipline. More art than science really. Anyway I have recommended an antidepressant and will start on some Cognitive Behavioural Therapy. Let's hope that does the trick.'

And that is just what happened. She was discharged a couple of days later. Three weeks later, when she was seen in the outpatient clinic her mood had lifted and her pain had gone.

Had the pain gone because she was no longer depressed or was she no longer depressed because she was pain free? Dr Starling was resigned to the fact that, as with many of his patients, he didn't really have a clue.

But you don't Win them All

It was a busy clinic, so the Senior Physician's heart sank when he saw Maria Ramos's name on the list. It wasn't that he didn't like her, or have sympathy for her problems, but it was that she was complicated, her notes were thick, her mind was slow, and he knew it would be a protracted and demanding interview. His clinical instincts told him he would neither diagnose her problem nor help her with it.

Mrs Ramos was a Spanish maid. As usual she looked emaciated and washed up.

'How's the pain, Maria?'

'It's the same, doctor, thank you.'

He sighed. It had been the same for months, and it had failed to yield to his investigations, and had resisted a handful of painkillers. He was beginning to despair; she looked resigned to her fate.

'And how are you in yourself? Apart from the pain, I mean.' He had long suspected she was depressed and that her pain was caused by that.

'I'm okay Doctor.' It's what she always said.

'Not unhappy?'

'No doctor.'

'Well, I'd better have another look at you.' The nurse took her behind the screens. 'I'll just need to feel her tummy and her back, Nurse.'

He flicked through the voluminous notes. She had been complaining of pain for three months. There was nothing to find on the physical examination. By stages she had had a barium meal and enema, an ultrasound of her abdomen and a radiograph of her kidneys and urinary tract. All were normal. She had seen the gynaecologists, who found nothing abnormal.

He examined her. 'Show me where the pain is, please.'

'Here doctor.' She pointed to a place to the right and below her umbilicus. 'And it goes right through to my back.' He thought of her appendix, but it was hardly acute appendicitis.

Gingerly he laid a hand on her abdomen. She tensed. 'Around here?'

'Yes doctor.'

There was nothing superficial to feel. He watched her face for signs of pain, and pressed deeper. She winced.

'Perhaps you could sit up, Maria.'

She moved with exaggerated caution.

'Tender around here?' He touched her lightly in the small of her back on the right and she jumped. 'Very tender!'

'Yes doctor.'

She was too tender for any useful palpation. 'Okay, Maria, please get dressed.'

She came back and sat down at the desk, and as before he noticed that she leant back in the chair without apparent discomfort, though she seemed to be leaning on precisely the same place that he had just touched and was apparently so tender.

'I'm sorry, Maria, but we are running out of options. I don't know what other tests would help, or how to make you feel better.'

'Yes doctor.'

A week later a large and important-looking letter slapped down on his desk. It was from Social Services and concerned Maria Ramos. They were concerned about her son, David. He was quite unaware that she had a son, let alone that he presented the authorities with difficulties. He read on. Maria had a gentleman friend, a Mr Masters who was married but separated from his wife. He usually stayed with Maria on weekends. Social Services' problem with this (and they didn't say how they found out) was that Mr Masters liked to cross dress, and apparently Maria allowed him to flounce around the place dressed as a woman. They were worried for David's moral development. There was a possibility of forcibly removing him from this environment, and the matter was coming to a tribunal to consider. They wanted to know whether he, as her physician, had any observations to make.

He did. He wrote to say that in his opinion they were worrying unnecessarily, and that his patient, who was frail physically, and probably mentally would be badly affected. It would be more than she could stand.

He asked his secretary to make me an earlier appointment to see Maria.

'Thanks for coming to see me so soon, Maria, but I've had a letter from Social Services about David. You must be very worried.'

'Yes, doctor...' She burst into tears.

'I had no idea.' He offered her a tissue.

'Please help me doctor! He is all I have.'

'Maria, I have written back to them saying they should leave David with you, but my voice will just be one amongst many.'

She nodded.

'Are you sure all these worries are not getting you down?'

'They are, Doctor. I am very worried and I cannot sleep.'

'It's very natural. What I'm wondering is whether being so worried and miserable is causing the pain in your tummy and back.'

'I don't think so, doctor.'

'I know that it sounds silly, but you have to take it from me that pains can have their origins in the mind. Some patients who are depressed don't complain of being sad but of a physical symptom, often a pain. I've seen it many times, and they usually get better when their depression is treated.'

'I'm not depressed, doctor, just worried and I have this pain.'

'That's the way it seems to you, but I still think you might be wrong. I would like you to take some tablets for depression to see if they help. There are many types available, and I could give you one that will help your anxiety, though it might make you a bit sleepy. I know you have doubts, but I would like you to give it a try.'

She shrugged her shoulders. 'I don't like to have depression, doctor; it is not a nice disease. Strong people don't get depression. No one in my family is mad. We good, strong people.'

'I'm sure you are, and I'm not for one moment saying you are mad or weak. Depression isn't madness. Strong people can get depressed. Winston Churchill got depressed.'

She looked blank. He realised he was far from convincing her and he knew there was a risk she wouldn't take the tablets.

'Maria, no one likes to think they have mental illness. I know that in your country that idea is very strong. Here people are beginning to accept that mental trouble is common and can affect anyone. They are able to be more open about it. I know you don't think you are depressed, and I admit you may be right, but I am at a loss to know what to do about your pain. It is possible, despite what you think, that anti-depressant tablets might help.'

'I don't want to take, doctor.'

'I know, but would you none-the-less accept my advice and take them, say for one month?'

She thought for several minutes. 'I not mad, doctor.'

'I agree. Of course you're not mad, but maybe your spirits are low. Maybe antidepressants will lift your spirits and make you feel better -'

'Okay, I'll take!' she said.

'Good!' He wrote out the prescription. 'Let's see how you get on with these. They may make you a little drowsy to start with, your mouth may be dry and you may find you are sweating more than usual. If anything more serious occurs, or you are unsure you should stop them and see your GP or call me.' He smiled.

'Thank you doctor.'

'And perhaps you will come and see me in one month.'

He was uncomfortable. His training and common sense taught him to expect a physical cause for a physical problem. Blaming a mental process felt like a cop-out. He was blaming the patient, telling her she was weak or defective in the mind rather than accepting his responsibility to find the real cause. He couldn't imagine how, if he became depressed, it could manifest itself in this way, but the books and his own clinical experience told him it could. The psychiatrists talked about conversion reactions – converting the mental distress into a physical one, but these usually involved neurological symptoms. There was no doubt it occurred, but was it occurring in Maria Ramos?

He had a keen sense of anticipation when he saw her name on his clinic list, but this was replaced by concern when she failed to show up. He asked the appointments clerk if she had cancelled, but there was no record that she had.

'Apparently her notes are with surgery, doctor.'

This was worrying. He hurried back to his office and got his secretary to make some enquiries.

'She was admitted four days ago to Ward C2, and she has had a laparotomy.'

'Oh, my God!'

He hurried out of the office, down the stairs and down the long busy corridor. He barely acknowledged the greetings of colleagues and patients as he hurried by. He bounded up the stone steps to the women's Surgical Ward. Sister could not hide her surprise at seeing the Senior Physician stride into her office.

'You have my patient, Maria Ramos on the ward, Sister.'

'Yes doctor. She's doing well.'

'She's had an operation?'

'Yes, she came in with colonic obstruction and she was found to have a tumour arising from her caecum.'

'No!' He collapsed into a chair. 'I've been investigating her abdominal pain for months. I couldn't feel anything, and all the tests were negative.'

'Oh dear!'

As Sister led him to her bed she was lying with the bedclothes pulled right up to her chin. On her bedside table was a picture of the Virgin Mary, but it seemed no one had brought her flowers or even a card. Her cheeks were wet with tears. She turned her head away from him.

'I'm sorry to see you here, Maria. This must have been a great shock for you. I don't know how we could have missed what was wrong with you. Our tests should have found it. I will need to talk to my colleagues in the X-ray department to see how this was missed.'

She turned her head to glare at me. Her face was red. 'I don't care about that, doctor. I have nothing to live for any more. You tell me I mad. You tell Social Services and they take my David away and put him in home! I never see him again!'

A Clinical Conundrum

It was a Wednesday morning and so Dr Starling, the Senior Physician, was in clinic. He worked his way through the usual drudgery, but smiled in pleasant anticipation of his final patient, Mabel Collins. He had been following her in his clinic for the best part of a decade, and as usual, she came in with her husband, Ted. Mabel was sixty-three years of age and chronically overweight, originally due to myxoedema (an underactive thyroid gland). He had been treating her with a small dose of thyroxine, on which she had perked up and returned to her previous cheerful self, and even lost some weight.

But he was shocked when they traipsed into his consulting room. Neither of them looked too well. She moved slowly, had put on weight and her complexion was pasty. She appeared to have reverted to her old myxoedematous state.

'I'm not so good, Dr Starling. I can't hide that from you. I've not got so much energy.'

'You've been taking your tablets?'

'Yes, doctor.'

'You don't forget?'

'No, Ted puts them out for me every morning and makes sure I take them.' She looked at her husband who grinned.

'She takes them, doc. I make sure of that.'

'And you've not been vomiting? Your tummy's okay.'

'I'm a bit constipated, Doctor.'

That fitted the picture. Her body was slowing down again. He guessed that for some reason her body's demand for thyroxine had increased. He examined her notes. Her development of myxoedema – thyroid hormone deficiency, had been spontaneous and she had a small nodular goitre (thyroid swelling). There had been little doubt about the diagnosis – the plasma bound iodide had been low; the I^{131} uptake of the thyroid gland low. Her symptoms and signs were typical. For the past five years she had been well controlled, only taking 100 micrograms of thyroxine, which was a low dose, but she had responded well, and it was much better for a woman of her age to take too little than too much. Tests didn't help much.

He examined her. Her pulse was down to 62; her facial features had coarsened; her tendon reflexes were slow-relaxing as you see in patients with an underactive thyroid.

So, what had happened? The most plausible explanation was that her thyroid gland had been producing significant amounts of thyroxine and that further damage to the gland had reduced this. Still, it didn't entirely make sense.

'Is your breathing alright, Mabel?'

'I'm a bit short on the stairs.'

Considering her weight, that was not surprising.

'No pain in your chest?'

'No doctor.'

It would be dangerous to increase the dose if she was getting angina due to narrowed coronary arteries. Thyroxine would place more demands on the heart.

'I'll tell you what I want to do. I'll arrange a blood test and a cardiogram, and I'll see you in four weeks when we will consider whether we need to increase the dose of your tablets.'

'Thank you, doctor.'

When he saw her again a month later she was much the same. Very slow, and her voice had become croaky. She was wrapped up in a heavy overcoat although the weather was mild. The tests suggested her myxoedema was being under-treated. Her cardiogram was satisfactory. He opted for caution and increased the thyroxine dose by just 25 micrograms.

But the following month her condition was no better. None of the features of thyroxine deficiency had improved and his clinical subconscious nagged him that she was deteriorating.

'I've been feeling a little sick, doctor.'

'Have you vomited?'

'No, doctor.'

'Okay, Mabel, we'll give you a little more.'

'Thank you doctor.'

'Where's Ted today?'

'His a little poorly, doctor. He didn't have a good night. It was his breathing, doctor.'

'I'm sorry to hear that. Get him to see his GP.'

'Yes, doctor.'

A week later he was on his ward round on Ward A2. Sister was conducting him past the beds of patients under the care of Dr Bruce when he noticed someone he recognised. It was Mabel's Ted. He waved.

'Good afternoon, Mr Collins, I'm sorry to see you in here.'

Ted grinned.

'Mr Collins is married to one of my old patients, Sister.'

'Are you doing alright?'

'Thank you doctor, much better.'

'Mr Collins was admitted two days ago, Sir, with left ventricular failure and pulmonary oedema. He was in fast atrial fibrillation (a fast irregular heart beat). He's a lot better now.'

'Excellent! I guess they'll get you home soon.'

'I hope so, doctor.'

But the following week Ted was still there.

'It's taken a little longer than Dr Bruce expected,' explained Sister. 'He developed a touch of pneumonia, but he's on the mend again now.'

In the clinic, Mabel was much better. She was livelier and had lost a little weight.

'Coping alright without Ted?'

'Oh, he's back home now, doctor. He's much better.'

'And you've made a lot of progress yourself, Mabel.'

'Yes, doctor, I'm feeling much better, though the warmer weather helps too.'

So it was with a lighter heart that Dr Starling left his clinic that afternoon. He did not understand what had happened, but there, how often did he fully understand his patient's diseases? He didn't give Mabel Collins another thought for several weeks, apart from dictating a letter about her to her GP recommending the new thyroxine dose. Then, six weeks later he got a phone call from his registrar.

'Dr Starling, we have an old patient of yours in the ward and I wanted to ask you about her, as your round is not until the day after tomorrow. Her name is Mabel Collins, and you've been treating her for myxoedema. You recently increased her dose of thyroxine because she's been slowing down, feeling the cold and putting on weight, but I think the present dose may be too high because she's been brought in with fast atrial fibrillation (AF). She's also been vomiting.'

'So she's gone from appearing to have not been taking enough thyroxine to appearing to be on too much now. She wasn't in AF before, so I guess we have to put that down to the increased thyroxine dose.'

'I must say Sir, she doesn't appear to be hyperthyroid.'

'No, I agree. And why is she vomiting?'

'I don't know, Sir. She's been nauseated for a couple of weeks.'

'Do you think she has gastritis?'

'She has no abdominal tenderness.'

'Difficult. Either way, you should stop the thyroxine for the present.'

By the time of his ward round she was feeling much better. The nausea had gone and her heart had snapped back into its normal sinus rhythm.

'You're a puzzle for sure, Mabel. What are we to do with you?'

'I put it down to all the worry, doctor.'

'What are you worried about?'

'It's Ted, doctor.'

'Surely he's not in here too?'

'No doctor, but I think he ought to be. He's wasting away. He's been losing weight for months, doctor.'

'What about his heart?'

'He's breathless, doctor but it's not as bad as before.'

He turned to his registrar and house officer. 'It's often the way with married couples. One gets ill and then the other follows suit. I've seen it many times. The delicate balance of their lives is disturbed by illness and stress or depression in the other party leads to them both being below par.'

But even as he pontificated thus he realised this wasn't an adequate explanation of their illnesses. It was too trite. He supposed that Ted could have developed heart failure because of stress, and he might be losing weight for the same reason, or because Mabel was no longer able to cook. He turned to the patient.

'Is Ted getting his food?'
'Yes, doctor. I see he gets three meals a day.'
'And does he eat them?'
'He'd eat more if I gave it to him.'

This was an important clue, but just at that moment there was a commotion further down the ward and Sister hurried away. The train of thought was broken. It wasn't until he was driving home that evening that the penny dropped.

Ted Collins looked alarmed as Miss Greaves ushered him into Dr Starling's office.
'Good heavens! I wasn't reckoning on there being so many of you.'
'Do come in, Mr Collins! Welcome! Please don't mind this crowd, but I thought it important to have my colleagues here in our attempt to learn what's been going wrong with you and your wife. You'll remember your own consultant, Dr Bruce.'
'Good afternoon, Mr Collins.'
'And these doctors are working on my team and Dr Bruce's. Now, the background you know. You and Mrs Collins have become ill at more or less the same time, but in different ways. Mrs Collins' old trouble has come back at the same time as you have developed heart trouble and have been losing weight. Latterly she has also become sick and developed an irregular heartbeat – something that you suffer with yourself.'
'That's right doctor.'

131

'Now, you and I have figured out how this has happened, and I'm grateful to you for coming here to tell my colleagues. It's an important lesson. But rather than have me just tell these doctors I want them to see if they can work it out for themselves. That's the way we like to teach each other.'

He turned to the Registrar. 'Now, yesterday, Jane, Mrs Collins told us Mr Collins has been losing weight, and she said something about his appetite.'

'Sorry, Sir, I cannot remember.'

'I suspect you do not remember because you have not fully appreciated the question. Mrs Collins told us he was losing weight despite a good appetite. That is extremely significant, is it not?'

'Err, yes. I guess so.'

'Tell me about it.'

She thought for several seconds. 'It happens in diabetes.'

'Quite right! Now then, Mr Collins, are you a diabetic?'

'No, doctor.'

'No hint of diabetes, Dr Bruce?'

'None that we have found.'

'Right then, Jane, you've drawn a blank. Another suggestion?'

'Malabsorption, Sir.'

'Yes, I guess so. Malabsorption, where the patient is unable to absorb nutrition from their gut is, of course, a type of starvation. That increases the appetite, of course.'

'You're not starving, are you, Mr Collins? Three meals a day we heard. And there's nothing wrong with your tummy?'

'No doctor.'

'Well then, Jane, what are we left with?'

'Thyrotoxicosis, I suppose.'

'Does he have thyrotoxicosis?'

'I don't know, Sir.'

'Dr Bruce, was there evidence of thyroid problems?'

'It's not the sort of thing you think of in a man of this age. He has no goitre and his weight has been stable for years, though it has recently fallen. It has to be said that when he was admitted last month he was in fast AF, which should always make you think of thyroid overactivity, but I guess we felt there were more plausible explanations in a man of this age and with a heart problem.'

'Quite so, but now we have raised the question, is there any evidence of an overactive thyroid? Tom, perhaps you could perform a cursory examination for evidence of thyroid overactivity. I assume that's okay Mr Collins?'

'No problem.'

Tom took the patient by the hand and felt his pulse. Then he asked the patient to hold his hands out in front of him.

'Please follow my finger with your eyes.'

He raised then slowly lowered his finger in front of the patient's face while the patient's eyes raised to the ceiling and slowly dropped to the floor. Finally he got the patient to sit forward and he felt the thyroid gland in the front of the neck.

'Well then?'

'He's still in AF, with a rate at the wrist of about one hundred, so control is less than perfect. His palms are slightly sweaty, and there is a fine tremor of his outstretched hands. He has no eye signs and no goitre.'

'Excellent! What do you make of all that?'

'It's difficult to be sure, Sir. The sweating, tremor and tachycardia might just be because he is nervous, but it could be due to thyrotoxicosis.'

'Absolutely! It is very difficult to diagnose thyroid overactivity from clinical signs. I don't know whether anyone is in a position to make sense of all this, and in particular can you tie his features and recent history with the fact that Mrs Collins was admitted a few days ago, nauseated and like her husband, in AF, which now has resolved?'

Blank looks prevailed.

'I'm quite sure these two good people's histories are causally linked.'

Still the penny did not drop.

'Mr Collins, I think you will have to tell them.'

'I'm very sorry, Dr Starling. The whole thing is my fault.' He pulled out two pill bottles from his pocket and laid them on the low table. 'You see, Mabel is a bit forgetful nowadays so I give her her tablets. It was very simple. I would give her one from this bottle, and I would take one from this one. I got it into my head

133

that this was the right way round, but my eyesight's pretty poor and I got them the wrong way round. The writing's too small, you see. I must have originally looked at them with my reading glasses on, but after that I just reckoned I knew. I never thought I'd got them the wrong way round until Dr Starling came round to see me last night.'

'Thank you, Mr Collins, for being so frank with us, but you mustn't blame yourself. It was an honest mistake, and the two types of pill look very similar. It is for us and the pharmacy to make sure mistakes like this don't happen.'

'So, I see now,' said Jane. 'Mrs Collins' hypothyroidism got worse because she was no longer taking thyroxine, and by the same token, Mr Collins developed fast AF and weight loss because he was inadvertently taking thyroxine that he did not need.'

'Yes, and Mr Collins was admitted in heart failure that was primarily caused by the rapid irregularity of his heart, partly as you have said due to the thyroxine but also due to the fact that he was no longer taking the digoxin which might have brought his heart rate under control.'

'But why did Mrs Collins get sick and develop atrial fibrillation like her husband?'

No one wanted to venture an explanation.

'Shame on you! Remember she was accidentally taking digoxin. Nausea is the most common side effect of that drug, particularly in overdose, and you'll remember that digoxin is also perfectly capable of causing atrial fibrillation, as well as being used to control that condition.'

The Miracle Cure

The patient, Mr Chen, was in his early fifties and had been sent to Dr Starling's outpatient clinic by his GP. The referring letter said the patient was having difficulty moving about and using his hands. Of late he had developed a tremor of his hands but was otherwise well. The GP believed he was suffering from early Parkinson's disease.

It was obvious as the patient entered the consulting room that his gait was quite abnormal. He walked with small steps, stiffly bent forward and with little associated swinging of his arms. The medical history was that he was 52 years of age and worked as a supervisor in a store. He had come to England as a young man from Southern China. He had been generally healthy throughout his life though he suffered a severe road traffic accident in his twenties with a head injury with loss of consciousness.

His symptoms had come on gradually over about 6 months, and had been commented upon by his wife and by colleagues at work. He was finding it increasingly difficult to get around, and his handwriting had changed for the worse. Over the past few months he had noticed he had a tremor of his hand - the right more than the left. He denied ever taking recreational drugs and did not smoke cigarettes. He had taken very few prescription drugs, just the occasional course of antibiotics for chest infections and anti-inflammatories for backache.

Talking to him, Dr Starling noted the rather slow tremor of his right hand and his rather expressionless face. On examination his arms and legs were rather stiff and his tendon reflexes were brisk, but he was otherwise physically normal. The features were strongly suggestive of Parkinson's Disease but he wondered whether the past history of head injury was relevant.

He explained his thinking to the patient.

'Yes, Dr Martin say the same.'

'Yes, I don't think there can be much doubt about the diagnosis. You will probably need drug treatment in due course, but since none of the treatments are without side effects I don't advise we start now.'

135

'Actually doctor I think I'm getting better anyway. I can walk better than I could a couple of weeks ago and my wife thinks the tremor is less.'

He felt like explaining that Parkinson's disease generally gets worse, though short-term improvements might be seen. Instead he asked: 'Have you had any treatment?'

'You would probably not approve, Doctor, but my wife persuaded me to go to a Chinese herbalist.'

'And what did he do?'

'He gave me acupuncture around my head and he gave me some Chinese medicine.'

'Well, let's hope it continues to make you better.'

'You don't object, Doctor?'

'I might if I thought it harmful or dangerous, but acupuncture is harmless and sometimes helps people. Basically if you want to try traditional medicine you are free to do so. A lot of people swear by traditional cures. So I hope you continue to improve. Perhaps I could see you again in two month's time.'

Dr Starling reflected that many people believed in traditional cures and often found them useful. For himself he was sceptical as were most doctors brought up on science based medicine, and evidence based treatments, but he knew that the placebo effect was important.

So it was with considerable astonishment that he observed the condition of his patient at his next appointment. The patient came in, walking quite normally. His face which previously was mask-like was now normally animated, and the tremor had disappeared.

'I much better now, Doctor. I think I'm normal now.'

'That's remarkable. What happened?'

'I carried on with Chinese medicine with acupuncture every week and taking herbs every day. I just gradually got better.'

'Recovery like this is very unusual.'

Dr Starling had never seen such a development where the diagnosis had been so clear-cut.

'You don't know what was in the medicine he gave you.'

'I think it's a secret, Doctor. He train in China. Maybe he don't know himself. China has cures for all diseases. They are very advanced.'

'So it seems. Do you know whether he has treated anyone else?'

'A lot of people are getting treated now. You see when I got better my wife told her friends, and soon everyone knows about my cure. Now we know three other Chinese people whose Parkinson's Disease got better.'

'That's quite amazing!'

'Yer, he pretty smart fellow!'

'I am very curious about this, Mr Chen. I can't say I have ever seen such a complete recovery even using modern Western medicines that have been shown in scientific studies to be effective.'

'They say Chinese medicines very effective, Doctor. They've been around for thousands of years. I don't know for myself, but every Chinese person believes in them.'

That was clear. It was often difficult to persuade oriental patients to take Western medicine. Often they only went to their GP when their traditional medicines had failed to deal with the problem. Sometimes the delay meant it was too late. Other times they would agree to take Western medicine but would stop them prematurely, often at the advice of a relative or friend.

'Perhaps you could tell me where this healer works.'

'You plan to send patients to him? Seems like a good idea.'

'No, I'm afraid the rules prevent me from doing that, but I would be very interested in knowing what he has given you.'

'He won't tell you.'

'None the less I might gain a little insight, or perhaps I might be able to persuade him to keep detailed records of the patients' conditions.'

'Best of luck, but he speaks only bit English. He has shop on the High Street in Biston. You can't miss it.'

But Dr Starling decided to sit on the problem. The following week he was eating lunch in the canteen when he was joined at his table by Dr Williams, the visiting neurologist. He decided to pick his brains.

'Alan, I have recently had the strangest case, very much in your territory.' He described the problem. 'I'm really puzzled. I've never seen anything like it.'

'It's certainly very unusual. Early on the symptoms can fluctuate, but they don't disappear. I suppose he could have been taking a drug that can cause Parkinsonism and then stopped it.'

'Yes, I thought of that but he was adamant that he hadn't been on any drugs. The only possible causative factor was his head injury years ago.'

'But that's not likely to resolve whatever treatment he has. And you are completely happy with your diagnosis?'

'Yes, completely. It was not a busy clinic and I had plenty of time to take a full history and to examine him thoroughly. I had no doubt what I was looking at, and I am equally confident that he absolutely had no Parkinsonian features when I saw him the second time. As you can imagine I was very surprised at the transformation so I looked extremely carefully for any residual signs of the disease. There were absolutely none.'

'That really is very surprising. I can't say I have an explanation.'

'And I'm told we aren't going to get anything out of the Chinese herbalist.'

'So I'd better be on the look-out for more miracle cures.'

Dr Starling had given Mr Chen a three month follow-up appointment. He was fascinated by what had happened and eagerly anticipated seeing his patient when he saw his name on the clinic list. To his surprise, on this occasion the patient attended with his English wife. As was his habit, Dr Starling closely observed Mr Chen's movement as he came in and sat down. He seemed to move normally.

'How are you?' he asked.

'No problem, Doc.'

'No return of the tremor or the movement difficulties?'

'Nothing at all, Doc. I think I'm cured.'

'That's certainly the way it looks. It's an excellent outcome, and not what I expected.'

'You not used to seeing how Chinese medicine works. Much better, I think than your Western meds.'

'Well, that's certainly the way it looks. Since I last saw you I had the opportunity to discuss your case with Dr Williams, the nerve specialist who does a clinic here. He was very interested, but had no explanation. The only thing he wondered about was whether you had been taking a drug that can cause these symptoms - some drugs used for mental illness can cause Parkinson-like symptoms. But I remember I asked you about medication and you told me you hadn't been taking anything.'

'That's right, Doc. Dr Martin can tell you that. I take nothing.'

'But what about those pills from your Chinese medicine man?' asked his wife. 'You take a lot of his pills and potions.'

'They only herbs. They're traditional Chinese stuff. They have no side effects. They're natural.'

'Yes, but some herbs have profound clinical effects,' said Dr Starling. 'What were you taking these medicines for?'

'Oh, I often go to see him. He give me medicine for colds or backaches. Things like that. They make me feel better.'

'Do you remember if you were taking any of these medicines when you developed the tremor and stiffness.'

'I don't think so, Doc. I'm not sure.'

'Yes you were, Vernon. I remember. You went to see him because you were anxious. Don't you remember? You couldn't sleep, and you were worrying over silly things. I told you to go to Dr Martin, but as usual you knew better and saw your mate.'

'And he gave you something?' asked Dr Starling.

'Yes Doc, I told you before. He did acupuncture. That made me feel better. He's a real expert.'

'But what about medicine? Do you remember if he gave you anything?'

'He did, Vernon. I remember. They made you quite sleepy at first, but you were a lot less anxious. I remember I was quite surprised.'

'Yer, I remember, he gave me some very strong herbs. Nearly knocked me out, but made me better.'

'When was this?' asked Dr Starling. 'Was it before you saw me the first time?'

'About six months ago I think.'

'No, Vernon, it was before that. It was just before Christmas. Don't you remember? You were too drowsy to put up the tree, and David had to do it.'

'So that was about six months before you saw me?'

'I guess so, Doc. Wife's alway right.'

'And then you began to have difficulty moving around, you got the tremor, while you were taking these herbs?'

'Yes, Doc.'

'So, you went back to see your Chinese medicine man, and what did he say?'

'He say he understand problem. He said he know how to cure with special medicine. He says it's very expensive but it will make me better. So I brought new medicine. Cost me £200.'

'And I said it was a waste of money,' said his wife.

'And what about the original tablets you were taking?'

'He told me to stop, so I did.'

'I see,' said Dr Starling, but in truth he didn't. Surely he would have heard of a herb that could cause Parkinsonism, or come to that, one that could cure Parkinsonism. 'Mr Chen, do you have one of these tablets left that you could let me have for analysis?'

'You want to steal his secret?'

'You shouldn't say that to the doctor, Vernon. He's trying to understand what's happened to you. He's just doing his job.' She turned to Dr Starling. 'You really should look into this, Doctor. I've heard all kinds of stories from Chinese relatives about what goes into these pills. I've heard they adulterate pills with steroids, anti inflammatories and antibiotics. I'm sure he has some pills left.'

'Could you bring them to my office and I'll see if I can get them analysed?'

'He's not going to be pleased with you.'

'Maybe not, but I need to know what's going on. It would be best if we keep this to ourselves. I promise you I will not steal his secret cure, if there is one. I'll send the tablets to the lab and when I have the results I'll give you a ring and we can discuss the findings.'

Three days later, the plot took another twist when Dr Starling received a call from Dr Williams, the neurologist.

'Tom, I'm phoning about that case you told me about a few months ago over lunch - the man with Parkinsonism who spontaneously recovered.'

'Ah yes, I saw him a few days ago. He remains well without any sign of the condition.'

'I seem to remember you told me he was a Chinaman.'

'That's right, though he's been in the UK for decades.'

'Well, Tom, the thing is that over the past couple of weeks I have seen four Chinese people - three men and a woman, all with recent onset Parkinsonism, and in two cases, by the time I saw them, they seemed to be getting better. We have very few Chinese people around here, and Parkinsonism isn't that common, so I'm very puzzled.'

'Well Alan, I think I've made a little progress on my case. Though my patient wasn't taking any medication prescribed by his GP, he was taking pills for anxiety from a Chinese herbalist in Biston. When he began to develop Parkinsonism this herbalist told him to stop the original pills and then charged him a small fortune for another pill to make him better. Now, thanks to his wife I have samples of both of these meds and I've sent them to our Chemical Pathology Lab for analysis.

It was four days later that the hospital's chemical pathologist, Dr O'Leary, phoned Dr Starling.

'I'm sorry it took so long Tom, but I did a few tests in addition to our usual toxicologic screen. The tablet you labelled '2'...'

'That's the one he was taking when his Parkinsonism recovered.'

'Well, that's a blessed miracle to be sure. We couldn't detect any pharmacological active substance. It's just lactose.'

'Good heavens! The patient was charged £200 for a supply of those!'

'A fellow has to make a living, I suppose. The other tablet, the one you labelled '1' was more interesting. Chromatography showed a number of alkaloids, many of which I can't identify, but they included low level nicotine and morphine, but there was a large peak of something else. We can't identify it precisely but

I'm pretty sure it's something related to Stemetil - prochlorperazine. It's certainly in that class of drugs.'

'Is that all?'

'I'm pretty sure, yes.'

Dr Starling felt let down. Stemetil was used to alleviate nausea. You could buy it over the counter. It was harmless.

'I don't think that's going to do him much harm.'

'I don't know, Tom, there's a lot of the stuff there.'

'How much do you think?'

'Roughly 50mg in one tablet.'

'Wow! That's about ten times the usual dose.'

'Exactly! I looked it up. Drugs of this class are still occasionally used as antipsychotics - in schizophrenia and the like, but their use is limited by their extrapyramidal side effects.'

'Of course!' A very large penny dropped. 'And those effects include Parkinsonism.'

'Quite right! That's what the web-site says. Not only that, if you stop the drug the patient generally gets better.'

'My God!' said Tom Starling as the truth sunk in. 'What a racket! You poison your patient and then charge them through the nose to make them better, when all you have really done is to stop poisoning them.'

'What are you going to do about it?'

'I have to inform the authorities - the Community Physician. He'll have to deal with it. I suppose this is a criminal matter.'

Dr Starling had promised to tell his patient the results of the analysis, but he spoke to his Public Health colleague first.

'Well, thank you for informing us about this, Dr Starling. We've had our suspicions about this guy, and have suspected he adulterates his preparations with steroids, but the Chinese community is pretty reluctant to cooperate. We've had a couple of reports from GPs with their suspicions, but no proof. Perhaps you could give us something in writing - an email will do, and we'll get the police involved. This is really quite a serious offense, so we are grateful for your investigation. Of course we'll need a statement from your Chemical Pathologist.'

The next day he phoned Mr Chen and told him the findings.

'I think it's wrong Doc.'

'What's wrong?'

'I think your analysis is wrong. This herb man. He's from China. He's a good man and very clever. He too good for your English medicine. You frightened he take your business. That's why he's gone.'

'He's gone?'

'Yes, Doc. He shut up shop a couple of days ago. I think he may have gone back to China.'

He should have expected this. He had no doubt his patient had told the herbalist of his investigation. He supposed that he hadn't returned to China, but that this lucrative scam would be played out amongst Chinese communities elsewhere in England, and that the Chinese faith in their traditional medical methods would remain as strong as ever.

He Gets it Wrong

It was a busy clinic. His clinics were usually busy, at least in part because he liked to pass the time of day with his patients, and often because he was teaching. The patients were shared out, pretty much at random between himself and his registrar who worked in the adjacent room. The registrar could come through to discuss problems with him, and sometimes he would go through to see one of the registrar's patients. The patients were from two sources; those referred to him by local GPs and patients who had been under his care in the wards and were being followed up after discharge. Most patients had just one or two clinic visits, but some, with chronic problems requiring specialist input, were regular attenders who he had known for years.

He had seen a couple of newly referred patients and a couple of follow-ups. His next patient was a man in his mid-fifties who he recognised. He had been in the ward a couple of months before and this was his third follow-up visit. The Registrar had seen him previously and had adjusted the doses of his diuretics (to aid the kidneys in excreting salt and water) and statins (to lower blood cholesterol). Dr Starling patiently looked through the notes, reviewed the drugs and blood results. The ECG taken on the last visit showed the pattern of a healing myocardial infarct (heart attack). He asked the patient how he was.

'I'm doing fine, doctor.'

'Taking all the tablets?'

'Yes, Doctor.'

'No problems with them?'

'No, Doctor.'

He was scribbling a brief note when he noticed the patient's weight. All the patients were weighed by the nurse when they arrived in his clinic.

'I see you've lost some weight, Mr Clark.'

'That's what the nurse said, Doctor.'

He noted that the patient had stopped smoking cigarettes after his heart attack. In his experience people usually put on weight after they stopped.

'Maybe it's a mistake.'

'No, Doctor, she checked it.'

'You're eating okay?'

'Fine, Doctor.'

'No problems with your stomach or bowels?'

'No, Doctor.'

'No cough?'

'Well, a bit of a cough over the past couple of weeks.'

'Coughing anything up?'

'No, Doctor.'

'How's the breathing.'

'It's okay, Doctor, but not as good as it used to be.'

'I guess I better have a look at you.'

The patient stripped to the waist and got onto the couch. Dr Starling felt the abdomen and then listened to the chest. There were some definite crackly noises over the right lung.

'I'd like you to go down and have a chest X-ray, Mr Clark and perhaps you will bring it back and I'll have a look at it.'

The patient left and Dr Starling saw his next patient.

Half an hour later the nurse said Mr Clark was back and the nurse brought the X-ray film in for Dr Starling to view. To his surprise there was an area of shadowing over the upper part of the right lung. The appearances were suggestive of acute pulmonary tuberculosis. He found the packet of his previous films and examined one taken when he had been an in-patient. The shadowing was definitely new, and this could explain the weight loss. He called the patient back in and explained that he would have to do more tests, and made an appointment to see him again in two week's time.

The following Wednesday afternoon Dr Starling was in the Minor Ops Theatre to do his bronchoscopy list. Bronchoscopy was a technique whereby the doctor could examine the bronchial tree using a flexible fibrescope inserted through the nose and larynx under local anaesthetic. It was particularly important in investigating lung cancer, but was useful in understanding many other problems. Dr Starling had added Mr Clark to the list in order to investigate this new shadowing on his chest X-ray. He suspected tuberculosis, but to prove the diagnosis he had to find

145

the organism, the tubercle bacillus. Usually this was obtained from the patient's sputum, but Mr Clark just had a dry cough. Dr Starling planned to wash some saline into the affected area of the lung and suck some back. Hopefully they would contain bacteria that could be cultured.

The first case done, they brought in Mr Clark. Dr Starling explained what he wanted to do and checked that the consent form had been signed. Then he began by anaesthetising the patient's nose and throat with a local anaesthetic spray.

'We'll allow a few minutes for that to take.'

'Do we have his X-rays, Sister?'

She gave him a withering 'I'm not your hand-maiden' look and pointed to the table.

He took out the top film, checked the date and put it on the light box. To his surprise the film was clear. He couldn't see the area of abnormal shadowing that he had noticed in clinic. There were other films in the folder, but they were older. None of them showed shadows in the right upper zone of the lung. The patient's case notes were on the end of the trolley. He opened them and then realised what had happened.

It was two days later and the medical staff had gathered in the Education Centre for the weekly clinical and audit meeting. Dr Findlay had prepared a case presentation about Crohn's disease, but Dr Starling pulled rank and started the meeting with a short presentation of his own.

'I would like to present two patients who were seen in this week's outpatient clinic. One was seen by myself, the other by my registrar, Peter Broom. The patient that I saw, a Mr Charles Clark aged 53. He had been in the ward with a heart attack two months previously. He made a satisfactory recovery, though he did have a little fluid retention requiring diuretics. But the thing that struck me when I opened his notes was that he had lost 4 Kg weight. It wasn't clear why. He was eating well and had no digestive problems, but he did have a bit of a cough. When I listened to his chest I heard crackles over his right upper chest, so I sent him for a chest film. This is the film. Robert, perhaps you could come up and tell us what it shows.

Robert scrutinised the film. This is a PA chest radiograph of Mr Charles Clark dated 5/10/95. The film is well centred and decently penetrated. The only abnormality I can see is an area of opacification in the upper part of the right lung.'

'Excellent! Now I don't want to labour this as Dr Findlay has a presentation to give, but the patchy nature of this shadowing and its distribution is very suggestive of tuberculosis.'

The other patient I want to tell you about, the one seen by my registrar was being followed up for tuberculosis. Do you remember the case, Peter?'

'Yes, there was a man like you describe. I can't remember his name, but he was doing very well. His cough had cleared and he had put on weight. Despite that I ordered a chest film which showed a really good improvement.'

'Did it still show any shadowing?'

'I don't think so.'

'And did that strike you as strange?'

'I suppose it did a bit, but I haven't seen much Tb.'

'It is decidedly unusual.'

He put the film on the light box.

'Before I ask Jane to come and describe the film, has anyone got an explanation for how one patient lost weight and seemed to have developed Tb while another put on weight with an improving X-ray appearance.'

'Could the first man have caught Tb from the second man when they were both in hospital?'

'I suppose that could have happened, Tony, but it didn't. Any other thoughts? No? In that case, Jane please come up and describe the film for us.'

'This is a PA Chest radiograph of Mr Charles Clark taken on 5/10/95. It is well centred and penetrated. The mediastinal contour shows slight cardiomegaly. The diaphragmatic shadows are in the normal position, and the lung fields are clear.'

'Excellent description, Jane. I don't disagree with your findings. Have you any thoughts to clarify the situation?' Jane stared at the film and shook her head. Dr Starling turned to the audience 'Anyone?'

'It's the same patient!' said an SHO sitting at the front.'

'That can hardly be right. What do you mean?.

147

'The two films have the same name - Charles Clark.'

'Well observed, Steve.'

'So their X-rays got swapped in Radiography,' said Jane.

'No, they're the correct films. Swapping the films does not explain the weight change.'

'You had the wrong notes!' said Robert.

'That's it! Not only were the patient's names the same, their hospital numbers were similar. The nurse weighed and brought the patient in with the wrong set of notes. I had a Charles Clark with known Tb, but the notes said he was Charles Clark recovering from a MI. Peter had the notes of my patient and therefore thought he was looking at someone with Tb but in fact his Charles Clark was recovering from an MI.

The message, obviously, is that you have to check that the notes and the patient match up. It's not usually a problem, but with common names like Smith, Jones, Brown, Green, and as in this case, Clark, you have to be more careful. The clinic nurse may have made the primary mistake, but Peter and I should not have been fooled.

'Now, just to complete matters, the Charles Clark recovering from a heart attack in fact had not lost weight and his chest film shows a slight reduction in heart size in line with his diuretic treatment. So that's fine. It's just as well I realised my mistake before I bronchoscoped him. The other Charles Clark, with Tb had put on a little weight and his chest film shows perhaps a little clearing of the Tb shadows, more or less as one might expect.'

Living with Disability

Asthma and Psychology

Roger Altounyan would often give talks about what it was like to live with asthma. Asthma is now almost universally viewed as a physical disorder, usually due to allergy, but until quite recently it was often thought to be a psychosomatic condition, where the mind somehow narrows the bronchi. Roger used to describe and illustrate a consultation he had with a GP when he had an asthma attack as a medical student.

'Well, what is the trouble, young man?'

'(gasp) My asthma is playing up.'

'I see.' The doctor turned away and appeared to be rummaging in a drawer of his desk. Suddenly he looked up, glared at Roger and brought his hand down on the desk with enormous force

CRASH!!

'STOP IT AT ONCE!' he shouted.

Needless to say, Roger illustrated this encounter with maximum decibel sound effects, always guaranteed to wake up his audience!

If only understanding and treating asthma was that easy!

The idea that asthma was a psychological condition persisted and was still mainstream when I was a medical student. We were taught by Dr Hugh Jolly on my Paediatric attachment, that one cause of childhood asthma was a dysfunctional relationship between mother and child. Mum's fault again! Jolly was a great communicator, and was often on the radio on the Jimmy Young Show dispensing wisdom about child rearing, like a British Dr Spock.

The evidence for this strange hypothesis was that if a child with poorly controlled asthma was admitted to hospital, the asthma would invariably improve, and this improvement was put down to separating mother from child. Later it was shown, however, that adult asthma also improves similarly during a prolonged stay in hospital without any change in treatment. The reason for this turns out to be nothing to do with psychology, or bad parenting, but was connected with allergy. The principal cause of the allergy that causes asthma is house dust, and specifically the protein of the house-dust mites that live in our bedding and carpets. By contrast to our mite infested homes, hospitals and hospital beds are pretty well devoid of house dust and mites. Stop the allergic stimulation and you stop the asthma!

Well, well, not Mum's fault after all! Or maybe you think she should have been more thorough with her dusting? Actually to rid the domestic environment of house-dust mites is close to impossible. Hospital beds have rubber covered mattresses and the wards don't have carpets or soft furnishings to harbour mites. You can vacuum a regular mattress until you are blue in the face, and hardly dent its massive mite population!

The Carer

It had been another tough day. They were more-or-less all tough days. She had showered him and put him to bed. It was only 9 pm and she felt like bed herself. It was difficult to take, but take it she had to. She was the devoted wife of an invalid. It was just her bad luck. It had been the same with her old father after her mother had died and he had suffered a stroke. She was the oldest and the only one still at home. There was nothing for it. She had got on with it with little complaint, and little help from her siblings. They had their excuses. She could find none.

She would usually flop in front of the TV with a glass of Pinot grigio but that evening she decided to give her sister a ring. Since her marriage to Gerald she had moved away from the London suburb where she had grown up, but Christine still lived there, or more exactly she had returned there from a spell in Australia. She was married and had two kids. Isobel envied her sister's normal, rich, fulfilling life. Christine envied Isobel's wealth and large house.

'Isobel! How lovely to hear from you! How are you?'

'Not so bad, Chris. Thought I'd catch up with your news.'

'How's Gerald?'

'No better, but no worse. At least he got over his last relapse without much deterioration.'

'He's still able to get about?'

'Mainly in his wheelchair, but he can walk a little with crutches.'

'He's bearing up?'

'Yes, I suppose so, considering everything. He's usually quite cheerful. He's not so good when he's in pain with the spasms, but the painkillers help. His worst problem is fatigue. The doctors say it's part of the disease.'

'And what about you? Are you coping?'

'Just about. We have a girl who comes in 6 hours a day and generally helps around the house. Otherwise I do everything.'

You sound tired, Isobel.'

'Oh, do I?'

'You do. Very tired.'

'It's been a long day. We had a trip to the hospital this morning, and nowadays that's quite an expedition. Then I did most of the work for lunch and supper, and then I put him to bed. It's good to be active. I doubt you have it easy with your two.'

'I'm sure you need a break, Isobel. When did you get away last?'

'I can't remember. At least a couple of years, I suppose. Gerald's not too keen. He was always a home-body, even before he got disabled.'

'Why don't you get away without him?'

'I'm not sure I would enjoy that even if it were possible to arrange.'

'I know what! Come down here! Come and stay with us. I'm sure you'd like to renew your acquaintance with your old hometown. There must be people you could catch up with. See how the old place has developed.'

'That would be really nice, Christine, but I don't think you have room.'

'We'll find space, Isobel. The kids can double-up in Jamie's room and you can have the little bedroom. Not up to your palatial standards, of course Sis, but cosy.'

'That's very kind of you. You know, a few days away could make all the difference. I certainly need a break, and to go back home would be lovely. I'll think about it, I promise and see if I can make the necessary arrangements. I'm afraid Gerald won't like it.'

'He'll have to lump it! He demands too much of you. It should be him that's suggesting you have a holiday, not me.'

So it was that three weeks later that, after what had seemed to be a gargantuan act of organisation, Isobel anxiously and apologetically kissed her sullen husband on the cheek, gave the maid some final instructions and stepped out of the front door and into the waiting taxi. On the way to the station her mind raced over the various concerns she had to deal with. Did the maid know about his soft-boiled eggs? Would the nurse know where to find his injection and remember to give it on Tuesday? Had she left the GP's number?

But by the time she was standing on the platform her worries began to recede. She knew she had been very thorough. She had typed out sheets of notes for the maid and the nurse. They both had her contact number, as did Gerald. She had met the nurse and had confidence in her.

Soon she was speeding through the countryside. The sun was streaming through the windows on the opposite side of the carriage. She had a double seat to herself and a book to read. She leant back and stretched out her legs. Ahead of her was a week of freedom when, more or less, she could do exactly what she wished. She had already arranged to meet up with a couple of old friends. It would be good to spend time with her sister and to get to know her nephew and niece.

Two hours later she was in a taxi to her sister's house, driving through the familiar but unfamiliar streets of the town she grew up in and had barely left for the first 20 years of her life. Christine's house was on a pleasant tree-lined road, not too far from where they had grown up. Isobel got out of the taxi and took a deep breath. It was good to be back.

She had got used to the size of the mansion she lived in with Gerald, so Christine's place seemed tiny and cramped, but her little bedroom was fine. She unpacked her things, and finding her mobile in her bag she phoned home. The maid answered.

'Hello, Mary. It's me. Is everything okay?'

'Of course it's okay, Mrs Johnson. You needn't worry, Mr Johnson's fine. The nurse phoned and she'll be here at five.'

'I just wanted to make sure.'

'There's no need. We can always phone you if need be, we'll try not to. You need to have a proper break, Mrs Johnson.'

They had a simple lunch of cold meat and salad at the kitchen table overlooking Christine's neat, pretty garden. Christine talked about her kids and her husband, Jon. They all seemed to be happy and successful. Jamie was a bit slow with reading, but was a smart decent boy, and her daughter Kate was very keen on sport. Jon, who was Australian was happy working in the City and was doing well. Christine had a part-time job in a local insurance office.

'Isobel, I had to do a couple of hours in the office this morning, so before the kids come home I need to do some grocery shopping. Would you like to come with me?'

'If you don't mind, Christine after being cooped up on the train, I fancy a bit of fresh air. I think I'll go for a wander around these old streets and refamiliarise myself with the area.'

The town had not changed much. The houses, garden, roads were more or less the same, but it was strange and rather disconcerting to realise that she no longer belonged there. No one knew her. Her past was irrelevant. She had walked for an hour before she saw anyone she recognised, and now about one in ten faces were brown or black. It seemed the mother had forgotten her child, and had adopted some new ones. She walked to the top of the hill and then turned and made her way down Queens Road, looking at the shops, most of which had changed hands. The tobacconist had become a nail bar. The paper shop was a Tandorri restaurant. Further down the Wesleyan Methodist church had gone and in its place a small but incongruent office block.

At least the baker's was still there, more or less as she remembered it. She would go in there with her mother to buy a loaf and if she was lucky her mother would let her choose a cake. On impulse, she found herself pushing open the door, and ringing the very familiar bell, and immediately like Pavlov's dogs she was salivating. The cakes looked a bit up market from what she remembered, and at one end there were now a couple of small tables and chairs.

There was a man in front of her buying buns, chatting and laughing with the girl behind the counter. His voice was familiar. He turned to leave.

'Isobel! Good Heavens!'

For a second she didn't recognise him. His hair had receded, he had put on a little weight and had grown a small moustache. 'Michael!' Strangely, coming here with all her worries and arrangements, she had hardly given him a thought. She had no reason to expect that he still lived here, so her surprise was complete.

'Fancy meeting you, Michael! I only came in out of nostalgia for my lost youth, and cake of course.'

'Well, I'm glad you did! Well well well!' He smiled broadly and she felt he would have hugged her had he not got a bag of cakes in one hand and a briefcase in the other.

'I never dreamed I would see you. It's been a long time, Michael.'

'I'd love to have a chat. Perhaps we could have a cup of tea.' He waved in the direction of the tables. 'Tracy, are we too late for a pot of tea?'

'Well, yes Mr Evans, you are, but as I can see you've just met an old friend, I'm sure I can bend the rules.'

So they shared the stories of their lives since they had lost touch. He had married Molly, who she remembered. She thought he could have done better than that. He had known about Gerald, but not that he had developed multiple sclerosis.

'That's really bad luck, Isobel. It must be so hard.'

'I try to be philosophical. These things happen. It's not his fault, but our life is very restricted, and most of the time I am a nursemaid or a housekeeper. Not quite how a girl wants to spend her days.'

'Didn't he have a bit of a limp when you first met him?'

'Yes, a horse-riding accident, but it didn't stop him getting around or doing all the normal things.'

'But you haven't had kids?'

'No, we wanted to get to know each other for a couple of years before taking the plunge, but no sooner had we decided to try and he fell ill with MS. After that it seemed crazy to start a family.'

'I'm sorry. Molly and I were a little more impetuous. She was three months pregnant when we got married. We had just got back from our honeymoon and she had a miscarriage. Since then she hasn't managed to conceive.'

Isobel shook her head. 'That's very sad. Poor you.' And she found herself reaching across and squeezing his hand. He laid his other hand on top of hers.' She felt like crying.

'Look Isobel, I have to get back now, but I would really like it if we could meet up one evening and spend time together. Are you here for long?'

'Just a week.'

'Maybe I could phone you?'

'I'd rather you didn't. Gerald scrutinises my phone. He's a bit of a controller. I'm sure he remembers that you and I were close in the distant past. Can't we arrange something now?'

'Why not? Let me think. I could make it on Tuesday evening, but no, I have a better plan. I'm due to go on a business trip on Wednesday. I'll cancel it, then we could have more time.'

'Where shall we meet?'

I could pick you up from your sister's.'

'No, I would rather we were a little more discreet.'

'Of course. How about here? Not too far to walk?'

'Fine.'

'Seven-thirty Wednesday?'

'I'll look forward to it.'

And she did. It was amazing! She was like a teenager again, walking on air. She told herself it was nothing. Just an old friend, but for a brief moment she could have fun, she could again be able to feel desire and to sense that she was desired. So it was a more lighthearted, happier Isobel who arrived back at her sister's house.

'What's with you?' asked Christine. 'You look as if you've won the lottery.'

'No, I've just been enjoying a stroll down Memory Lane, but so much has changed.'

'Yes I noticed that when I came back from Australia, but now nothing seems to change. It's a really dozy place.'

The kids were back from school and she enjoyed playing aunt. She had bought each of them a small present and listened to them telling her about school and their friends. After tea, when Jon came home, the three of them shared a bottle of wine over the kitchen table while the children watched TV. She had always liked Jon. He was boyishly uncomplicated and quite amusing. She thought they were well suited and seemed happy in each other's company. But she found it difficult to really get into the conversation. Her mind kept flitting off and enjoying itself in happy contemplation. Suddenly her sister was asking her something. She hadn't heard the question or what had led up to it.

'Hey, Isobel! Where are you?'

'Oh sorry!'

'Off with the fairies.'

'I'm a little worried about Gerald,' she lied. 'I'm wondering whether I should call the nurse.'

'Oh yes?'

'Actually Jon, Christine, I'm really quite tired after the journey and all that. If you don't mind, I think I'll go to bed.'

'So early?' Her sister looked at her quizzically. 'Are you sure you're alright?'

'I'm fine. Just tired.'

She lay on her bed, looked at her phone, and reflected that for once in her life she had no immediate responsibilities, and something pleasant or even exciting to look forward to. She sort of knew in her heart that Michael would prove a disappointment. He would no doubt bore her, and she was uncomfortable with the thought that she was, even if trivially, encouraging him to cheat on his wife.

The following day Christine had the day off and drove her to Brent Cross for shopping. Gerald gave her a decent allowance that she usually didn't spend. She had never been as obsessed with clothes as her sister, and anyway she usually had little need for new outfits. They never went anywhere. She had become depressingly beige but now she browsed the clothes racks with renewed interest.

'Okay Christine, here's a project. I'm free for a few days. I want to feel free and look my best. I want something bright. Something to make the most of my fading looks.'

'What's got into you? You almost seem like a different woman since yesterday.'

'It's such a relief to be away.'

'Yes? Right. I see, but you don't just need new clothes, you need new makeup, a better hairdo, and your nails could do with attention.'

So they set to. Two hours later they were ready for lunch having purchased several tops, two skirts and a dress that Isobel was sure was too clinging and young.

'No, it's fantastic. You'll really turn heads in that!' Her sister giggled.

Actually she only wanted to turn one head.

After lunch they continued with enthusiasm. She allowed Gerald to buy her sister an expensive dress. She had her hair cut a good deal shorter than was her habit.

'It takes years off you!'

They decided to forgo the nail bar and bought her a pair of shoes. The heels were a good inch higher than her norm.

'I don't think I've worn anything this high for a decade or more.'

'They'll look great!'

'Make me look like a slut, rather.'

'Better a slut than a frump. At least sluts have fun.'

'I think they come to a sticky end.'

That evening she phoned Gerald.

'How are things?'

'I don't like the nurse you organised.'

'What's wrong with her?'

'She's bossy, ugly and fat.'

'All nurses are bossy. For the rest I didn't think you cared.'

'Can you come home sooner. I need you.'

'No Gerald, we agreed. I need a break.'

'I wouldn't mind one myself.'

'Well maybe we'll go away after I'm back, but usually when I suggest a trip you don't want to go.'

The following day she donned a selection of her new clothes, put on her high heels, ventured out and caught the underground to London. She hadn't thought of what she would do or where she would go. The possibilities were endless. She was not completely shopped out and Oxford Street was a possibility. To wander in a park would be relaxing. Then she thought of the Tate. She loved art galleries but she hadn't been to one for years. Soon she was on the Tube to Pimlico, observing, with pleasure, that men were gazing at her more intently than she was used to. She felt pretty and confident.

Tate Britain was wonderful - more so than she remembered. The Bacons were horrible, if memorable. She stood in front of the Singer Sargent of the little girl in a white smock with white lilies and marvelled, She loved the Lowrys and the Hockneys. She went to the cafeteria for lunch and then took the Tube to St James' Park. She enjoyed the flowers and sat for a long time watching the ducks and the endless stream of people. Then she found a sunny spot and lay down on the warm grass and listened to the sounds of the great city.

In the morning her sister asked her to give the kids their tea.

'I'll be home a little late.'

'No problem. What do they eat?'

'Oh, something simple. You'll probably need to go to Waitrose. Have a look in the freezer.'

'Hamburger and oven chips?'

'You'll be a popular aunt!'

'I'll be going out later.'

'Really? Where to?'

'Oh, nowhere much, just supper with an old friend.'

'What kind of old friend?'

'I thought you might ask me that.'

'So you have a prepared answer?'

'Not really. It's just someone I knew when I lived here, who I met by sheer chance in the Bakers.'

'It, you say. Gender undetermined? Your transsexual friend, is it? A hermaphrodite of your acquaintance?'

'That's about it. And remember, little sister, that I am a very respectable married lady.'

'Well, let's hope you bear that in mind too and that you manage to stay that way.'

She went for a walk over the railway line and across the meadows to the cricket field. There was a bench facing the wicket where she and Michael had snogged as teenagers. He was very handsome but a bit full of himself, which she didn't like. She thought of her date. Her silly excitement had evaporated and been replaced by apprehension. It was bound to be a disappointment. There was something lacking in him when they

160

were young, and though he had been very keen on her, she had not allowed their friendship to progress. Maybe she had been too choosy, but a life with Micheal would have turned out better than her life with Gerald. Her decision to marry Gerald had seemed wise at the time, and at first they had been happy until his illness had intervened.

Then she walked through the strip of oak woods and down the hill to the lake where sometimes they had hired rowing boats. It seemed like a long time ago. Then she was free. Now she wasn't.

She made her way back, getting a few things at Waitrose on the way, and as predicted the tea she provided for her nephew and niece was greatly appreciated. When they had finished she sent them off to do their homework while she went upstairs and got ready. She knew her sister would tease her and draw conclusions, but she put on the 'slut' dress. With a light jacket over it, she looked respectable. She regretted that she had not bought a matching handbag.

She heard her sister arriving home and went through to the bathroom, where there was a mirror and she spent a little more time and care on her face than was her usual habit. The sun had given her cheeks a healthy glow, and she agreed with her sister that her shorter hair made her look younger and almost girlish.

She crept downstairs in the hope of avoiding her sister's gaze.
'I've got a key. I don't know when I'll be back.'
'Sometime tonight I hope.'
'Of course!'
She crept out and shut the door. It wasn't just that she didn't want to be teased or asked more awkward questions, she was now feeling guilty. Whatever she might try to tell herself, she wasn't just going out with an old friend to share reminiscences and catch up on each other's lives. She was going on a date! Her invalid husband who provided for her and loved her in his own way was alone at home. She was undoubtedly cheating. She reassured herself that although she might flirt and enjoy his interest and attention she had no intention of doing anything she would regret.

A silver Mondeo was parked outside the bakers. As she approached he got out, and opened the passenger door.

'I'm glad you came,' he said. 'I wasn't sure you would.'

Seemingly he had lost some of his old cockyness.

'Of course I would come. I said I would.'

'You could have got cold feet. We are both being a little naughty.'

'Only a little,' she echoed.

'I thought we would go to the Griffin in Chingford. They have a pleasant restaurant and it's usually quiet.'

'This is where you take all your young ladies.'

'Only the nicer ones.'

'But we can go for a curry or tapas if you prefer.'

'No, it's fine, I'll go with your recommendation.'

She reckoned he had chosen the place for its cosy intimacy. It wasn't busy and that probably said a lot about the food, so she viewed the menu in the light of what was most difficult to ruin and most likely to be fresh.

'I'd go for the fillet steak if I were you,' he said, reading her mind. Then he smiled at her. 'No, it's not what you're thinking.' He was reading her mind again. 'I quite often bring my clients here. Male in the main. Doctors in the main. So this place values my custom. It makes a difference.'

'Filet steak sounds fine.'

'And they're not exactly speedy so I suggest a starter. The smoked salmon is the best bet. What about something to drink? They have a decent Malbec, if you fancy a wine. Maybe a gin and tonic?

'The wine would be enough for me, but by all means you have something else.'

'No, no! Malbec will be fine for me too.'

They talked about their lives. He worked for a large pharmaceutical company, and this involved a lot of travelling and a lot of study, but he was happy with his job. He showed real sympathy and understanding for Gerald's illness and its effect on her life. She thought he would remind her of their teenage romance and their snatched moments of passion, but he didn't. Neither did he muse on how it might have been if University had not supervened and they had not married others. He did talk about Molly and how she had thrown herself into her career when she realised they probably would not be starting a family.

'We both have our separate lives now, but we remain fond of one another. She had a lot of work friends that I have scarcely met.'

'So neither of us has the relationship that we hoped for.'

He nodded. 'But I don't complain. I don't 'what if'. I have a good life and I think Molly does too.'

They were silent for half a minute, then she smiled at him. 'There's something though that I do not understand about you. I've been puzzling about it.'

'Yes? I am an open book. Allow me to shine light where there is darkness.'

'It's not something big. It's just something I observed.'

'Well, get on with it - you've detected the fatal flaw in my character!'

'I doubt that. It's just that when you were in the baker's you bought cakes - quite a lot of them, and I wondered who they were for.'

'Oh dear! My secret is out. I am undone! My cake problem!'

'That's what I thought.'

'I'm sure you didn't. You see, Molly has a sister, Rachel who lives quite near us. She has three small children - the oldest is eight. Rachel has no husband - he left, and consequently little money. So we try to help her. I'm often round there and try to impose a semblance of order. The cakes are a reward. The oldest two have to read to me and the younger one has to paint me a picture, and if I approve, the cakes can be eaten.'

'And if you don't?'

'The cakes are still eaten, I'm afraid.'

'That's very sweet.'

'I love the kids in moderation. I suspect I make a better uncle than I would a father, I think I lack the patience.'

Then with obvious joy he told her about each of them, their interests and their foibles. He showed her pictures of them and their artwork on his phone.

'You talk almost as if you are their father.'

'Kids need a father.' He looked solemn and put his phone away.

They talked about their lives. He told her about his work and their holiday in Thailand. She talked about Gerald's illness and his disabilities. She realised, with more force than previously, just what a boring life she had. Fate had been cruel, but now at least she was on a date with a very nice man. She slipped off her jacket and noticed as his eyes flicked towards her breasts. She smiled at him, but he seemed embarrassed. She waited.

'Isobel, I had a hard time as a boy. Like my nephews and nieces, my father wasn't around. He was a philanderer, a womaniser. He did a lot of harm to us all, and when I became a man I was determined not to follow in his footsteps. I don't philander, though God knows I have plenty of opportunities in this job.'

'You're not philandering now?'

'I'm trying not to, but you are different. You're an old friend. You were my first love.'

'But we do rather seem to be on a date. This is a romantic setting, is it not?'

He nodded and looked serious again. 'I've often thought of you over the years and often regretted that things didn't work out for us. I have thought of you, even, to my shame, when I'm making love to Molly...no, sorry. I shouldn't have said that.'

'I've often thought of you too, though not quite in that context.'

Then she had an idea. 'Have we done here?'

'Well, but what's the rush? Wouldn't you like a coffee, or something?'

'I've never wanted coffee less in my whole life. Let's go! You need to take me somewhere.'

He paid up and they left. As they walked to the car she took his hand.

'So, where are we going?'

'Just drive back. I'll direct you. It needs to be a surprise.'

'A pleasant one I hope.'

'Oh, I hope so too.'

He drove. She rested back, content and excited. She rested her hand on his thigh. They drove through the dark valley, past the boating lake and up the hill. At the High Road at the top she told him to turn left. There was St John's Church and the school where she went when she was five. There were big houses.

'Okay, slow down.' Ahead the road descended steeply. 'Pull in here Michael.' It was a rough track that ran part way round the cricket field. 'I guess you know where you are. Stop here.'

They walked hand in hand along the path by the side of the field.

'I was here this afternoon. The old place hasn't changed much, and I particularly noticed that the bench is still here. I thought we should check that it is still in working order, we are, after all, on a date.'

He brushed the seat for her with his hand. They sat down and immediately she was in his arms and they were kissing, at first with tenderness and then with passion. For several minutes they said nothing. For a moment he laid a hand on her breast. Then they were sitting back, Her head on his shoulder, looking at the distant yellow lights of the High Road and the ghostly grey trees of the forest that surrounded the ground.'

'Well, good Sir, if memory serves me correctly, your kissing has improved, as has your patience, even if your moustache prickles me.'

'And you are even more gorgeous.' He kissed her again. 'Joined at the lips, weren't we in those days.'

'Oh yes, and your hands also show improvement. Much less wandering. I seem to remember spending half my time fighting you off.'

'No, I think that must have been one of your other lovers.'

'Nope, it was definitely you.'

An owl hooted and a red bus passed in the High Road on its way to London. The stars were struggling to make themselves visible against the orange glow of the sky.

'We'd better go,' she said at last. 'If I'm much later my sister will know I am a fallen woman.'

Her return to Gerald and to her humdrum lonely life was a dreadful anticlimax. Gerald seemed resentful of her brief week of freedom, or perhaps he suspected something had happened. They barely spoke. He spent his time locked in his study while she managed the house and his every need. She had few friends and rarely went anywhere that wasn't a shop or the doctors. Over the four years of their marriage Gerald had been antagonistic to any friends she brought home. He seemed jealous of any activity that was not connected to his needs and care, but now she could not settle to his restrictive regime. She had to get out. She drove to local beauty spots and went for solitary walks. She sat alone in cafes and read a book. She spent time in the local library.

She was desperate to see Michael again. They had agreed to meet when his job next took him to her part of the country. At last, after three weeks he sent her a brief text message.

'Comfort Inn, Hentington, Wed 4 after 3pm'

She texted back:

'I'll be there.'

She had to wait five days, which passed glacially slowly. Fortunately Gerald seemed to have got used to her going out more, or at least he said very little.

Hentington was twenty-five miles away, and it was a pleasant drive through the countryside. She was excited, for she was confident of his love and of her own, so she knew what was going to happen. She drove quickly and arrived at 3.15, and with some nervousness she entered the place and went to Reception. She was about to ask for him when she found him at her side. They kissed and then he led her by the hand upstairs and to his room.

They kissed some more, and then in silence they helped each other undress and then they were in bed. He was the wonderful gentle lover of her dreams, and he marvelled that a woman could be so fantastic and how he could be so lucky.

They had tea together in the little dining room and then they parted. She would have dearly loved to stay, but prudence dictated that she ought to get back and not arouse Gerald's suspicions.

As she drove back her happiness was tainted by a rising sense of guilt. She prided herself that she was a decent and trustworthy person. She thought of Gerald, stuck at home, alone and disabled. He had trusted her and she had betrayed his trust. She told herself that Gerald was selfish and was neglectful of her needs, but her sense of guilt remained and bothered her.

Over the following couple of weeks her longing was painful, and the boring restrictions of her life even more unbearable. She dreamed of being with Michael, of walking in the countryside with him, of pottering in the shops with him, of cooking him a meal and making love. Each day she checked her phone for a text from him, and at last one came, and a few days later they were again in each other's arms. If anything, their second afternoon of passion was even more wonderful than the first, as now they had more understanding of one another.

When they had done, and she was lying in the bed in naked contentment, and he was making coffee she asked him:

'Can we go out, Michael and take a stroll together?'

'No problem.'

They were in an ancient market town with its big central square and medieval church. They ambled hand in hand down the pretty streets and came to a small park.

'I only wish we could be together more,' he said.

She squeezed his hand. 'That would be nice, but I'm feeling pretty guilty about Gerald. He's a decent man, even if there's no longer much love between us. He provides for me, and I guess I should be grateful for that.'

'Do you think he suspects?'

'He shows no sign of it.'

They walked on. She had thought endlessly about it. 'From what you said about you and Molly, I guess you're quite free, but I could never leave Gerald, you know. I vowed to care for him in sickness and health. I would hate myself.' She didn't continue, but if she had she would have said that MS was a disease that disabled the sufferer over many years, but was usually slow to kill. Her thankless career as a carer was a life sentence.

Over the next two months they met on three occasions. Her love for him, her desire for the joy that he brought her grew more intense. She was becoming desperate, but what could she do?

167

She suggested she could travel down to London, allowing them to meet more frequently, but he was reluctant. She realised that increasingly she wanted him to herself. She did not like the idea of him in the same house, perhaps the same bed as Molly. She asked him to leave her, but he said that anyway they were very distant, albeit in the same house, and they no longer slept together.

Two day after their latest tryst Gerald called her into his study. He was sitting at his computer as she came in. He swivelled round and looked at her impassively.

'Isobel, I had hoped that when you started your affair that it would not last. I note that it is still continuing and it could prove embarrassing for both of us, so I have to discourage it as best I can.'

She was shocked. She sat down.

'You have nothing to say? Well, I am having your car sent back to the garage. If you need to be taken anywhere around town, and he's not otherwise occupied, Derek can chauffeur you in the company car. I've however given him strict instructions not to take you further afield without my permission. Also, I'm reducing the maid's hours so that you will have more to keep you busy. Oh yes, and I am halving your allowance.'

'You bastard!' She stormed out, slamming the door behind her.

She sent Michael a text:

'Gerald knows. I have no car. Next time pick me up from here.'

Two weeks later Michael picked her up from outside Tesco Extra, five minutes from her house. They drove to Hentington. Her passion for him was intense. She loved him and now she saw that her only hope of lasting joy was with him. After they had made love they went for a walk and then he drove them to a country inn that he knew where they had supper. Neither of them had raised the subject of their future together, and when she had mentioned her changed relationship with her husband, he

168

changed the subject. Now over their desert she could wait no longer.

'I know I have done wrong, but Gerald's actions have made me feel quite different about my responsibilities towards him.'

'I'm not surprised.'

'I said I would never leave him, but I don't think I owe him any more. Maybe he has a right to discourage me from seeing you, perhaps to punish me, but he shows me no affection. He shows me no concern for my happiness. We've not had sex for eighteen months. What I do for him could be done by a hired hand. He doesn't love me or need me.'

'I see.'

'So, what I'm saying, Michael, is that I am prepared to leave him, and I see no need to delay. We can be together, Michael!'

'Hold on! Hold on! You're rushing me. It sounds wonderful, but it's difficult.'

'What's difficult? You told me that you and Molly were distant from each other and leading separate lives.'

'That's true, but still it's difficult.'

'Are you thinking of your sister-in-law's children?'

'Certainly. They need me.'

'But there's no reason why we can't live near them so that you could see them just as much as you do now.'

'Yes, but...'

'I thought we wanted this, Michael. I thought you wanted it. I thought you loved me.'

'I do love you, and I do want to be with you, but it's not straightforward, and it needs thinking about. Molly and I may be distant, but we are still married and we are fond of one another. We are friends.'

'But you can still be friends. I don't see why if you are leading separate lives it matters if you marry someone else.'

'It's more complicated...'

There was something not quite right. Something she had not been able to put her finger on. The cakes, his devotion to the children...It came to her as a shattering revelation.

'They're your children, aren't they? You don't live with Molly, do you? You live with your sister-in-law and your three children, don't you!'

He looked down at the table and nodded. 'I didn't think you needed to know, as there was no possibility of you leaving Gerald. I wish I had told you at the beginning instead of making up stories.'

'You should have told me. I wouldn't have dreamed that I might find happiness. It's so unfair!' She began to weep.

'I'm sorry.'

'I'm sorry too.' She wiped her eyes and stood up. 'Michael, you must take me home now, and we must never meet again. I love you and it's all too painful. You must go back and at least be faithful to your sister-in-law and be a proper father to your children.'

Gerald did not comment on her late return, but she sensed quiet satisfaction in his manner. They continued to ignore each other where possible and it wasn't difficult for her to hide her misery from him. Did he know the affair was over? If he didn't she was not going to tell him. For weeks she thought her heart would break. She wanted, despite everything, to see Michael again, but she resisted the temptation to contact him. But amid her unhappiness, she had a little hope. Now she knew that she could leave Gerald. There was a possibility of another life, a better life, even if she had to live it alone. If she could divorce him she could be a rich woman.

Life had again settled in a boring pattern of routine chores. Gerald had gone out to a business meeting and she was running the vacuum cleaner around downstairs. She went into his study and began her cleaning duties. Gerald was very secretive, and she knew nothing of his business affairs apart from what he had told her. She was therefore surprised to see one of the filing cabinet drawers pulled slightly out. Usually everything was locked. She switched off the cleaner and shut the door, pulled the drawer out and looked at its contents. It all seemed to be business stuff. She then tried the top drawer, and her eyes fell on several files labelled 'Medical'. She pulled out the first of these. It contained appointment notices, letters and statements about his medical problems neatly classified by date. He had seen several doctors, including at least three neurologists. He had many appointments with the Physiotherapy Department at the local hospital. Near the beginning she found a long letter from a Neurologist in Harley Street. It was headed *Diagnosis: Multiple Sclerosis*, and started '*I saw Mr Gerald Johnson in my rooms today and discussed the above diagnosis with him. The medical history, physical examination findings and the tests I have performed all point to this as the correct diagnosis. The illness seems to have started one year ago when he developed weakness and clumsiness of his left leg. He has also had a period of blurred vision of the right....*'

Isobel looked at the date at the top. She couldn't believe her eyes.

'My God! The complete bastard!'

Her heart was beating fast. She felt faint at the enormity of what she now realised. The letter was written nearly two years before their marriage! He had known that he had MS and kept it a secret from her! He knew he was going to become disabled, but he had not told her! He had married her under false pretences!

How could he have done such a thing?

She thought quickly. What he had done was a clear ground for divorce. The letter was important. She photocopied it and put the copy back into the file. If he discovered the swap he would demand the original back and he might destroy all the evidence of what he had done. She found a couple of envelopes, and put the letter in one of them, sealed it and wrote 'Private' on the envelope. She put this in the second envelope and addressed it to her sister, adding a note: '*Dear Chris, Please put this somewhere safe for me. Love Isobel xx*'

She cleared away the cleaning things, put on her jacket and went to the post office and sent off the letter by Registered Post.

Two days later they were sitting in silence, eating lunch.

'Gerald, I've had enough. I want a divorce.'

He looked at her without expression. 'Really? But I thought your little friend had returned to the bosom of his family.'

'It's nothing to do with him. It's to do with you and me. We have neither love nor interest for one another. I have grown to hate you, and you are indifferent to me. I am basically your servant, nothing more. We have no sex life and do nothing together.'

'What are you going to do for money?'

She had only thought vaguely about how she would support herself. She had no real trade or skill, though she had done a little secretarial work before she was married.

'This is my home. I will stay here until my divorce comes through, then I will have a financial settlement on which I can live.'

'Well yes, I suppose you could do that, but it won't be easy for you. If you take that course I will immediately stop your allowance, and you will have to come to me for all expenses, and I warn you that I am unlikely to feel generous. Also, I will ensure that the process of the divorce is as protracted as possible. I have excellent lawyers, while you don't.'

'You're a bastard!'

'Yes, I suppose I am, but because I am I'll see that you take away as little money as possible from this marriage. You may think I am a rich man. In a way that is true, but the vast majority of my money is in the firm, and will not be included in any settlement. My lawyers will see to that. Of the rest, of course my financial needs will far outweigh yours. I face a life of increasing disability. To care for me will be extremely expensive. I'm afraid, dear Isobel, that by the time you have paid your lawyers you'll maybe have enough to buy a sandwich.'

-o-O-o-

For years she had been intending to go through the boxes of her father's things that had lain in the loft for years. When he had died everything was boxed up and the boxes had travelled with her to her marital home. Now she decided that this task could wait no longer. Previously she had hoped to salvage memorabilia, but now she had a far more practical mission. Her father had died in great pain from prostate cancer. The doctor had prescribed morphine a couple of months before he died. The dose was progressively raised as the cancer advanced, and as his body got used to the medication. At the end he was on the top strength morphine tablets and the highest strength morphine liquid. Of course, on his death these ought to have been returned to the chemist, but she couldn't remember that happening.

-o-O-o-

It was four weeks later that the police called. She was not surprised, and in fact had expected them earlier, and because she expected them she was prepared. She wore no makeup and her hair was a mess. She wore a black cardigan over a beige blouse, and a black skirt. They wanted to ask her some questions.

'What is this about, officer?'

The detective looked embarrassed. 'I am very sorry to bother you, Mrs Johnson in this time of sadness.' He fiddled with his notebook. 'But we have received information that shortly prior to his death, you may have had cause to harm Mr Johnson.'

'Goodness me, where did that come from?'

'Actually madam, from Mr Johnson himself. You see, three days before he passed away your late husband wrote to his solicitor stating that he suspected that you may wish to do him harm after a dispute between you. We would have acted on this earlier if we had been informed, but unfortunately the solicitor, Mr Bentley, was taking a two week holiday at the time the letter arrived at his office. When Mr Bentley returned from his vacation he saw the letter and immediately contacted us.'

'I see.'

'Do you have anything to say about this?'

'Yes, officer, quite a lot. In the first place my husband was seriously paranoid. I would never have harmed him. He was a severely disabled man who I have looked after for nearly five years.'

'Why do you think he wrote to his solicitor in this way? I mean, there must have been something that sparked such a letter.'

She didn't know what other information they had. She decided she needed to seem honest and open. 'I had told him I wanted a divorce.'

'So your relationship had broken down?'

'Yes, officer, for the past couple of years.'

'And what did Mr Johnson say when you told him you wanted a divorce?'

'He said he would make it difficult for me and that I would not get any money from him.'

'It seems to me, Mrs Johnson, that you had an excellent motive to harm your husband.'

'Kill him, you mean.'

'Er yes…'

'I suspect that would apply to many married couples, don't you think?'

The officer smiled briefly. 'Mrs Johnson, I believe your late husband was prescribed some strong painkillers by his GP a couple of weeks before his death.'

'Yes, he was prescribed a small dose of morphine to deal with painful spasms that he occasionally got.'

'And did he need to take that medication?'

'Once or twice I believe.'

'So you have most of the prescription left?'

'I believe so.'

'Would I be able to see how many tablets remain?'

'Er, yes. I think I know where they are. I had been intending to take them back to Boots. You'll excuse me for a moment.'

To her relief the bottle of liquid and the tablets were where she had last seen them in the medicine cabinet. She returned downstairs and handed them to the officer.'

'I would be grateful if I could take these away.'

'Certainly, but please give me a receipt.'

'Mrs Johnson, we know from our investigations that approximately five years ago you nursed your father through his final illness, and that during this period he was prescribed very large doses of morphine.'

'Well, well officer, you have been doing your homework!'

'The records of his prescription suggest you must have had quite a substantial amount of the drug unused. Now, there are no records of where that residue went.'

'I'm afraid I cannot help you with that. I cannot remember what happened to his unused drugs. I guess they went back to the chemist, but I'm not sure. My father's effects are up in the loft here, and you are at liberty to look through them.'

'You do not have that morphine in your possession?'

'Not knowingly.'

'And you did not administer any of it to the late Mr Johnson?'

'Of course not, officer!'

'Mrs Johnson it would save us all a great deal of time and effort if you cooperated with us a little more. It seems to us that you had the motive and means to murder your husband, Mrs Johnson. Morphine is a drug that persists in the body long after death. We can easily order the exhumation of your late husband's body, and if you administered morphine to him it will be easily and quickly detected.'

'Look Officer, there are aspects of my husband's case that I suspect you have not quite caught up with. Mr Johnson was a sick man. He was disabled with extensive brain damage. I told Dr Williams, his GP, that he had been having occasional fits at night. They were part of the illness. You can confirm that for yourself on Wikipedia. Of course you understand that it was only I that had witnessed them, but I told Dr Williams about them at least a week before my husband's sad and untimely death. Such fits are dangerous, and if stomach contents are aspirated into the lungs death may result. It was natural therefore when my husband did actually die in his sleep that the good Dr Williams concluded it was likely to be a natural death. When I requested that my husband's body be cremated, he was happy to sign the necessary forms confirming that this was not a suspicious death. One of his colleagues countersigned the form and Mr Johnson's body was duly cremated. He's right there on the mantelpiece, Officer. You are welcome to take him away and examine his ashes, but I suspect you will find no morphine in them.

My Mum

I think I had more of an orientation towards medical matters than my peers because I had a sick mother. For years she had been unable to cope running her family and home and later developed brain damage and dementia.

She suffered from severe high blood pressure, and in those days there wasn't much the doctors could do about it. At one point she was admitted to hospital for a few days. I think it was this chronic hypertension that caused widespread hardening of the arteries and subsequent brain damage.

At medical school I learnt the rule of thirds. This stated that of the total population of hypertensive people only a third are diagnosed as such, only a third of those are treated, and of those only a third of those are properly controlled (ie 1:27). I believe things are much better now with more health screening and much better drugs, saving ten of thousands each year from strokes, heart attacks and death. I guess there's still room for improvement.

But there wasn't much more that could be done for her. When I was about fifteen her gait changed and she became unsteady on her feet. She walked with short hurried steps, rather like someone with Parkinson's disease, and also like sufferers with that unfortunate condition she began to dribble. As she walked down the road to the shops she had difficulty walking straight and would tend to collide with fences and other stationary objects. Fortunately she didn't fall or hurt herself.

She also developed emotional lability - that is, with the slightest provocation she would begin to laugh or cry. This is something I have seen quite often in brain damaged people, but never have I witnessed it to such a degree. It would happen at home if, for instance, there was something emotional on the radio, but more embarrassingly would occur when we were out. So, if we were getting onto a bus she would invariably burst out laughing with the effort of climbing on board. It goes without saying that a staggering, giggling, dribbling woman was taken to be drunk. I was mortified, but I guess she was more so.

On several occasions my mother had what seemed to be small strokes. I think these must have involved the lower part of her brain - the brain-stem. She would become very dizzy and nauseated and couldn't eat or drink for days. She had to lie still in bed or she would get terrible vertigo.

Her condition slowly deteriorated and matters came to a point when it was dangerous to leave her in the house alone. By this time I had qualified as a doctor and was working on the other side of London. My younger sister was training to be a nurse and my older sister had moved to the Midlands. So my mother's last years were spent in a pleasant nursing home in the Oxfordshire countryside close to where my older sister lived. I think she was happy there.

At least she managed to outlive my father. He had moved out when I was sixteen. He had a job he loved as a High Court judge's clerk. My father was an intelligent man but had been deprived of the formal education he deserved. He was a self-educated academic and his lifelong fascination was with the law. His judge was on assize in Winchester when my father was taken ill in court. He was sent back to the Judges' Lodgings and was later found dead on the floor. He had had a heart attack. He was only 59. He was, I believe, a victim of the 20th Century pandemic of cigarette smoking. This was the year I qualified in medicine. My mother died five years later.

Love Amongst the Ruins

The Senior Physician had been a widower for a couple of years and was yet to entirely adapt to being alone. Fiona, his wife of thirty years, had died of breast cancer and he missed her dreadfully. His daughter was often around, sometimes to cook him a meal, sometimes to spend time with him, and for the first few months his friends and colleagues had rallied round and invited him out for meals and drinks. People were very kind, but the invitations had tailed off. People were generally more comfortable inviting a couple to a dinner party rather than an individual.

Of course there were ladies who would have been more than happy to take on the wifely role. The man obviously needed caring for and needed female company. Many noticed the rather run-down condition of his attire and the excessive intervals between haircuts. He was obviously comfortably off; he had a nice house adjoining a small farm. He was a pleasant gentleman, and though wedded to his work and to the hospital, several ladies thought him an attractive proposition and tried, each in their own way to woo him. He received their approaches with the greatest politeness, their cakes and cards with genuine appreciation and their invitations with caution. He looked with scant interest at the fat worm wriggling on the look and was not inclined to swallow it. He actually didn't mind his own company. He probably hung around the hospital for longer than he should, and dreaded that he would have to retire in a couple of years. He spent longer in the pub than was good for him.

On this particular evening, his daughter had just left and he was planning to settle down and watch a bit of television. He was just looking for his pipe, when the phone rang. It had been a long day and he was tired, so he dreaded it was a problem at the hospital.

'Is that Dr Starling?' It was a woman's voice. 'Thomas?'
'Speaking.'
'Thomas, this is Rachel, Rachel Bailey that was.'

'Good heavens!' His heart was thumping, his mind in a whirl. He hadn't seen her or heard her voice for thirty years. 'Good heavens!'

She seemed to have fuller control of her emotions. 'I was sorry to hear of Fiona's death. It must be a great loss for you.'

'Yes, a great loss, and one I suspect I will never get over.'

'You had a happy marriage?'

'Very. I was very fortunate, considering...'

'It was a long time ago, Thomas. Thirty years I guess. A lot of water under the bridge.'

'An ocean.'

'Look Thomas, I'm not too far away. I live in Harrogate. I know I've got a cheek but I would love it if we could meet up for a drink or a meal some time. I guess we have a lot of catching up to do, but actually I would just love to see you again.'

'Are you sure?'

'Quite sure. It was a long time ago.'

'I am amazed. Of course, I would love to see you again, but is it wise?'

'Who knows? Don't be so serious Thomas. I just want to see you.'

'God, It would be an absolute delight. I've thought...'

'Okay, Let's do it. I know a nice little place over here, and it'll be an easy drive for you.'

So they fixed on an evening of the following week. She promised to book a table.

'I will see you then Rachel and meanwhile I'll really look forward to our meeting.'

He put down the phone. He was still shaking with shock and excitement. In the brief few minutes of their call his tranquil life had been turned upside down. He paced to and fro in his sitting room, excited and quite unable to settle. He thought of the girl he had known all those years ago, her pretty face, her full lips, her big brown eyes and her raven hair. She was smiling and laughing at him, she was holding his hand, she was in his arms. How he had loved her and how she had loved him! And if it hadn't been for his stupidity...

He knew he would not settle. He needed to get out. He needed a drink and preferably someone to talk to. He decided not to take the car but to walk. It was only half a mile.

It was chilly outside and pitch black. He lived amongst fields. The lane meandered down to the village. The great moonless canopy of the sky was brilliantly studded with stars. A breeze rustled the leaves of the hedgerow and the trees. He imagined her as she was all those years ago when his love for her was overwhelming. They were walking along the beach at Scarborough, or was it Whitby? They laughed at the clockwork sanderlings and she suddenly charged off down the beach after them, and he ran after her. He wondered how she had changed...

'I didn't expect to see you down here tonight Tom,' said the barmaid as she pulled his pint of bitter.

'And I didn't expect to come down here, Debbie. I'm here on impulse. I'm here because I didn't want to stay at home.'

'Nothing much on the telly I suppose.'

'That's more or less it.'

He looked around the bar. There was usually someone with whom he liked to spend the time of day. At one end furthest away from the fruit machine was one of his oldest friends George Jenkins, a local GP. They had been at medical school together. He was sitting with Tony Williams who was a farmer out at Beltby. They caught sight of him and beckoned him over.

'Hi!' said George. 'I didn't expect to see you here tonight Tom. You know Tony, of course.'

'Nice to see you again, Tony. No, it's not one of my usual nights, but I fancied a bit of company.'

'Well, I'm sorry to be antisocial Tom,' said Tony standing up, 'but I just dropped in for a quick one and then I ran into this fellow. Jane's expecting me back for supper and I'm already late.'

'Never mind. I'll see you around.'

The Senior Physician sat down. 'Are you okay George? Work not too overwhelming?'

'It's warming up as the weather cools down.'

'Much the same at the hospital. Actually, George, I had hoped to find you here. I've just had a bit of a shock.'

'Oh dear! ! Not too bad a shock I hope.'

'No, far from it! Quite a pleasant one. You probably remember Rachel, Rachel Bailey.'

'Oh yes! Wow! That's a name from the past! You were crazy about her, weren't you? How long ago was that?

'I was married to Fiona for twenty-five years, so we're going back the best part of thirty years. Half a lifetime.'

'Yes, I remember. It was before you went to Australia. You brought her to a mess dinner and we were all very impressed. She seemed to light up the place!'

'She was quite something!' He thought of her dreamily. 'She was amazing.'

'I think we all wondered how a hopeless git like you managed it.'

'True. She was a bit out of my league, but she seemed to like me for reasons I never properly understood. She could have had anyone.'

'But then you went and married Fiona. We assumed Rachel had ditched you.'

'No, it wasn't quite like that and actually it is still bloody painful to think about. I'm amazed she's contacted me again.'

'Oh I see! So that's the shock?'

'Yes, she phoned me this evening and asked me out to dinner. I'm gobsmacked. I didn't even know that she was still alive.'

'I don't quite understand Tom. Okay, an old flame contacts you after a lot of years. It's a surprise, and probably a pleasant one, but you are not telling me you are overjoyed. You are shocked. This is something quite different.'

'Very perceptive of you George. I am actually very happy, but my predominant sensation is of shock. It has quite knocked me off my emotional balance.'

'I still don't understand. It was decades ago. What's the big deal? Okay I can see that you'd forgotten her and then she suddenly rears her head, but what of it?'

'No George, I have never forgotten her. She has never been out of my mind. I have thought of her every day I was married to Fiona. Every bloody day! She has haunted me throughout my marriage.'

'Gawd! I thought you and Fiona were very happy together. You were a lovely devoted couple. I envied you.'

181

'Oh, absolutely, and I miss her dreadfully. It has been like losing a limb. I grew to love Fiona very deeply. She was a wonderful wife and friend.'

'You grew to love her. You didn't love her to start with?'

'No, we were colleagues to start with, and then just friends.'

'So you married Fiona on the rebound, when Rachel broke up with you?'

'No George, it wasn't like that.' The Senior Physician looked down at the table between them and their drinks. He picked up a beer mat and fiddled with it. He was reluctant to share this confidence, but he wanted his friend to understand. 'I have never told you this before simply because I was so ashamed! It was the greatest mistake of my life.'

George stared at him while the Senior Physician took a large gulp from his pint.

'You'll remember that I won that scholarship to do a year of medical research in Melbourne. I was quite prepared to forego that opportunity for the sake of Rachel, but she was adamant that I should go, so I did. All well and good. But when I got there I met Fiona, who had come from Glasgow, also on a research fellowship. We found ourselves working together, and that led naturally to socializing together and becoming friends. We got on well and shared our interest in medical science and we also had a similar sense of humour, but I didn't feel romantic towards her. She was a colleague who I liked; a sister perhaps. My heart was full to overflowing with Rachel and anyway Fiona said she had a young man in Glasgow. Whenever I had a spare moment I would be writing to Rachel. We were planning our future together.'

'Despite that I suppose what happened wasn't that surprising. Fiona and I had some success with our research. We were undoubtedly a great team. We went out one evening after work to celebrate, we had too much to drink and we ended up in bed. It was just the once, and we regretted it immediately, at least I did, but the harm was done. The die was cast. She became pregnant.

Maybe this wouldn't have been such a disaster, but as you know, she was a devout catholic. Abortion was out of the question. I couldn't see how she could cope in her close catholic family and community as an unmarried mother. Nonetheless she said I ought to marry Rachel, as she knew how much we meant to each other, but this seemed wrong. It wasn't as if Fiona and I could not be happy together. We had a responsibility to the unborn child, and I had a duty to both of them. So Fiona agreed to marry me on the condition that I went back to England and told Rachel in person, which is what I did.'

'Can you imagine how awful that was? Rachel was shocked to see me back from the other side of the world. I had dreaded that there would be an awful scene and that she would be as distraught as I was, but somehow it didn't happen. I guess I had told her about Fiona in my many letters, and maybe she was forewarned that this might happen. I don't know. I spent just a few minutes with her. I apologised profusely. We hugged and wept and then I left. Until tonight we have had no contact. How she learned about Fiona's death I do not know. Years before I heard from a friend that Rachel had married, but I don't know whether that marriage continues.'

'Well, my dear Thomas, you are going to find out pretty soon. Are you sure you want to see her?'

'Of course. Though I'm pretty apprehensive. Actually I'm very excited. I have to wait a whole week to see her and that's too long.'

'You will both have changed pretty much beyond recognition. '

'Thanks very much. If you don't mind, I still consider myself in my prime.'

'I'm not sure that's how she will view you, and I guess she'll be a bit worse for wear. What would you think if she's twenty stone and has a moustache?'

'There's a thought.'

'You went out of her life and she just started eating and has never stopped. Maybe she wants to eat you too.'

'Very funny. I know she'll look different and be different. I'm telling myself that the old magic won't be there, but...'

'Of course it won't! How old are you?'

'Maybe it'll be a different magic.'

'I wouldn't count on it.'

The days passed painfully slowly for the Senior Physician. In the morning when he woke she was there at his side, and she was sitting opposite him, smiling as he ate his solitary breakfast. She was next to him as he drove to and from the hospital and she interrupted his logical trains of thought during his ward rounds and outpatient clinics. He would drift off mid-sentence. His secretary, Miss Peggs would find him in his office, staring into space. All noticed he was unusually benign and in constant good humour. The topic of the Senior Physician's distraction was much discussed around the corridors, offices and wards. However unlikely it seemed, it was universally concluded that he was in love. He had all the symptoms. Intense speculation, however, failed entirely to discover the object of his infatuation.

At last the day arrived. He had planned every aspect, but felt a lack of female advice on the details. Asking anyone of his acquaintances could have been fatal so he had to do without. The day before he went to town for a haircut, and invested in an expensive bottle of aftershave. He wandered the shops hoping to find a small gift for her, but without success. After he had given up he saw a flower shop, and he and the florist decided that a small corsage of freesias might do the trick. He would pick it up on the day.

He agonised over a suit or a blazer, and decided on the latter. He chose a tie that was casual, colourful but tasteful. He was all set.

He left the hospital early, called on the florist, went home and got dressed. He set out, and driving carefully he was in Harrogate in good time. Parking was always difficult but he found a space near the restaurant. It was a chilly, draughty evening and already dark. He put on his overcoat and walked to the restaurant. Trattoria Luigi was a small place down a side street. Through the window he could see there were only a few tables and she hadn't arrived. He was almost ten minutes early and didn't fancy going in and waiting so he opted to take a stroll until the appointed time. He liked Harrogate and had often come here with Fiona to eat and shop. He liked its twisty old streets, its interesting shops, its hundreds of restaurants. They had often walked in the parks and gardens.

The road wound uphill to a corner with a slightly wider road. He turned right and continued upwards, stopping and gazing into the window of an antique shop. Fiona loved to browse in these places, hoping to find an unrecognised masterpiece or a nice piece of pottery to gather dust around the house. The next turning would have taken him back towards the restaurant, and he would still be too early. He wondered again what she would look and be like. It had been a very long time. He couldn't expect her to still be the vivacious beautiful girl of his dreams. He thought yet again what he would say to her, and what she would tell him. There was actually too much to say - a whole lifetime of it, but he also had to listen. She wouldn't want to hear about his good life with Fiona. What would she like to hear?

There was a woman walking down the hill towards him. There was something about the way she carried herself. He glanced at her. Even after all these years she was unmistakable, the slightly upturned nose, the big eyes. He stopped. Her eyes were averted.

'Rachel!'

His greeting startled her. She stopped and stared, and for a moment failed to register it was him. Then a big smile spread across her face.

'Tom!'

For a moment they stood there, neither of us quite knowing what physical contact was appropriate. Then she stepped forward and kissed him on both cheeks.

He held her at arm's length and looked at her. 'Rachel! As lovely as ever. God, it's wonderful to see you again!' There were suddenly tears in his eyes. He was an emotional man.

'And lovely to see you again Tom.' As before, she seemed more in control of her emotions than he. 'Come,' she said. 'It's chilly. Let's get into the warm.' She took his arm and they walked, neither knowing what to say to the other, down to the restaurant.

She seemed delighted with the corsage and happy to be with him. He allowed her to guide his choices of food and he ordered a far more expensive bottle of Amarone than was his custom. They talked about their lives, she more than he. She was divorced five years before from Jonathon and she had a grown up son who

185

worked in London. He felt inhibited talking about his life with Fiona. She asked him about his children and his work. Their conversation was easy. They were both smiling and laughing. He was amazed at how little she had actually changed, for all that she had the face of a mature woman and a few streaks of grey in her hair. She was still slim and beautiful, though he thought she appeared tired and a little pale. He had lost his boyish lines years ago and was a stone or two overweight.

They finished their main course, which was excellent, and he was contemplating a sweet, but she became more sombre. She frowned and fidgeted with her wine glass.

'Look Thomas, I have to ask you something.'

'Fire away. I have little to hide.'

'Good. It's been bothering me all these years. I truly don't mean to be offensive or to pry, but I do need to put this to you, but it's difficult.' She paused, seeking the right words. 'I've thought a lot about what happened between you and Fiona in Australia. The more I thought about what you told me the less sense it made.'

'But it was exactly as I told you at the time. I hid nothing from you. There was no mystery.'

'Not for you, maybe, and not for me when you told me, but subsequently I began to think and doubt.'

'What was there to think about apart from the fact that I had let you down dreadfully and destroyed our future together?'

'I have been tormented all these years by the thought that she did it deliberately.'

'No, of course she didn't. That's ridiculous!'

'Look, I'm sorry. Remember Tom, I never met Fiona. I never had a chance to observe what sort of a woman she was.'

'Well, I can tell you Rachel, she wasn't that sort of person. We made a mistake, that's all.'

'Please hear me out Thomas and try not to take offence. Please let me get this off my chest. I have to understand this if we are to be friends.'

'But what is it that isn't clear?'

'You two went out to celebrate your research success. You had a bit too much to drink and then had sex. All understandable, except that your Fiona was a good catholic, to the extent that abortion was out of the question.'

'So?'

'Well, she wasn't such a good catholic that she refused to go to bed with you, was she? She was a doctor, like yourself and presumably she knew it was her fertile time. She didn't insist you use a condom and being a good catholic she wasn't on the pill. Are you sure there wasn't a bit of deliberate carelessness?'

'I never thought of such a thing. She wasn't like that.'

'Like what?'

'Well, scheming. She knew all about you. I had banged on endlessly. She knew I was in love with you.'

'Look, I'm not saying she was a bad person, just that she wanted you and used the only method known to her to get you. All's fair in love and war, after all.'

'I don't think so, Rachel. I think it was a simple accident, that's all. We had too much to drink. We were young and stupid, and we were both horrified at what we had done.'

'At least you were.' She smiled at him. 'I'm sorry, that's not kind.' She looked away and appeared on the edge of tears. 'These thoughts have bothered me, that's all. I had to ask you and you have reassured me, at least to some extent. It is easier to live with the thought of an accident rather than a scheme.'

'It was an accident, I assure you.' But as he said this, the Senior Physician reflected that he had never been a person to look beneath the surface, to seek to understand, or suspect the inner workings of the minds of others. He was a straightforward sort of person and he tended to think others were more or less the same. For several minutes he was lost in thought and she noted the change in him and wondered whether he was just annoyed, or was reflecting on her hypothesis.

'Thomas, we mustn't let the past mar the present, must we?' She reached across the table and took his hand.

'No, quite,' said he. 'Life's too short.'

'I'm just very happy to be with you at last.'

He nodded. 'After all this time...It is remarkable.' There were tears in his eyes again. 'I have thought of you just about every day since we parted. I loved Fiona, but even at times when we were blissfully happy, I thought of you. You were always there with us, or at least with me.'

'I hope that doesn't mean what I think it might mean.'

'Yes, even then, to my shame.'

They finished their meal and had coffee.

'I hope you're sober enough to drive me home Tom.'

'Oh, I assumed you had come by car.'

'No, I came by bus. It stops right outside my house and I know the times. I like the bus.'

'Well my car's not far away.'

They walked down the road hand in hand while he wondered what, if he was to take her home, what else was on the evening's menu.

They drove down a road beside a park and into a district of detached Edwardian houses, set around with large trees and overgrown gardens.

'Okay, Tom, slow down. I'm just down here on the left...this one by the street lamp you can park in the drive.'

He stopped the car and turned off the ignition.

'Look, Tom, I would like you to come in and have another coffee before you drive back. If you don't mind, I would rather you don't stay too long as I'm very tired.'

'No, honestly Rachel. It's been a lovely evening, and I feel fine to drive back as I am. I don't want to be a burden.'

'Come in for half an hour Tom. I would love that.' She laid a hand on his arm.

The house was more or less what he had expected, tastefully decorated, in a style he recognised as popular amongst owners of properties of this age. The furnishings were colourful, some pieces of strip pine furniture, some bright hangings on the walls. He followed her into the kitchen.

'How would you like your coffee?'

'Oh, I suppose it had better be black in the circumstances.'

She filled the electric kettle and took a couple of mugs from a cupboard. 'Go and sit down Thomas. I'll bring this through.'

He went through to the sitting room and looked around. There were photographs on the mantlepiece of her with her son as a toddler, a schoolboy and as a young man. There was a picture of her with an older couple, who he took to be her parents. He saw no pictures of the ex-husband.

'You know Thomas,' she said as she brought in the coffee. 'I am a little worried about you driving back. You had more of the wine than me. I actually have a spare bedroom, and I would gladly have you stay but for the prying eyes of my neighbours. I guess they keep an eye out for me, living alone in this big place, and they are sure to ask whose car was parked in my drive.'

'It's no problem. I'll be fine, but I appreciate your concern.'

'No, it's good of you to drive all this way just to see an old lady.'

'Old lady nothing! You are remarkably like the young woman I thought I was going to marry. You still look wonderful, though I can see you're tired.'

'Thank you. You're not so bad yourself.'

'I hope we can repeat this in the not too distant future, Rachel.'

'I would like that very much. I have really enjoyed this evening.'

But as he drove back north there were shadows over his happiness. His expectation that they might just continue where they had left off after so many years had been naive. They were different. She had a degree of reserve that was predictable, but she also seemed sad. Was that because of what had happened between them, or because of her divorce, or was there something else?

He thought about Fiona. He imagined her sitting next to him in the car as she had on countless occasions of the years.

'So what are you thinking, love?' he asked her. 'I hope I've not upset you. I do miss you terribly. You did tell me on that last day to find someone else and I said I would never find anyone to compare with you. She thinks you were a naughty young woman. She thinks you worked it all out and trapped me. What do you say about that?'

'No, stupid,' he imagined her saying, 'I had my young man in Glasgow.'

But he reflected that Fiona was a well organised woman. She made long-term plans for them and their children much more than he did, but she was not a risk taker. Would she have deliberately got pregnant if she hadn't known for sure that he would marry her?

The more perceptive among those at the hospital who were well acquainted with him, and were used to his ways, noted another change in the demeanor of the Senior Physician. Much of his dreaminess had evaporated, and though he was usually in a pleasant mood, there was a return of the occasional tetchiness they expected of him. It was concluded that although his affair of the heart continued, it had clearly moved on into new territory.

The following evening he phoned her. She sounded pleased to hear from him.

'I'm hoping we can meet again soon.'

'Of course Tom, but I would prefer it if you could give me a few days...It's just a little difficult at present, Tom.'

He wanted to ask her why. He wanted to tell her that he felt empty and frustrated without her and that he longed to be with her again, but he sensed he had to respect her reticence, her reservations.

'I'll tell you what Tom. Give me a ring on Friday and we can plan then.'

Friday was three days off. It seemed like an age. He was like an impatient teenager.

'I'm not sure I'll live that long,' he said ruefully.

'I'm sorry to be difficult Tom, but I think you might just make it.'

'Why are women so bloody complicated?' he asked George in the pub the following evening.

'They have to be because you are so simple.'

'But if it is difficult, why doesn't she tell me what it's about? Why so mysterious?'

'There are probably things she doesn't want you to know about. She's lived for thirty years since you two were an item and she may have accumulated any number of people and issues she would rather you don't know about. We are not all as innocent and blameless as you, Tom. Maybe she's got one or two other lovers on the go, and you just have to take your turn. Did you find out why she got divorced?'

'No, I kept clear of that, and she didn't mention her ex-husband.'

'And she's been divorced for 5 years?'

'More or less.'

'A lot of time for hanky-panky. An attractive divorcee, living alone...'

'I know. Of course, but I would rather not think about that.'

'The jealous lover. Either way Tom, I reckon you are a lucky sod and you should appreciate that fact. For God's sake, you spurn the poor woman for thirty years and then she comes back and asks you out, and when you get to meet her you find her beautifully preserved and still interested in a boring old git like you.'

'You have a point, George.'

It was as if she had heard their conversation, for it was a rather different Rachel who phoned him on Friday. She got straight to the point.

'Tomorrow evening, if you are free.'

'What for?'

'Come round to my place and I'll cook you supper.'

'Great. That's very kind of you. I could come early and help you.'

'I suspect I'll do better by myself if you don't mind. You can bring the wine.'

'Red or white.'

'It doesn't matter. How about one of each?'

He left early, bearing two of the better bottles from his cellar. He drove through town and called on the florist and again sought her advice.

'What are you trying to say to the lady, Sir?'

'I haven't really thought. A bunch of flowers to show appreciation - she's cooking me supper, you know.'

191

'I always feel it's nice to receive something that lasts - like one of these beautiful orchids, but perhaps you want to make a statement of love. Is she that kind of lady for you?'

I suppose she is.'

'You don't sound very sure.'

'No, it's red roses all the way.'

'They're expensive, mind and you'll need at least a dozen.'

'Do I look as if I'm on the breadline? Make it two dozen!'

'She'll love them!'

He found the house by the streetlamp and decided to park in a sidestreet a little way down. She greeted him exuberantly at the door, planting a kiss full on his lips before rapidly retreating to the kitchen.

'Sorry Tom! Things are at a crucial stage. Come in!' she shouted as she retreated to the kitchen. He wiped his feet, took off his overcoat and followed her. Enticing smells were emanating from the kitchen. 'Go away! Go away! You'll be under my feet. I've left drinks on the sideboard. Go and help yourself and make yourself at home.'

'Okay, okay! Can I pour you something?'

'No, I'm fine.'

He dumped his things on a side table and poured himself a dry sherry. Then he remembered the Sauvignon blanc and took it through to the kitchen.

'This needs to go in you fridge'

'Fine. Over there.'

He went back and looked around her sitting room. There was a vase in pastel pink and green on the window sill that looked about right. He measured it against his bunch of roses. He took it through to the kitchen and without speaking to her filled it with water, went back and arranged the roses in it and placed them at the centre of the table. It might not have been the most artistic arrangement but they definitely looked good.

A few minutes later she came through, untying her pinny. 'They're beautiful! Thank you so much. She came across to him and they embraced. 'Red roses eh? Is there a message?'

'Definitely.'

They kissed.

'That's a lovely message. Now, are you ready to eat?'

He opened the white wine and she served leek soup that she had made. He was amazed at how much stronger and vigorous she seemed. She had more colour in her cheeks. She looked younger and happier.

He held up his glass. 'To us!' They clinked glasses.

'To us!' she repeated, smiling.

'You are a new woman, Rachel.'

'Yes, I guess I am. I'm afraid I wasn't quite myself last time. I wasn't entirely well, but I'm fine now.'

They finished the soup.

'Now Tom, I remember you are a traditional sort of bloke, so I've not tried anything too exotic. I've just roasted a shoulder of lamb. Perhaps you could carve?'

'Delighted! He carried the joint through to the table while she brought the vegetables from the oven. He sharpened the knife and began to slice the tricky joint. He reflected that there was something almost symbolic about what he was doing. He was doing the man of the house thing. How many times had he carved the joint at the table with Fiona and the kids? He supposed Rachel's husband must similarly have stood here and carved. He looked at her and she smiled up at him. He wondered whether she was having the same thoughts.

'You know,' he said, once they were set, 'You've told me nothing about your ex-husband, and there's no photo of him.'

'That's because I neither want to think about him or look at him.'

'Well, it's okay. You don't have to tell me about him. I'm naturally curious.'

'What do you want to know?'

'Oh, you know, general stuff. His name, what he did for his living, what went wrong between you two, whether he's still part of your life. That sort of thing.'

'I met him at a veterinary conference, and he quite swept me off my feet. I guess I was still on the rebound so I guess I can blame you and Fiona for my susceptibility. My ex husband, Graham, is nothing if not charming and pretty nice looking. We had a whirlwind romance. It was wonderful! It took away the pain of losing you. I felt love and appreciation, rather than loss and rejection.'

'I sense there is a 'but' coming.'

'Yes, and it wasn't very long in coming, but unfortunately not before we were married and I was expecting. He was lazy and untrustworthy. I think he probably had several affairs before the one I discovered that led to the divorce.'

'That must have been difficult to take. More rejection.'

'It wasn't all bad. I loved him for a few years and we had some happy times. He provided quite well so I only needed to work part time, which suited me. Our son, Clive, is a lovely young man - good looking, clever and decent, and he's doing well in London. I feel very lucky.' She smiled at him, as if acknowledging that he too was part of her good fortune.

'Where is Graham now?'

'He moved down to Bristol and I believe now lives with a woman half his age, so, to answer your other question, no. He is no longer part of my life, thank God.'

'And you get to see Clive often?'

'Yes, pretty much. I like an excuse to go down to London, and he's happy to put me up and lets me cook for him. Of course this is where he grew up and he has quite a few friends here so he's often up here keeping me company.'

The roast was wonderful and he ate too much, as usual. She, he noted, was far more restrained. His best claret did not disappoint. The Senior Physician was feeling mellow. They sat and chatted and then he helped her clear the table and in the process of maneuvering in the tight space of the kitchen he put his arms around her and pulled her into a tight embrace. She giggled and they kissed with youthful passion.

'Unhand me Sir!' she protested. 'There is yet more food to eat.' She tried to push him away.

'I'm already stuffed.' He kissed her again. She replaced her arms around him. His hands were on her bottom. Then he released her, took her by the hand and led her back into the sitting room where he collapsed onto the sofa, pulling her down beside him.

'Tired are we?'

'Very.'

He held her close and they kissed some more. They stopped and looked at each other. 'You're so beautiful,' he said.

'You're not too bad yourself, but as you're so tired, I suppose we better go to bed.'

'I was hoping you would see my need.'

They hadn't made love for thirty years, though they had both dreamed of it during that long interval. Now their love making was more tender and gentle, but none the worse for that.

And afterwards, as they lay in each other's arms, the Senior Physician was a happy, fulfilled and contented man. He had the sense that a miracle had happened and that he was its beneficiary. She had come back into his life when he needed her. At last he had the woman that he had always wanted, the woman who had for thirty years been in his dreams. Fiona had come between them, accidentally or, now he ceded perhaps deliberately, but he couldn't regret it. They had had a good life together and he was inordinately fond of their children, and he hoped that Fiona was now looking down on them and smiling that her guilt was assuaged.

He opened his eyes and looked at her. She was looking at him, but to his surprise her expression was anguished and there were tears in her eyes.

'What's the matter, love?'

'Oh, I'm sorry. It makes me sad, that's all.'

'But why? Here's me, overwhelmingly happy and you are crying your eyes out.'

'I'm sorry. I do love you Tom, and making love with you again is wonderful, but it is too late. We are old. We have missed out on thirty years of happiness together. I wanted to have your children, to build a life with you. Now I'm... It's too late Tom!'

'What were you going to say?'

'No, it's nothing. I just feel it's too late.'

'It's not too late, and it's silly to think like that. We can do nothing about the past. We have the future and we are just at the beginning of something wonderful.'

She attempted a smile. 'Of course you are right. I'm sorry Tom.' She sat up and dried her eyes. 'Let's go and finish our meal. Maybe you've worked up an appetite.'

She put on a dressing gown and went downstairs while he dressed and wondered about what she had said and not said.

She had made a meringue covered in whipped cream and raspberries, which they ate in silence, thinking their thoughts.

Afterward they sat together and sipped coffee. She seemed happier and relaxed.

'Would you mind awfully if I stayed the night. I've taken the precaution of parking my car down the side road.'

'So cunning! You plotted your wicked purpose from the start!'

'Guilty as charged.'

'Who cares about a reputation? I suppose I'd rather be viewed as a scarlet woman than a sad old lady.'

'Was that a yes?'

'I suppose it was.'

He poured himself a scotch and a Baileys for herself and they chatted. She talked about her son, and how happy she was that he had found a nice girl and was in a good job. He talked about his daughter and the farm, and a bit about the hospital.

'You're going to miss that place when you retire,' she said.

'I guess I will. Medicine is what I seem to have done forever. Sometimes that hospital feels like my baby. It needs my love and dedication.'

'I think it gets it too.'

'I suppose it does. I've been there for thirty years and we seem to have grown up together, though now she seems to be outgrowing me. Medical science is really taking off and I fear it is leaving me behind. Every day there are new treatments and protocols, new scans that I can't read, and new diseases even. The juniors try to keep me up to date but it is a losing battle.'

They slept together, and in the morning made love again, gently and sensually. It was a sunny morning and she suggested that after breakfast they should go out walking.

'We could go to Harlow Carr. I like that place and the colours will be beautiful at this time of the year.'

'I guess you must have been there with Fiona.'

'Yes, a couple of times I think.'

'Well I don't want to go there then. I don't want you thinking of her, or telling me about your trips with her.'

'Oh. Okay...' He frowned, slightly taken aback.

Her face crumpled. 'It's not fair, Tom! I'm with you and I love you, but I can't get her out of my mind. I think of you with her. I think of you making love to her. She's always there! She's laughing at me because she won, and I think you are comparing her and me.'

'But...'

'I know you loved her. I know you miss her. I can't help thinking about these things. Maybe she's prettier than me, maybe you prefer her cooking, maybe she was better in bed. I dreaded that when you came you would call out her name!'

'Oh, I'm so sorry.' He folded her into his arms.

'I feel I have to perform, to compete with a dead person who I have never met.'

'No, no Rachel. Remember, you are my first love. Even after I had been married to Fiona for several years and we had children I still yearned for you. I have told you how I have thought of you throughout my marriage. Now you are my only love. I'm not making comparisons. I just want to be with you and love you. I'm a very simple man.'

'It's so difficult.'

'You're making it difficult. What if she did something better than you? Who cares? We're together now and no one else counts. I love you. Anyway, I guess I could be tormenting myself that in some regards I don't come up to the standard of your ex-husband. You tell me he was good looking and charming, qualities that I am not famed for. Maybe he was funnier, more interesting, better in bed. I mean, it's pointless to think like that.'

'I know you're right Tom. Of course I know and tell myself these things. I will try not to think of her.'

'Okay, where would you suggest we go?'

She wiped her eyes and sniffed. She looked up at him and smiled. 'What about Bolton Abbey?'

'Isn't that miles away?

'No, It's not far. It'll only take us about half an hour. You've not been there with Fiona?'

'Not as far as I can remember.'

197

'Well okay. It'll be a pleasant drive and we can toddle around there happily. I don't want to walk too far. I'm feeling a little tired from my exertions yesterday.'

She felt the prying eyes of her neighbours as they left the house together and walked down the road to his car. As they started out her mood seemed to lift and she chatted happily about her neighbours and about Harrogate.

The countryside was looking at its best in the bright autumn sun. He drove at a leisurely pace.

She laid her hand on his thigh. 'It's lovely being with you Tom.'

They ambled together, arm in arm around the ruins of the Priory choir, imagining the life that once filled the place, and admiring the elegance of the ancient walls and arches. He was surprised that the western end of the building was still intact and was the local parish church. Inside it was a large and impressive space to serve that purpose for such a small community. They walked on the banks of the river and he tried and failed to persuade her to cross it on the stepping stones that stretched across to the opposite bank.

She was feeling the cold, so they retreated to a cafe for tea and cake. She talked about her work as an advisor for an animal charity, and the veterinary research she had done before that.

'I regret that I gave up full time work when I was expecting Clive. We didn't really need the money, and I wanted to be the perfect mother, as I suppose most mothers do. I didn't keep up with the enormous expansion that was occurring in biology at that time - you know, molecular biology, immunology and all that stuff. I've never managed to catch up, and now I never will.'

'Look Rachel, I have always worked full time - more than full time actually and I'm hopelessly out of touch as I told you. Actually I've never felt it particularly important. We're surrounded by specialists, and my juniors are usually up to date on these things. I just stick to the basics, and I still seem to contribute.'

'Would you like to go somewhere else, Rachel?'

'No Tom, thank you. I'm a little tired and it's a little chilly out. Let's go back and we can have something to eat before your long drive back.'

They strolled, hand in hand back to the car while the Senior Physician felt a twinge of anxiety about her apparent delicate physical condition. He remembered how she was when he first knew her - full of energy and up for anything.

They drove back and as they approached her home he said:

'I think the neighbours are going to have to get used to me being around.' And he turned into her drive.

She leant across and kissed him on the cheek. 'I'll be happy to tell them all about you, if they ask.'

She busied herself in the kitchen, refusing his help while he sat in the sitting room and read the Sunday paper.

She had prepared an avocado salad that she spiced up with crispy bacon which they ate with smoked salmon. Then they finished the meringue from the day before. By the time they had drunk coffee and chatted it was dark.

'I guess I ought to be on my way. I have a busy day tomorrow.'

'Let's have a cuddle before you go,' she said, leading him across to the sofa.

They hugged each other tight.

'It's been lovely,' she said.

'It has. A dream come true.'

They kissed.

'I can't believe how lucky I am to have found you again,' he said.

'I found you, stupid.'

'You're right as always. I'm so lucky you found me.'

'I'm sorry to have been a little feeble this weekend. I'm not the girl I was.'

'Well, I'm not much better. Falling apart, and anyway you're still gorgeous. You have nothing to apologise for.'

'I'm an old ruin, like that bloody old Priory.'

'Love amongst the ruins.'

'I guess that about sums us up.'

It was a happy and ebullient Senior Physician who went into work on Monday. The world was a beautiful place, his secretary of ten years seemed particularly efficient, the nurses in outpatients were lovely and helpful, and even his patients pleased him with their progress and gratitude. The morning passed quickly, and his colleagues at lunch in the canteen were impressed by his cheerful good mood. And in the afternoon his team, with whom he had been a trifle harsh at their previous meeting were relieved to see the boss arrive for his ward round wreathed in smiles.

It was widely assumed by those around the hospital who were interested in these things that the Senior Physician's affair of the heart had progressed substantially and that it was a near certainty that he had had his end away.

He got home from work. His daughter had been round and left him his supper that he just needed to heat up. He helped himself to a small glass of wine, sat down, put his feet up and turned on the TV. He had watched the news for a few minutes when the phone rang. It was Rachel:

'Tom, I trust you have had a good day.'

'I have indeed. I've gone around the hospital with a stupid grin on my face all day. They must think I've gone gaga.'

'No, they know you too well. I'm sure they know you are in love.'

'I'm sure they don't. How could they think an ancient crusty old git like me could be head-over-heels in love.'

'Why not, for heaven's sake?'

'It must be unusual at least.'

'I suppose. Look, Tom, I've phoned you early because I'm feeling a little tired and thought I would have an early night, so I'm phoning to say 'Goodnight' and to tell you how happy I am and how in love I am.'

'That's wonderful to hear. No, you go to bed and I won't disturb you, but I'll be thinking of you. I love you.'

The following evening he phoned her several times but she did not pick up. He worried that something had happened to her, but reassured himself with the thought that she had gone out or perhaps that she had gone to London to see her son. He didn't like to phone first thing in the morning, but when he got to work he phoned her number again. Still there was no reply. The Senior Physician was beginning to panic. He toyed with driving to Harrogate, but he could hardly cancel his bronchoscopy list; there was no one else to do it. He consoled himself that there was probably a logical explanation, or even an illogical one, and that he would go there in the afternoon if he hadn't heard.

The list seemed to go on forever. Nothing was simple. Two of the patients were difficult and needed a lot of sedative. Biopsying a lesion in an upper lobe bronchus was exceedingly difficult with the patient coughing so much. He was not back to his room before one o'clock. As we walked in the phone rang:

'Is that Dr Starling?' It was a male voice he did not recognise.

'Speaking.' His heart was pounding.

'This is Clive, Rachel's son.'

'Oh, is there anything wrong?

'I'm afraid there is. She's in Harrogate District Hospital and is seriously ill.'

'Oh God! I was with her this weekend. She seemed well, if a little tired. What has happened?'

'She's been ill for years.'

'She didn't tell me.'

'She was diagnosed with aplastic anaemia several years ago. You would understand it better than me, but basically her marrow has stopped working. She has to have blood transfusions every few months, and I think she has a bit of a problem with iron accumulating in her liver. The doctors say she's got pneumonia. She's had it before. She was found semi-conscious by her cleaner yesterday. I got up here last night. This morning she came round for a little while and she told me to contact you. I think you had better come over as soon as you can.'

'You mean she is in danger?'

'That's what I've been told.'

'Oh my God! Oh, this is terrible! I'll come now. I'll be as quick as I can.'

'She's in Intensive Care.'

Afterwards he could hardly remember the drive to Harrogate. He remembered speeding, sweeping past cars and lorries, horns blaring. His world was crashing around him. He did not care. His only concern was to see her; to be at her side.

He parked his car without a thought to legality and rushed into the hospital and followed the signs to Intensive Care.

A nurse conducted him into a waiting room.

'I'm afraid there's already someone in there with her. We only allow one person at a time at the bedside. I'll go and tell him you are here.'

A moment later a young man came into the room wearing a gown and facemask. He pulled off the mask and looked glumly at the Senior Physician. He had his mother's likeness. He forced a smile and held out his hand.

'I'm Clive.'

'Thomas. How is she?'

'Not good, I'm afraid. She's sleeping or unconscious. They tell me her blood pressure is low and that they are having difficulty getting on top of the infection. Her white blood count is very low and hasn't responded to treatment. When I spoke with the doctor an hour ago he didn't hold out much hope.'

The Senior Physician shook his head. 'This is so shocking.' He felt like weeping. 'She never told me, but I should have realised there was something wrong. She was very tired the first time we met, but then at the weekend she almost seemed like a new woman.'

'I believe she had a blood transfusion last week.'

'That makes sense. We went out on Sunday to Bolton Castle. I guess she must have met a virus.'

'She phoned me after she had dinner with you in Harrogate. She was over the moon. She told me all about you. I think you were the love of her life and she never recovered from losing you when she was younger. I think her marriage to my father was doomed because she was always comparing him with you.'

'I'm sorry. It is my fault. My stupidity. My selfishness. We should have married, and would have done had I not got someone else, who I did not love, pregnant.'

To his surprise the young man stepped forwards and hugged him. 'You'd better go in there and see her.'

He put on the gown and found a facemask.

She was lying with her eyes closed. An intravenous infusion dripped into her arm. Electrodes were attached to her chest. Lines marched across monitors and varied in time with her breathing, her heart beat and blood pressure. A naso-gastric tube protruded from her nose.

'Are you the husband?' asked the nurse.

'No, I'm an old friend. I am very close to her.'

'You can sit there, but it's best not to touch her. She's got no resistance to infection.'

He looked at the lips that he had kissed so recently and at the bruised arms that had so recently hugged him.

'How is she, nurse?'

'I'm afraid I'm not permitted to say Sir, but I'll ask the doctor to have a word with you when he is free.'

The Senior Physician lent forward bringing his masked lips close to her ear. 'Rachel!' he said in a loud whisper, 'it's me, Tom.'

There was the slightest flickering of her eyelids.

'It's Tom!'

No response.

'Does she respond at all, Nurse?'

'She goes up and down. She said a few things to her son a couple of hours ago, but I don't think she made much sense.'

'She told him to phone me. That can't have been more than two or three hours ago.'

'I don't think I was here then.'

He looked back at Rachel, and to his surprise her eyes were open, staring at the ceiling.

'Rachel! It's me, Tom!'

Her eyes slowly turned towards him. For several seconds she stared at him without seeming to recognise who or what she was looking at.

'It's me, Tom.'

Then she smiled. 'Tom...Tom, it's lovely of you to come,' she mumbled. 'Lovely...'

Her voice trailed off and she shut her eyes, but the smile lingered.

He waited. She was very tired. He was relieved that she was conscious and able to recognise him. The nurse smiled at him and then turned away to look at her charts. He squeezed Rachel's hand.

She looked at him again. 'I'm sorry Tom. We had so little time…'

'No Rachel we'll have lots more time. You're going to get better.'

She shook her head. 'I'm sorry, Tom...I should have told you....I'm sorry.' There were tears in her eyes. He took her hand again. The nurse saw, but said nothing.

'You mustn't upset yourself Rachel.' He noticed on the monitor the rising rate of her heart, blood pressure and breathing.

'No. It was selfish, but I had to feel your love.' She opened her eyes wide and squeezed his hand. 'Your passion… Not your pity. I needed to be a mayfly, to be young with you, to flutter my wings if only for a day and to be overwhelmed by my love for you.'

She shut her eyes; her mouth was open a little. It seemed the effort had exhausted her. The vital signs declined again. Her blood pressure, he noted, was dangerously low.

The nurse looked concerned. 'I need to get the doctor. Perhaps you could leave for a moment. He gazed at his lover. Something told him he was with her for the last time. This was not the time for protocols or procedures. It was a time for him and her. He stood up, lent forward, put his hands on her shoulders and kissed her. her eyes opened a fraction and there was a flicker of a smile.

'Please Mr…' started the nurse.

He looked at the monitor. Her vital signs were declining fast. From his long bedside experience he recognised the inevitable that was approaching.

'I think, nurse, you had better get her son.'

And as tears welled up and ran down his cheeks, the Senior Physician held her limp cold hand as her breathing and pulse slowed, her blood pressure declined.

'Don't go Rachel!' he pleaded.

There was the slightest flickering of her eyelids, the slightest hint of a smile on her pale lips.

'Please Rachel, stay with me! I cannot…'

Clive came back into the room with the nurse.

He looked round at them in anguish, but when he looked back at her she had slipped away.

Medicine and Society

Sickness Benefits

For twenty years I was involved in a judicial capacity deciding who should and who shouldn't get sickness-related state benefits. These benefits are administered by the Department of Work and Pensions, but if a sick person's claim is rejected there is a right of appeal to the Department of Justice. The claim will then be considered by an independent appeal tribunal. I used to sit on these tribunals.

At the tribunal it is the doctor's job to interview the appellant to identify the medical conditions, and the degree of associated disability, and to interpret the medical information in the papers. Then the tribunal decides whether the identified disability fulfils the legal requirements for the benefit. This is often difficult because the wording of the legislation is open to various interpretations. There is also the problem of credibility. The appellant has an incentive to lie or exaggerate, though I believe most are reasonably, if not exactly honest. This problem is made much worse by the fact that with many of the common causes of disability, for instance, depression and back pain, there are few objective ways to gauge severity, apart from analysing what the sick person is claiming..

It is predictable that tribunal members differ in their beliefs about the credibility of claimants. From my experience, tribunal judges with a background in criminal law tend to believe everyone is lying. Those who have a background in family law tend to be more trusting and sympathetic.

The DWP says that the level of fraud is around 3%, but I have no confidence in the validity of that figure.

So whether a benefit is awarded or not depends in substantial part on who you meet at the tribunal. No surprise there I guess.

Sometimes we can be certain. The appellant was claiming severe respiratory disability. He was breathing heavily as he came into the tribunal room and used his inhaler a couple of times during the hearing. The tribunal thought he was significantly disabled and awarded the benefit. Later we heard that he had left the tribunal by taxi and said to the driver:

'Thank God that's over! It's bloody difficult pretending to be breathless when you're not!'

Unfortunately for him the taxi driver knew someone who worked in the tribunal centre and reported back what he had heard.

On other occasions appellants don't manage to join up the dots. I have witnessed this sort of thing at tribunals several times. An appellant is claiming his walking is limited to about 50 metres slowly, say due to arthritis or backache.

'So, have you been on holiday recently?'

'Yes Doctor, we went to Cyprus.'

'How did you get there?'

'We flew, Doctor.'

'From Newcastle?'

'Yes Doctor.'

'Did you make any special arrangements?'

'How do you mean?'

'With Newcastle Airport.'

'Er, no.'

'You didn't order a wheelchair or any help?'

'No, Doctor.'

A reasonable conclusion is that he or she must be able to walk about 500 metres, possibly with luggage.

As part of my training I sat in on a couple of tribunals to get an idea of procedures. One case sticks in my mind. A school teacher had some sort of bowel problem that caused relatively minor incontinence. Nowadays you have to have pretty epic bowel incontinence to qualify, but then it was much easier. The Judge was attempting to define in embarrassing detail just what this incontinence amounted to. The appellant tried to explain. Then the Judge asked:

'You mean, it's more than a wet fart?'

'Yes.'

So the teacher got the benefit!

Then there was the woman with a claimed whiplash injury to her neck that had occurred years before and was apparently still causing extreme disability. Whiplash, typically caused when your vehicle is shunted from behind, used to be accepted as a legitimate cause of chronic pain and disability until it was noted that in countries where no compensation for this injury was available the condition hardly existed, and if it did it was transient - for a few months only. This appellant came in very slowly with her head on one side and looking upwards, so it was difficult for her to see where she was going. She was shepherded by her husband. It seemed her disability was almost total even to the extent of having to be fed and watered by this long suffering spouse. In trying to understand the extent of the disability the Chairman asked whether she would, for instance, be able to operate the remote control for the TV.

'How do you mean?'

'Well could you change channels?'

'What for?'

'Well, to watch a different program.'

The woman pulled a puzzled expression and gingerly shook her head. *'No, it's always on Channel 3.'* It was not clear to us whether she realised she had a choice!

We were reluctant to believe that this disability was as severe as she was claiming, or as severe as it appeared to be, but this leaves a nasty taste in the mouth. Did we get it right? Did she actually have a severe disability of an undiagnosed nature? Could we really have been witnessing some sort of charade?

Two people with a similarly severe disease or injury are unlikely to be disabled to the same extent because of their different levels of motivation, or support. Commonly depression decreases a person's drive to get things done, but the end result depends on where they start from. A person who was highly motivated before the illness may still be able to care for themselves and function reasonably normally, albeit not to their previous high standards. Life may go on with little disruption until they recover. A previously unmotivated person, whose previous coping abilities were marginal may stop functioning altogether when depressed. She may be unable to care for herself and, if she lacks help and sympathy from others she may become seriously neglected. She may stop washing or dressing, becoming housebound or even bedroom bound.

Self seclusion is also due to associated anxiety. There is particularly a fear of being outside and meeting people. The curtains are drawn; there is the fear of a knock at the door. The sufferer may have panic attacks if they go out, particularly if they are alone, or in a crowded place. They often feel that people are looking at them and judging them.

This social isolation tends to aggravate the depression that caused it. People enter a permanent state of housebound disability from which they cannot escape. If the depressed person turns to alcohol, or drugs their situation will become even worse. The longer this goes on, the more likely it is that they will never recover. Even if their mental state does recover they may find, after a prolonged period of disability, that they have lost the skills and aptitude to return to work.

The irony is that the unmotivated, unsupported person is effectively more disabled and therefore gets the benefit. Coping does not pay in the world of sickness benefits! If you cope, even if you struggle to do so, you're not disabled. This seems unjust and in many cases it is unjust, but you get sickness benefits because of what you cannot do (like walking, using hands, meeting people, controlling anger) as against the pain or distress involved. There are huge grey areas here. In my experience tribunals do take into account the effort an appellant seems to be making to overcome their difficulties, within the limits the law imposes. Disability has to be due to their problems with physical or mental health and in general proportional to the health problem, though that is often pretty impossible to judge.

I guess that before there was the Welfare State, if you became depressed you just had to carry on or starve. If the person continued to be active and to interact with people their depression would tend to lift after weeks or months. The provision of out of work benefits for depression, though well intended, may allow a short lived mental discomfort to become a permanent state of misery, disability and unemployment.

But this is not necessarily all it seems. The self-neglecting recluse may still be motivated to do what they consider to be essential. An appellant gave a story that he was too depressed to do anything, and hadn't left the house for months due to anxiety and panic. So I asked:

'So how have you managed to come here today by yourself?'
'Oh, I had to! It's about money!'

This attitude is common, and I had many exchanges like this. The tribunal would often ask why, if the depressed person was motivated enough to seek a sickness benefit they hadn't motivation to fight the disease, find a job and get on with life. If they could leave the safety of their home and come to face a tribunal, why could they not leave their home and engage with the world in other ways that they were claiming were impossible? I guess the likely rewards from striving to get better may be less tangible than the likely rewards from striving to get money from the state.

Another unsatisfactory aspect of the benefit system is that it discourages those in receipt of benefit from getting better. Once you get the benefit you want to keep hold of it so you don't want to be seen to get better. I felt sorry for a gentleman who did the right thing and paid for it. He had been overweight with severe backache to the extent he was awarded the highest rate of the mobility component of Disability Living Allowance on the grounds that he could only walk a short distance. This gave him a motability car, which was of great utility to him and his family. Later he (foolishly?) listened to his doctor's advice and managed to lose weight so that his back became much better. When he came back to a tribunal to be reviewed it was found that now he was able to walk much further and he therefore lost the benefit and the car. He was not pleased.

It is annoying if the bloke next door boasts that he has a sickness benefit when you know from personal observation that he is not disabled. To help you with your righteous indignation the Department of Work and Pensions provides a hotline for you to shop your neighbour. If they decide there is a case to answer they send someone round in a car with a video camera to hang around with the aim of filming him doing what he has claimed

211

not to be able to do. Then at a tribunal we get to view these video recordings and come to a judgement about what is shown. People who are shown to be fraudulent have to repay the benefit and sometimes face criminal charges.

I used to particularly enjoy sitting as a respiratory disease expert on Industrial Disease Tribunals. Usually these concerned more clear cut interpretation of data and occupational history. The majority of the appellants were men who had previously worked in coal mining, shipbuilding, chemical and construction industries. A frequent concern was occupational exposure to asbestos dust. For many years after it was known that asbestos was harmful to health, men, particularly in shipbuilding and in large chemical plants, continued to be exposed and were not even supplied with face masks. Asbestos is really nasty stuff. It consists of very fine needle-like fibres and if these are inhaled they get trapped in the lung. The tissues cannot rid themselves of the material which therefore sits in the tissues causing inflammation. Over years this inflammation causes scarring and cancer.

However, the commonest effect is more benign. Fibres find their way through the lung tissue to the membranes that cover the lungs - the pleura. Here they form scars that over many years take up calcium from the blood and become visible on a chest x-ray film. They are known as pleural plaques and confirm previous asbestos exposure. Usually they cause no discomfort, but their finding on a routine X-ray film causes worry and often prompts a claim for Industrial Injuries compensation. However, because plaques usually cause no disability, no compensation is payable. I suspect it might be different if this was a disease of legislators.

People become very anxious about their pleural plaques. They realise that they have been exposed and they know they are at risk of cancer.

On one occasion we were dealing with a situation in which the diagnosis of an industrial disease was open to interpretation. The DWP had turned the appellant down several times because they said he hadn't got the industrial disease in question. He therefore appealed. After seeing him several times and obtaining all the available occupational and medical evidence I decided he was, on the balance of evidence, suffering from this industrial disease. So the case was sent back to the DWP for them to decide on the level of disability and benefit. At this point they had no right to demur about the diagnosis, but demur they did. Their doctors refused to agree he had the industrial disease and they referred the case to a higher court.

From this lofty legal pinnacle came back the following judgement:

'If Professor Halford says the Appellant has this industrial disease, that's what he has.'

It had taken me a long time in my professional life to attain infallibility, but it is satisfying to have gotten there in the end!

It's a Slippery Slope

'No, that's not how you do it you silly sod! How many more times do I have to tell you, Goddard? Are you really thick or are you deliberately trying to wind me up?'

'We've been doing it this way for years, Stecher. I know what I'm doing. I've always done it this way and until you came along I had no complaints. Dodds told me to do it this way, and it always worked. You're new here, remember?'

'Dodds ain't here anymore, is he? It's me you're dealing with now, and you'll bloody well do it as I tell you or you'll be out!'

The following day Dave Goddard, who actually valued his job and realised the foreman had it in for him, tried to assemble the goods in the new way that was demanded by the new management. As he feared everything went wrong. If you got things out of order it just didn't work.

'Christ, Goddard what the hell have you done?' Stecher had returned from a management meeting.

'I've done it the way you told me, and it doesn't work. I knew it wouldn't.'

'You stupid bugger!' He gripped the front of Dave's overalls and yanked him close and shouted in his face. 'Do it again and do it fucking right this time or else!'

Dave was a well-built ex-miner. With force he shoved the foreman away. Stecher stumbled backwards, fell over some bales and landed heavily on the concrete floor.

That afternoon Dave Goddard was dismissed from Walkers and was given a month's pay in lieu of notice.

That evening, Dave, mentally bruised and dazed, but flushed with cash, went down to his local, the 'Earl Grey'. His foreman was there and had already had a few pints. Dave thought about leaving, but ordered his drink and talked to his mates. After a few minutes Stecher came over.

'So you got what was coming to you, Goddard!'

'No!' said Dave, 'you've got what you've been wanting. No one had a problem with me until you came along. You're sick in the head, Stecher!'

'You're just a bloody psychopath, Callum Stecher!' said Graham who had known him at school. 'Come over here to gloat, have you?'

'No mate, I'm just pleased to see the back of this useless prick.'

Dave jumped up and squared up to the foreman.

'Say that again and I'll punch your head!' He gave every indication that he would do just that, but before they could come to blows Jo stood up and got between them. He was a head taller than either of them and big with it.

'I think it best if you bugger off out of here Stecher.'

The foreman could see he was outnumbered and outgunned.

'I'll see to it you never get a job around here Dave Goddard! I know people, I do. They listen to me!'

'Piss off!'

Walking back from the pub with a few pints inside him Dave felt a little restored. His mates would stand by him. He would soon get another job, and he had a month's wages in his pocket. Everything would be okay, and he had got shot of a really boring job that he was really tired of.

When he got back his wife Beryl was watching TV. He stood there with his coat on. She looked up.

'What do you want?'

'Oh, nothing much, it's just that Walkers have fired me.'

'What! Christ, what did you do?'

'Nothing much, it's that Callum Stecher. I told you about him. He hates me and deliberately winds me up.'

'What of it? That doesn't get you fired.'

'No, he wound me up and grabbed me. I pushed him away and fell. He wasn't hurt, but they decided to send me packing. He's in with the management. I told them he started it but they believed his lies.'

'My God, Dave Goddard, why are you such a hopeless prat? You can't even keep a lousy dead-end job.'

'It's all right Beryl, I'll get another job. No problem.'

'What planet are you on? There are young people with qualifications who can't get a job. Look at Jane's boy. He went to college and he's been looking for months. You're old and clapped out. Who'll want to employ you? I reckon Walkers are right pleased to have got rid of you!'

He awoke the next morning at 6am as he had for all his working life. It was still dark. Beryl was snoring gently next to him. Mentally he was preparing himself for another day's work. He would get up, trying not to disturb his wife. He would don his work clothes that were lying on the chair next to the bed. He would wash and shave and go downstairs and cook himself a bowl of porridge and prepare a flask of coffee. Then he would be out in the chill morning air as dawn broke above the silent streets. He could take the bus but he usually preferred to walk if he had time...

It came to him with a thud what had happened. He tried to adjust. What was he going to do? The day stretched before him. He wasn't ready for change and felt angry that there was no longer a point in following the familiar routine that had sustained him for so long. He got up, found his dressing gown and slippers and went downstairs to the cold kitchen. He put the kettle on and began the reassuring task of making his breakfast. Then he sat down at the kitchen table and began the familiar ritual of eating his breakfast while reading the previous day's newspaper. He ate very slowly because he had no idea what he was going to do when he had finished.

He stood up and looked out onto his back garden. Even in the half light it looked a mess. At least now he would have time to get it into shape, though he disliked gardening and Beryl wouldn't lift a finger. He went through to the sitting room and turned on the telly. He only ever watched breakfast telly at the weekend. He looked without seeing. His mates would be on the way to work. Maybe it wasn't too bad to be free. He stretched out and contemplated that he still had more or less a month's pay in his pocket. He would be able to go down to the pub at lunchtime. He would get lunch there as Beryl would be at work. He looked at his watch and realised the pub wouldn't be open for about 5 hours.

There was an item about horse racing. He liked the horses and liked to have a flutter. He reckoned he was pretty good at picking a winner, and the tips he got from Barry at the pub were pretty reliable. Barry had worked in a betting shop. Some people managed to earn a decent living gambling. Maybe he should think about it.

'What the hell are you doing?' It was Beryl standing in the doorway looking matronly and disapproving.

'What does it look like I'm doing? What's the harm in watching a little breakfast TV?'

'No harm I suppose, it's more about what you are not doing.'

'And what's that, Beryl?'

'Getting off your ass and trying to get your job back for a start.'

'I really can't see how I can do that, Beryl at this time of the day.'

'No, maybe you can't, but I can. You'll get yourself down to Dr Ali's and you'll be there before the doors open so you'll be at the front of the queue.'

'What do I want to see him for? I might be pissed off, but I'm not ill.'

'You are ill, Dave. Just get that into your thick skull. You're suffering from depression and that's why you fell out with that git of a foreman. You couldn't help it, you see. You're not yourself, not in your right mind.'

'How can I tell the doctor that when it's not true?'

'What does he care whether it's true or not? The only thing that bastard cares about is getting you in and out of the place in as short a time as possible.'

'But what's the point Beryl?'

'I would have thought a child of five could see that! He'll give you a note to say you're depressed, and not in your right mind and you can take it to Walkers, and they more or less will have to give you your job back.'

'I don't think it works like that, Beryl. They've been looking for excuses to fire people for months since business slumped.'

'We'll see Dave. Either way you need to get dressed. Don't bother to shave and practice looking miserable.'

'I'm not going.'

'You are if you want to stay married to me, and I'm coming with you!'

Dr Ali seemed a little more bright and cheery than she remembered from a couple or years before when she had seen him about hot flushes.

'It's you I'm seeing, Mr Goddard?'

Dave sat hunched, staring at the floor in the way she had told him to. He nodded.

'He's not been himself for the past few weeks, Doctor,' said Beryl. I've been worried about him. I think he's got depressed like my old mum.'

'I see. How do you feel Mr Goddard?' He spoke a little louder to the slumped man.

'Miserable, Doctor.'

'Anything else?'

Dave was stumped. He suspected depressed people were sad, that was the limit of his knowledge. He shrugged his shoulders.

'Are you anxious.'

'No,' he muttered.

'He's not sleeping well, Doctor, and I found him crying yesterday.' Her mum used to cry a lot.

Dave looked up, annoyed and appeared to be about to say something to his wife.

'And he has anger issues… and I think he's a suicide risk. He said he wanted to die.'

'No I didn't!'

'You haven't thought about harming yourself?'

'No doctor, I wouldn't dream of it.'

'Well, okay,' said the doctor, taking a prescription pad out of a drawer, 'I'll give you a prescription for just a few mild sleeping pills. I suggest you take them every other night. Meanwhile try and get out and have some exercise and do something you enjoy. Spend time with friends or family, go to the cinema, or bingo, or whatever might cheer you up. If you're no better come and see me again and maybe we will then have to take things further.'

Dave nodded, took the script and stood up.

'We want a note,' said Beryl.

The doctor noted the determination in her voice and guessed this was the main purpose of the visit. 'What sort of note?'

'One for his work to say he is depressed and angry and needs a week off work.'

The doctor smiled. He didn't know what she was after, but he was having none of it. The last thing he needed in this deprived community was a reputation as a soft touch. 'Mrs Goddard, I do not know whether your husband is depressed. If he is not, then his anger is unlikely to be a medical matter. For him to stop work at this stage is probably not a good idea anyway. It might be worth having a word with the nurse at work if they have one.'

'Doctor, we really need a note. We can pay you for it.'

'I'm sorry Mrs Goddard. It would not be appropriate.'

She glared at him and stood up. Come on Dave, we're wasting our time here.'

Dave shook his head. 'I'm sorry doctor.'

'Well, I'm off!' said Beryl outside the surgery. 'Some of us have work to do.' She stormed off towards the bus stop.

Dave turned for home, relieved to be free of Beryl's nagging and bullying and happy that he had a free day in front of him. He quickened his pace and was soon home. He put on the kettle, made himself a cup of tea, turned on the telly and sat down. He flicked channels and found something on car maintenance that interested him. Then he watched a game show. At midday the pub would be open. It would take him five minutes to walk there. He looked at his watch. It was nearly time. He went through to the kitchen and looked out on the back garden that he had neglected for weeks. It was difficult to see where the overgrown lawn ended and the weedy flower beds started. He resolved to have only a single pint and to spend the afternoon tidying up. Maybe that would get her off his back.

He was the first customer in the 'Earl Grey'. Angie, the bar maid came through from the saloon to serve him.

'Didn't expect to see you here at this time of the day, Dave.' She pulled the pint.

He could see no alternative but to tell her the truth. 'Walkers have given me the sack.'

'That's terrible, Dave. What are you going to do?'

'Oh, I'll find something.'

'And Beryl, what does she think?'

'She's pretty pissed off with me, to be quite honest.'

'Why? Was it your fault?'

'No! You know that Callum Stecher - he's often in here. Well he was my foreman and all the time he was getting at me about nonsense. In the end I kicked up and then I got the sack.'

'I'm really sorry about that Dave.' There was a sound from the Saloon Bar. 'I have to go through, Dave.'

He leant on the bar and drank his pint. After a few minutes Henry the landlord came through looking far from happy.

'I don't want you in here any more, Dave Goddard. I'm not having fighting in my bar.'

'I wasn't fighting.'

'That's not what I heard.'

'Well you heard wrong, didn't you?'

'How come Callum Stecher left without finishing his drink?'

'Because we told him to go.'

'You were threatening him.'

'He was deliberately winding me up.'

Henry looked at him sternly. 'Look Dave, I know you're a regular here and I appreciate your custom, but for the present stay away, okay? I can't afford any more trouble. A place gets a reputation. Go to another watering hole, and to show you there's no hard feelings I'll pour you another pint on the house.'

Dave emptied his glass and banged it down on the bar. 'Don't bother! I'm off!' He stormed out and stopped on the pavement outside and looked up and down the road, feeling slightly dazed having gulped his pint on an empty stomach. His life had revolved through work, pub and home. Now only one of those was available to him, and even that, if the previous 24 hours was anything to go on, home was going to prove a hostile environment.

Three hundred yards further down the road was the 'Holly Bush'. He had hardly ever been in the place. It was a foreign land. He turned the other way and headed for home and was nearly there when he realised he was hungry. The chippy was only a five minute walk away.

He was walking back with his lunch wrapped in paper when he ran into Beryl's friend Ann Frobisher. He had never liked her, and the feeling was mutual.

'I hear you've lost your job.' Her voice was thin and pinched, like her face. 'Fighting wasn't it?'

'No.'

'That's what I heard. And I see that now you're living the life of Riley with a takeaway lunch. I feel sorry for Beryl, I do. You were never much good for her and now you're just a millstone around her neck.'

'I'll get another job.'

'Pigs might fly!'

'Fuck you!'

Now he just wanted to get back indoors. He walked briskly up the road. Suddenly he didn't even belong in these mean streets with their grimy red brick terraces where he had lived all his life. As a kid he played in these streets. Everyone knew him. He was part of the furniture. But now they had rejected him. He imagined disapproving eyes staring at him through net curtains from darkened front rooms. The mother had spurned her child.

Someone was coming towards him down the street. He began to panic and dodged left into empty Lampton Street and then up Shinwell Street. He got home without further confrontation.

He sat down at the kitchen table, head in hands. He wanted to cry. He wanted to shout. He was a refugee from his work and his community. This was his only refuge. For the first time he realised the seriousness of his situation, but for the life of him he didn't know what he was supposed to do about it. He had said to Beryl that he would find another job, but he had not thought how he might do that. All his life he had gone with the flow. He went down the mine like his father and his grandfather and his mates. When the pits closed he went to Walkers. They were recruiting. A lot of miners went there. The pay wasn't nearly as good but the work was lighter, and he liked it. But now it was different. Unskilled work was hard to come by. There was a lot of unemployment around.

After he had eaten his lunch he thought about turning on the TV then thought better of it. Beryl would be home at about 4.30.

She would smell the booze on his breath. He wasn't clear how he was supposed to have spent his first day of leisure, but he suspected Beryl would want him to do something more than drinking and watching TV. Then he remembered the garden. With a heavy heart he realised there was nothing for it. He would do the garden.

It wasn't a large patch. He got the electric mower from the little shed, found the extension cable and got to work. The lawn only took ten minutes even counting raking the cuttings. Then he set to and attacked the weedy flower beds. After a few minutes he heard someone in the garden next door.

'I didn't expect to see you out here at this time of day, Dave.'

It was his nextdoor neighbour Tony. He liked Tony and they often chatted over the back wall.

'Have Walkers given you a half day or something?'

'Something it is, Tony. They've given me the sack!'

'No! Why for God's sake?'

'I had a row with my bloody foreman, Callum Stecher. He's been getting at me since he started. He said I started it, but I didn't.'

'That seems very harsh, Dave.'

'I think he's in with the management.'

'Haven't Walkers been shedding staff for some time?'

'Ai, but no one said my job was on the line.'

'Look Dave, whatever, you have to contact the Jobcentre. You'll need to get Job Seeker's Allowance to tide you over until you can find another job. Give them a ring.'

So this is what he did. The following day he went to the jobcentre, he talked to a jobs coach and with her help wrote a CV. He looked on-line for jobs, of which there were quite a few, and he applied for many. He tried to be useful around the house and to his surprise quite enjoyed the simple tasks that were required of him, and over the next several weeks, Dave Goddard, the man who had always gone with the flow began to battle against the flow. Having achieved no success with his job applications he decided on a bit of direct action. There were a lot of small firms locally - garages, a scrapyard, decorators, builders and the like. He took to walking around these places each

222

morning asking for casual labour. He was allowed to do a few hours of work without losing Job Seeker's Allowance, and to his surprise on the first day he tried this he achieved success. He earned £20 at Harrisons shovelling a load of building waste into a skip. A few other similar tasks followed over the next couple of weeks. He earned a pittance, and he knew he was being exploited, but it was better than nothing, and it got him out of the house.

After a couple of months, and about 50 job applications later he was losing hope, but as usual he went out looking for casual work. In the woodyard the surly foreman promised him a tenner if he sorted a pile of timber by length. It took him a couple of hours to complete the task.

'No! You've not done it right,' said the foreman.

'What do you mean? I've done it exactly as you told me.'

'No, you've done it wrong. I'm not paying you for that.'

'You bloody cheat!'

'You better get out, or I'll have you thrown out.'

'You pay me for what I've done. I've worked hard at this and you saw what I was doing. You owe me a tenner, and even that's little enough.'

'I won't tell you again. Get out!'

Two of his men were coming closer.

'Fuck you!'

He stormed off, blind with anger, outraged at the injustice. He strode up the road, hardly aware of where he was going or where he wanted to go. He found himself outside the Earl Grey and dearly wanted to go in to drown his sorrows, and to share his outrage with a sympathetic listener, but he knew there would be trouble. He walked on, but he needed a drink. He turned and walked the three hundred yards to the 'Holly Bush', marched in and ordered a pint of lager. He leant on the bar and looked around at the place. There were three men sitting at a table drinking and chatting, and at a neighbouring table a man sitting alone with his pint. Dave vaguely recognised him from the far end of his road. As Dave caught his eye the man raised his glass and smiled. Dave went over to him. He felt a desperate need to unburden himself to someone.

'Not seen you in here before,' said the man, who was a good deal older than Dave.

'No, I'm usually in the Earl Grey.' His voice was raised because of his anger. 'I've just been doing casual work down at the wood yard. The bastard offered me a tenner for sorting some planks. It was hard work and it took me a couple of hours and then the bastard refused to pay me. Said I'd done it wrong, though he had watched me all that time and had said nothing about me doing it wrong.'

'That's not fair, is it lad? I can see why you're pissed off.'

'Pissed off? I'm fucking livid! I tell you, I'm going to get my own back on that fucking prick you see if I don't!'

'Hey! Keep your voice down!' The landlord was glaring at Dave. 'We don't want any of that sort of talk here!'

'Nay Lad,' said the old man, quietly. That's not the way. You'll never win with those types. They know all the tricks and they've got no conscience. Forget it and get on with your life.'

'I just can't see how he could do that.'

'There's lots who take advantage of those who they think can do them no harm. It was different in my day when the pits were open. There was honour, and respect. We helped one another. It's all gone now. Dog eat dog!'

But Dave's anger was not that easily assuaged. He gulped the rest of his pint and stormed out. He thought to go back to the wood yard and give them grief, but he reckoned he would only get hurt. He strode up the road, past the Earl Grey to the Co-op. He went in and bought a 2 litre bottle of cider. He didn't like cider, but it was the cheapest. He got home, poured himself a large glass and gulped it down. He poured a second and drank that equally quickly. He paced up and down the hall. His anger was still as intense, but now he could deal with it. He hit on a plan.

He gulped some more cider from the bottle, unbolted the back door and went to his shed. He found a large adjustable spanner which had about the right size and weight to be a weapon. He slipped it down the front of his trousers and put his jacket on. After a further swig from the bottle he went out and marched purposefully towards the wood yard.

It was a ten minute walk, down two rows of terraced houses, across High Street and down a road of abandoned shops and premises. The area was due for redevelopment but nothing had happened for years. He rounded a corner. The tall corrugated iron gates of the wood yard were opposite. They were shut and padlocked.

'Come out here you fucking bastard!' He bashed on the gates with his hand. 'We have business to settle!' he shouted. He bashed some more until it dawnwd on him that if the gate was padlocked on the outside no one was likely to be inside. He pulled out the spanner and bashed the padlock, but it was large and unlikely to yield and so in his frustration he whacked the gates a few times before turning away.

An elderly couple carrying shopping were standing on the opposite side of the road watching.

'What are you looking at?' Dave demanded to know.

'Looking at you bashing the gate, mate.' said the man.

'Why the hell do you have to go crazy like that?' asked Beryl. 'People cheat all the time. What did you expect?'

He had bought another large bottle of cider and was pretty far gone. His anger had been replaced by self loathing and self pity. He sat on the sofa, head in hands weeping.

'I just can't do this, Beryl. They've done for me.'

She sat down next to him and put her arm around him. 'Come on lad. You can do it. Things will improve. You'll find another job, I know you will. You've tried hard, and I'm proud of you. People have seen how you've struggled, how you've tried. They admire you.'

He shook his head. 'This is the only place I've known. I belonged here. I was part of the bricks and mortar of the place and now I'm not. I'm garbage - thrown on the tip.'

When he woke the next morning it was still dark. He felt sick and his head was throbbing. He made himself a large mug of coffee. He went through to the front room and pulled back the curtains. Grey dawn was breaking, but already lights were on in several of the houses opposite as people prepared for a day of work. The world was waking and about to go about its business.

He closed the curtains and flopped onto the sofa. He no longer felt he could face that world. It did not want him. There was nothing he could face doing. He turned on the TV and watched, but could not concentrate. He made himself a black coffee, but it just made him feel sicker.

Beryl came downstairs in her dressing gown. She had not slept well but she, as usual, had an early start.

'How do you feel?' she asked.

'Like shit.'

'Look Dave, you've had it rough. Take it easy today. Maybe do a little gardening. If you can face it, how about trying to fix that shelf I've been asking you to do?'

'Maybe.' He didn't feel like standing up, let alone doing anything, and after she left for work he went and laid on his bed. He got up at lunch time, but he wasn't hungry. He made some tea and found some biscuits, but the tea tasted awful. He felt on edge, and even frightened, though he didn't know why. The curtains were still drawn. He didn't want to go out, but he craved a drink. He knew it would give him relief and take away his fears, but Beryl would give him a hard time. His father had been an alcoholic and she was terrified he would go the same way.

He had no booze. The Co-op was 200 hundred yards away down roads that now held terrors. He sat down and turned on the TV, and watched a game show that almost amused him for a couple of minutes, but his restlessness returned. If he just had a little drink, maybe he could settle enough to do some tasks.

He opened the front door and looked in both directions. Twenty laced curtained windows accused him from up and down the road. He knew they were watching him. There was someone walking away at the far end of the road. He stared back, defiantly at the windows, stepped out and walked briskly, with his head down towards the Co-op. He pushed the door open, but inside there were at least half a dozen people. He panicked, and propelled by fear half ran and half walked back. He had to wait. He paced up and down.. Half an hour later, and with the same anxiety he went again. There was only one other shopper, an old lady, and he did not recognise her. He went in and bought his cider, put the precious cargo beneath his jacket and hurried home.

He sat at the kitchen table and gulped down the first glass. Almost at once his anxieties were receding. After a second glass he felt almost human, and after the third he was an entirely new man. He put the screw cap back on the bottle, opened the back door and hid the bottle beneath his workbench in the shed. He looked at the garden. It was a bit of a mess again. The grass needed cutting, there were weeds all over the flower beds. Without a plan, and with energy born of guilt he set to ripping up weeds and piling them on the edge of the lawn. He had only cleared a small fraction of what needed to be done, when he felt bored and decided he needed to rest. He went inside, lay on the sofa and fell asleep at once, and he was still asleep when Beryl returned.

He had been on her mind all day. She was not naturally a sympathetic person, but she knew it was difficult for him, and she had decided he might respond to more encouragement and less criticism. He had, after all, been trying.

This worthy resolve went straight out of the window as soon as she smelled the booze on his breath.

'You've been drinking again!'

'Not much, Beryl, just to steady my nerves.'

'Enough to make you unconscious more likely. Dave Goddard, you really are the biggest idiot.'

'I'm sorry, like. I felt awful.'

'Pah! You're weak, just like that useless father of yours. So where is it?'

'Where's what?'

'Where's the rest of it.'

'I finished it.'

'Well where's the bottle?'

'In the shed.'

'That's a funny place to put it. The bin would be more usual. So let's go and find it, shall we?' She stormed out to the shed. He meekly followed.

'Where is it?'

'Under the bench there.'

She grabbed it, barged past him and into the kitchen. She began pouring the precious cider into the sink.

'Please Beryl, I need it. It makes me feel okay again.'

'You can't take it Dave Goddard. In no time you'll be like your father.'

He collapsed onto a kitchen chair and sat with his head in his hands.

'You have to fight it Dave. The booze will just make you worse. It can't help you.'

'I know, I know! I know about my dad. I want to be strong, but I can't do it. I'm at the end of my tether, can't you see?'

She put the bottle in the bin and looked at him. 'Okay, then we've got to do something. We've got to be positive.'

'It's all very well saying that. I've tried to be positive and look where it's got me.'

'Let's go out! Let's try to enjoy ourselves like we used to.'

'No Beryl, I can't face it.'

'Of course you can. Let's go to the pictures. We haven't been for years. Cheryl says the new Terminator film's good. It's on downtown at the Empire.'

He helped her make tea and ate in silence, dreading their outing, particularly as the alcohol was draining from his system. Fortunately, the bus to town was almost empty. He sat close to his wife, but he still felt threatened by the couple sitting near the back. He was sure they were looking at him and judging him. He hung nervously behind Beryl as she bought the tickets, but he felt safe in the darkness of the cinema. The film was good, and for a couple of hours he forgot his troubles.

'Okay, Dave, let's go for a drink.'

'But?'

'No, I don't mind you drinking in moderation with me. It's by yourself I don't trust you. We're just having one.'

She came with him to get the drinks and then they sat at a table at the back away from the crowds. He soon began to feel better.

'Thanks, Beryl, you're a good lass. I feel a lot better.'

'You've got your appointment at the JobCentre tomorrow, Dave. You mustn't forget.'

His heart sank. She really knew how to ruin a moment!

He woke early the next morning feeling very miserable, and he was immediately dreading his appointment at the JobCentre.

Beryl got up earlier than usual and they ate breakfast together, or at least he tried to eat, with no appetite. He was sure he couldn't manage to get to his appointment by himself.

'Could you go with me?'

'Where to?'

'To the JobCentre.'

'No, of course I can't. I'll be on the other side of town. We can't have both of us off work. You'll be fine!'

'I don't feel like going.'

'If you don't they'll stop your money, and then where would we be? We won't even be able to pay the rent. I know, you're already behind on job applications, and they have warned you. Those bastards would be only too pleased to stop paying.'

'I'm frightened Beryl.'

'A big strapping fellow like you? You weren't frightened after those fellows got killed down the pit. You weren't frightened when that bloke picked on you in the pub. You were like a lion! What are you frightened of for God's sake?'

'I don't know! I know it's stupid. People look at me. They reckon I'm a bad person and I suppose I am.'

'You're no worse than any of them. I don't know what's come over you.'

'Nor do I.'

His appointment was for 11.30. It was about half an hour's walk. He needed to allow plenty of time. He could cut across the park which would be pretty deserted, and with any luck he wouldn't meet anyone.

It was a chilly morning so he put on his anorak and pulled the hood up over his head. He stood at the front door, stealing himself to open it. He took a deep breath and grabbed the handle and yanked it open. He looked each way to see that the road was clear and then, checking again that he had his key, he closed the door and began to walk briskly. He crossed the park, avoiding a woman with a pushchair. He walked down a street on the other side and then he could see the JobCentre. Two minutes later he was at the door. He pulled the hood down as far over his face as he could, pushed open the door and walked in. There was a queue at Reception and people were waiting around and looking at computer screens. He stood in line. He felt scores of pairs of eyes looking at him and criticising him. He began to feel unwell. He could feel his heart pounding and he was sweating and feeling dizzy. He looked at his watch. It was only 11.00. He was much too early. He turned around and walked out.

There was a row of shops to the left. Whatever Beryl said, he knew he just couldn't do this without a drink. It had been okay before. This was his fourth time, and the previous occasions hadn't been bad. There was nothing to fear, but he feared all the same. There was a small store half way down. He peered in. There was no one inside. He went in. The spirits were behind the counter. He bought a quarter bottle of vodka and slipped it into his pocket and then walked quickly back to the park. He sat down on a bench and looked at his watch. He had twenty minutes. He took a large gulp of the awful tasting liquid and sat back, waiting for the magical effect. Five minutes later he grew calmer and began to look around at his surroundings. The park took on a beauty he had not previously noticed. The trees swayed in the cool breeze. He smiled as he watched a dog chasing a ball. He pulled the hood off his head and made his way to his appointment.

Three days later Beryl took him back to see Dr Ali. Reading the notes he had made at their visit, the wily practitioner was again sceptical about the true reason for the visit, however, as he listened to the story, this time it made clinical sense. The man was feeling low, he was anxious, particularly when he went out, and he had experienced what sounded like panic attacks. It was a pattern of presentation he had become used to, particularly in the newly unemployed.

'Look, Dave. I think you may have become depressed because you lost your job. Depressed people often get anxious. If we could find you a job tomorrow I think you would get better quickly, but that's not easy, is it? Now, I would like to see you in a couple of weeks. Meanwhile, I want you to try to get out of the house every day. Perhaps you could keep a record of your outings, and try to do a little more each day. As you are not sleeping well, I'll give you some more sleepers, but don't use them every night. I won't start an antidepressant pill today. They don't always work, and they have side effects.'

'He's drinking to give himself Dutch courage, Doctor,' said Beryl.

'Try to be strong without it, Dave. You'll become an alcoholic, and then you'll never get another job.'

But Dave Goddard did not make his next appointment with Dr Ali. Events took a dramatic and unexpected twist.

It was a night when he hadn't taken a sleeping pill. His shallow sleep was disturbed by the sound of emergency vehicles. He got out of bed and went to the window. It was difficult to make out, but something appeared to be on fire on the other side of the High Street. There was a ruddy glow reflected off nearby buildings and then flames would briefly shoot upwards.

Then he realised, with satisfaction, that the wood yard was in that direction.

The next morning it was on the local news. There had been a massive fire, needing six fire appliances to bring it under control. The cause of the fire was being investigated.

'You said they were a bunch of crooks, Dave,' said Beryl. 'They probably set fire to the place themselves to claim on the insurance.'

'Yer, maybe.'

That afternoon Dave was in the kitchen when there was a knock at the door. His anxiety was such that he usually did not answer the door. It was usually only someone selling something, or Jehovah's Witnesses. They knocked again, loudly. They were pounding on the door itself. Dave went to the door and stood behind it.

'Who is it?'

'Police! We need to have a word with you, Mr Goddard.'

'How do I know you are who you say you are?'

'Look out of your window. You'll see our car.'

He went through to the front room and pulled back the curtains. A police panda car was at the kerb, immediately outside. He opened the door. Two large police officers were on the pavement outside.

'Mr David Goddard?' The officer held out his ID.

'Yes.'

'Mr Goddard, we need to ask you some questions in relation to the fire last night at the wood yard in Mill Lane. May we come in?'

He led them through into the kitchen and the three of them sat at the table.

'Okay, Mr Goddard. Would you prefer it if we call you David?'

'Dave. Everyone calls me Dave.'

'Now Dave we've been given information that suggests you might have had something to do with the fire.'

'What information? I had nothing to do with it. Someone's lying.'

'Okay, Dave. Don't get worked up. Tell us what you were doing last night.'

'I watched the telly with Beryl until about 11.30 and then we went to bed. I didn't sleep well and was woken by the sound of the fire engines, so I went to the window and saw the fire. I don't know what time that was.'

'You didn't go out last night?'

'No.'

'You didn't go to the wood yard last night?'

'Of course not.'

The policemen exchanged glances.

'Look Dave, we know you had a dispute with the guy in charge of the wood yard.'

'What of it?'

'You were ranting about him in the Holly Bush.'

'How would you like it if you were promised a tener for some hard work, but he refused to pay?'

'And did you do anything to get your own back on them?'

'I tried. I went down there but they were closed, so I bashed on their gates. That's all I did.'

'When was this?'

'I don't know. A few weeks ago.'

'And you've done nothing since?'

'No. Beryl told me to calm down and then I got frightened of going out.'

'Dave, do you have any petrol or paraffin here?'

'No.'

'And what about matches or a lighter?'

'I don't know. We don't smoke and the stove's electric.'

'Could you have a look please? And where do you keep tools and things like that?'

'In the shed out back.'

'Okay, do you mind if we have a look in your shed?'

'Go ahead.'

Dave searched through the kitchen drawers and cupboards and in the end found an ancient box of matches.

'Do you mind if we take these, Sir?' Asked the constable.

'No problem.'

Ten minutes later the detective came back into the kitchen carrying the large adjustable spanner and a bright blue can with a spout.

'Have you anything to say about these items, Dave?'

'Yes, that's my spanner, but I've never seen that can in my life. It's not mine.'

'From the smell of it I think it contains paraffin.'

'I never use paraffin. We used to have a paraffin heater years ago, but that's long gone.'

'So you deny that this is yours.'

'Yes.'

'Even though it was in your shed.'

'That's what you say. It's not mine.'

'Well, how did it get there?'

'How do I know? Someone put it there, not me.'

The detective thought for a moment. 'Look Dave, I think we need to take this further. I would like to interview you under caution down at the station. You are not under arrest and therefore you can refuse to cooperate at this stage. In fairness to you I need to inform you that this afternoon, a local man has told us that some minutes before the fire last night he saw a man of your description walking towards the wood yard carrying a blue can similar to this one.'

'Whatever he says, it wasn't me and this isn't my can.'

'Will you come down to the station like I ask?'

'Yer, I guess. When?'

'Dave, we need to get on with this, but maybe you need to talk to a lawyer, or perhaps get a lawyer to be present when you are interviewed.'

'I don't have a lawyer and don't have money for one.'

'Well maybe a trusted friend or your wife. Come down to the station at 10.30 tomorrow. Hopefully we can eliminate you from our inquiries.'

Dave sat in his kitchen in shock after they had gone. He couldn't think straight. Someone was framing him for something he did not do. How could someone have seen him when he was in bed? Where did the can come from?

He phoned Beryl.

'Dave, you mustn't phone me at work!'

'Beryl, the police have been round. They think I did it!'

'What?'

'The fire at the wood yard. They think I started it! Someone says they saw me.'

'That's ridiculous! How could you have? You were in bed with me.'

'I know, but they think differently. Someone's setting me up. I have to go down to the police station tomorrow for an interview. They say I need a lawyer.'

'God!'

'What am I going to do, Beryl?'

'Honestly Dave, I can't talk now. I tell you what - go next door and talk to Tony. He's a decent bloke and quite smart. See what he says, and I'll be home as soon as possible. For God's sake don't start drinking.'

He knocked on Tony's door. He could hear talking inside.

'God man! You look as if you've seen a ghost. Come in!' said Tony.

Tony retreated back to the kitchen and turned off the radio. 'Come in and sit down Dave. I guess this has something to do

234

with the police. I saw their car outside. I can tell you I was puzzled.'

'They think I started the fire down at the wood yard.'

'Why do they think that?'

'I think I'm being framed. Someone said they saw me and they found a paraffin can in my shed. I haven't had a paraffin can for twenty years.'

'Why would anyone want to frame you?'

'I had a run in with them a few weeks ago.' Dave explained what had happened. 'That's the only reason I can think of.'

'If they're trying to set you up, it mean they know that someone else started the fire. Why would they do that?

Dave shrugged his shoulders'

'Maybe it's an insurance scam.'

'How do you mean?'

'You fill the place up with cheap wood and claim for expensive wood. This sort of thing happens all the time. If they can find a fall guy, so much the better.'

'Look, Tony, I need to ask you a favour. I have to go down to the police station tomorrow morning to be interviewed. They say I need a lawyer, but we can't afford one so I wondered if you could come with me and give me your advice.'

'I don't think I can be of much use.'

'You're a lot cleverer than me, and I just can't go there alone. I'll panic. I won't be able to cope, feeling like I do.'

'Can't Beryl go with you?'

'She can't take time off.'

'Well, okay, but maybe you should find someone qualified to help you.'

So the following morning he and Tony were seated at a table in the interview room in Regent Street Police station. Across the table were two detectives in plain clothes. The senior officer introduced himself as Detective Sergeant McClean and started the recording. He said for the record who was in the room and cautioned Dave that he didn't have to say anything, but what he did say would be taken down as evidence.

'Now Mr Goddard, we understand from our enquiries that you had a problem with the wood yard.'

'How do you mean?'

'You had some sort of a dispute with them.'

'Yes, I did some work for them. The boss guy promised me a tener for sorting some wood. It took me a couple of hours and I did it right, but he refused to pay me. He said I'd done it wrong, but I hadn't.'

'So what did you do?'

'I got pretty annoyed, but then a couple of his men came over, and I thought they were going to have a go at me, so I went.'

'You felt threatened?'

Dave nodded.

'Now, this boss of the wood yard, did you know him?'

'I've seen him around.'

'Where?'

'I'm not sure. Probably in the Earl Grey.'

'Right. But you hadn't had dealings with him before?'

'How do you mean?'

'You haven't done work for him before? You haven't talked to him? You haven't had arguments or fights with him?'

'No, I've only seen him around.'

'Okay, but I have to tell you that we have spoken to the boss of the wood yard, Mr Haas, and he says he paid you despite the fact that you didn't do a good job. He felt sorry for you because you're unemployed.'

'Well he's lying, isn't he?'

'He also told us you've been banned from the Earl Grey for fighting.'

'I wasn't fighting. I had an argument, that's all.'

'Who with?

'With a guy called Callum Stecher, who was my foreman at Walkers. He got me fired after we had an argument.'

'You seem to be always getting into arguments, Mr Goddard.'

'Not really.'

'Okay, let's move on. Where did you go after the wood yard?'

'I went to the Holly Bush. I needed a drink.'

'For the record the Holly Bush is a public house approximately 500 yards from the wood yard.'

'Yes.'

'And you had the money you earned in the wood yard.'

'No I didn't! You're trying to trick me.'

'Sorry, my mistake...and what did you do in the Holly Bush?'

'I had a drink, of course.'

'Did you talk to anyone?'

'Yer, to an old bloke from down our road. I don't know his name.'

'And what did you talk about?'

'I was pretty angry and was mouthing off about not being paid, and he told me to calm down and forget it.'

'We have been told that you were threatening to get your own back on the wood yard.'

'I dunno. I was pretty angry.'

'Did you threaten revenge?'

'Maybe.'

'That doesn't help us much, Dave, does it. You either threatened or you didn't.'

'I don't remember. I was in a state. I was livid. The landlord told me to quieten down.'

'Come on, Dave! Admit it. You were furious. You threatened revenge. It's obvious. You're wasting our time.'

'No lad, said Tony. 'Don't let them twist your arm. If you are not sure what you said, leave it at that. Don't play along with their little game.'

'I honestly don't remember,' said Dave.

'Now, Mr Goddard, what happened after that?'

'I went home.'

'And then what did you do?'

'I was still furious, like. I decided to go back down there and have it out with them.'

'To the wood yard?'

'Yes. So I went down there but the gates were shut and padlocked.'

'So?'

'I bashed on the gates and shouted for them to come out, but then I reckoned they had gone. So I went home.'

'That's it? You've nothing else to tell us?'

'No.'

'I think there is, Dave.'

'Like what?'

'Like something you took with you to the wood yard.'

'Dave shrugged his shoulders.'

'Shrugging your shoulders I think tells us there is something you should be telling us.'

Silence.

'Okay, we note that you are holding back on us.'

'Hey!' said Tony. 'The lad's told you a lot. He's not obliged to say anything, or at least that's what you said at the beginning.'

'Okay Dave, let's try to get real! A passerby has told us he saw you bashing the padlock on the gate with a large metal object.'

'Well he's mistaken, isn't he? I found a brick in the road and hit it with it.'

'I see. Now Dave, you recognise this?'

The detective drew out from under the table the adjustable spanner, now contained in a transparent plastic bag. He pushed it across the table towards Dave.

'I suppose it's the one you took from my shed?'

'That's correct. It was lying on your bench. Now, what we want to know is whether you took this with you when you went the second time to the wood yard.'

'No.'

'Only our witness says the object you were using to hit the padlock looked like a large adjustable spanner.'

'He was wrong.'

'Well, okay. In that case we'll move on and consider that other piece of evidence, the paraffin can that was found in your shed.'

'It's not mine. I'd never seen it before. I don't use paraffin or petrol, so why would I have a can?'

'Well, Dave, maybe so that you could set the wood yard on fire.'

'No way!'

'Well, let me tell you this, Dave. We have had a witness come forward saying he saw a man of your general description carrying a can like this down his road minutes before the fire started.'

'Well, it wasn't me. What was he looking out of his window in the middle of the night for?'

'How do you explain these things, Dave? It seems to us that you had the motive and the means to commit this crime, and we have a witness who is willing to testify he saw you on your way to do it?'

'He's lying. I never went there. I didn't do it!'

'There's nothing more you can tell us?'

'Just that I had nothing to do with it.'

The detectives looked at each other and nodded. 'Okay Dave, Tony, we'll wrap this up for now. My colleague and I need to confer. Wait here, we won't be more than a few minutes.'

'Can I go then?'

'Let's hope so. Interview suspended at 11.48.'

'So, what do you think, Collins?'

'I think he did it, Sir. As you say, he had the motive and the method. He was seen going there and had a can of paraffin in his shed.'

'Don't you think it's all a little too neat and tidy? Don't you feel we are being led?'

'How do you mean, Sir?'

'It's all too easy. People have come forward to tell us. It's almost as if they were told to.'

'Why not arrest him and question him further?'

'I don't want to unless we have to. Not yet. He's got no criminal record and I don't think he's going to run away. No, I feel that we've been directed to follow certain paths in this investigation. Let's choose some directions of our own. I want you to find out about these characters Callum Stecher, Kevin Haas and Darren White. See if they have a record. And then I want you to find out about wood yard fires over the past few years. Cast the net wide, and meet me here at 8pm. Oh, and you know that bright blue jumper you are always wearing? Bring it with you, and oh yes, send Goddard home.'

'Well, that wasn't too bad, was it lad?' said Tony as they walked home, but he could see that Dave was still trembling and frightened. He was walking so fast that he had difficulty keeping up.

'It was terrible. They think I did it, or at least they're going to pin it on me. They've got it in for me. Everyone's against me. How did that bloody can get in my shed? Someone put it there. I think I saw them!'

'How do you mean? I thought you said you were in bed?'

'Yer, I know. It seemed safest to say that, but actually I don't sleep much nowadays and I heard something out back. I thought it was probably just a cat but I went downstairs and looked out the back window. It was very dark but I was sure I saw something or somebody by the wall at the side where there's the alley. I should have gone out but I was scared.'

'You should have told them that.'

They were approaching the Holly Bush.

'Hey Dave, how about a drink to steady your nerves?'

'No, I don't want to go in there.' He needed a drink, but he still had some vodka hidden away.

At last he was indoors. He bolted the front door, went into the sitting room and drew the curtains. He went out to the back and he found the vodka in the shed. He went upstairs to his bedroom, shut the door and drew the curtains. He finished the booze and waited for its comforting effect.

He phoned Beryl.

'I'm home now, Beryl. I thought they were going to arrest me, but they didn't.'

'Okay Dave, that's good. There's stuff for your lunch in the fridge. No booze. I'll be back at four.'

Sergeant McClean decided he needed more local knowledge. He wasn't from these parts. He needed to visualise the neighbourhood. He drove the mile or so from the station and parked opposite the Holly Bush. There was a dismal parade of shops set back from the road, a small grocers, a unisex hairdresser and some men were standing around outside a betting shop. Further down was a hardware outfit with a lot of stock displayed on the pavement outside. He walked the 50 yards and went in. A huge array of goods was stacked from floor to ceiling to the extent that at first he could not work out where the proprietor was hiding. He found a man at the back of this Aladdin's cave.

'I'm looking for a paraffin can.'

Without a word the man scurried off between two rows of high shelves and returned with a shiny blue receptacle that appeared identical to the one they had found in Dave's shed.

He showed the man his police badge. 'I'm Detective Sergeant McClean from Regent Street station. May I know your name?'

'Arthur Groves. I'm the owner.'

'Right Mr Groves I am interested in whether you have sold a can like this in the past couple of weeks.'

'I don't recollect, I'm afraid.'

'You're always here?'

'Usually, yes, but my wife sometimes serves.'

'Well, could you ask Mrs Groves please?'

A few minutes later a worried looking, portly lady came down the stairs.

'I hope we've not done anything wrong, officer.'

'No, no, Madam there's no suggestion of that. We are just interested to trace the origin of a can that is very similar or the same as this one.'

'Yes, I do remember. Maybe a week ago. I thought it was a strange time of year to be buying such a thing.'

'Can you remember who bought it?'

'No, I didn't recognise him.'

'It was a man?'

'Yes. He was quite short and a bit overweight.'

'You're sure?'

'Yes, and he was balding.'

'Can you remember anything else about him - his clothes, his manner, his accent?'

'No, I can't really.'

'Do you think you could recognise him?'

'Maybe.'

Det Sergeant McClean turned left out of the shop and walked half a mile down the road before turning left into Keir Hardie

Lane that led downhill towards the wood yard. He turned right at the bottom into Church Road. Two hundred yards down the gates of the wood yard were open and there was a truck backed in and behind it a man was shouting. He walked round to the back of the lorry. A man was shovelling burnt wood and ashes into a skip. A large man with unruly ginger hair was standing by, looking annoyed.

'What do you want?' He was not welcoming.

McClean showed his badge.

'Can't you people leave us alone?'

'You must be Kevin Haas. I'm sorry to bother you, Mr Haas. I know my constable has already interviewed you.'

'So?'

'So Mr Haas, I wanted to see the place for myself and ask you a couple more questions. You told the Constable about how this guy came here looking for casual work. He claims you promised him £10 for sorting some wood, but you refused to pay him.'

'Yes, that's a bloody lie!'

'Okay, but what I want to know is whether you knew this guy.'

'His face was familiar, but I didn't know his name or anything about him.'

'If you paid him, why do you think he was so cross?'

'He said it took him so long, he wanted more, but it was only because he was so bloody slow. What I offered him was fair.'

'A last point. If this fellow, or someone else wanted to set this place on fire, he would have to get into these premises, wouldn't he?'

'Yer, I guess.'

'Well, how could he have done that? You are surrounded by a high corrugated iron fence. He would have to climb it somehow?'

'Look, I don't know. Maybe he had a ladder.'

'Yes, I thought of that. So he comes down here with a can of paraffin and a ladder. He gets over the fence with the can, jumps down the other side and then starts the fire. He has to get out smartish, yes?'

'Yes.'

'But how does he do that? The ladder is on the other side.'

'Look mate, I don't know! I've got work to do.'

'Okay Mr Haas. Are you the owner of this place?'

'Nar, of course not, I'm just the bloody manager.'

'So who owns it then?'

'It's a guy called Thompson. He's often around here.'

'Do you know where he lives?'

'No.'

'Or a phone number?'

'No.'

'Do you know anything about him?'

'Not really.'

'How do you communicate with him?'

'I send him an email, don't I?'

'Can you let me know his email address?'

'That's more than my job is worth.'

McClean turned to go. 'By the way, what sort of wood got burned?'

'Mainly hardwood. We'd only taken delivery a few days ago. The shed was full of the stuff.'

'How very unfortunate.'

By the time he got back to the station it was getting dark. Collins was at his desk peering at the computer.

'Have you found anything?'

'A bit, yes. The wood yard manager, Kevin Haas has previous. He did 6 months for GBH in 2009. Darren White, the witness seems to be clean. Nothing on him at all. The most interesting is Callum Stecher. There was a wood yard fire in Shotley Bridge in 2005 and Callum Stecher was the manager.'

'And don't tell me. The owner was a man called Thompson.'

'How did you know that, Sir? He was called Granville Thompson.'

'Just a guess. Did you discover anything about this Thomson,'

'I'm afraid not Sir. It's a pretty odd name so I thought our systems would come up with something, but no.'

'Okay, never mind. We need to get on and have a word with this Darren White.'

'Why don't we call him in for interview tomorrow, Sir?'

'Because I need to see him in the dark in his own place. Let's go and don't forget the sweater.'

They drove past the Holly Bush and the sleeping hardware store, past Keir Hardie Lane and then took the second left into Albert Road, leading downhill towards the wood yard. They parked at the top.

'Okay, Collins. No 17 is about a hundred yards down on the right. It's the house with the For Sale sign. I'll knock on his door. As soon as he answers I want you to walk past on the opposite side of the road carrying your jumper so that he can see it. Then come back and join us.'

Collins waited to perform his boss's mysterious instruction. McClean crossed the road. The small Victorian villas had small gardens in front. By the light of a street lamp opposite he could see McClean push open the gate and ring the bell. Ten seconds later the door opened and he began to walk down the road holding his sweater in his right hand.

The door had been opened by a shortish man with receding black hair.

'Good evening. I'm Detective Sergeant McClean from Regent Street police station. Am I speaking to Darren White?' The man nodded.

'You kindly made a witness statement down at the station. I have read it and want to ask you a few questions.'

'Come in, Sergeant.'

'That's kind of you, but I would like to understand the circumstances of your observation. I see you have a street lamp almost opposite, and I guess that helped you see the man. Which side was he walking on?'

'Opposite.'

'So he walked down right under the light.'

'Yes'

McClean could see Collins approaching. 'And he was carrying a can.'

'Yes.'

'Can you describe it?'

'Yes, it was bright blue with a spout.'

'And in which hand was he carrying it.'

244

'Er, the right I think.'

'Now this is very convenient, Mr White. You see the man coming down the road?'

Collins was approaching the street lamp.

'My colour vision isn't very good. Could you tell me the colour of the thing that man's carrying in his right hand?'

'White stepped out onto his front path. 'Yes, I think it's a piece of clothing in black or brown.'

'Agreed. That's very helpful, Mr White.' McClean glanced up at the estate agent's sign. 'I see you're moving.'

'Yes, I'm moving out of town to Hayly village.'

'Come into some money?'

'You could say that, yes.'

'For service rendered, I guess.'

'What do you mean?'

Now Constable Collins appeared at the front gate.

'Mr White, I'm sorry to play tricks on you, but this is my assistant who you just observed walking down the road opposite. Now, Collins, Mr Whte just told me that the thing you have in your hand was coloured black or brown, but if you would come closer Mr White can see the actual colour of your sweater by the light from his hallway. I'm sure you can now see, Mr White that he is holding a royal blue sweater. The colour is not too different from that of the paraffin can that my colleagues found in the shed of Mr Dave Goddard.'

'You see, Mr White it is very difficult to gauge real colours in the pure yellow light of a sodium vapour lamp. There is no blue light for a blue object to reflect, so it looks black, as you observed. But, of course you knew the can was blue, didn't you?'

'No I didn't, I saw it.'

'I think not. You knew it was blue because you had purchased it days before in Mr Grove's hardware store opposite the Holly Bush. You may deny this, but I suspect Mrs Groves will be able to identify you.'

'I never bought it.'

'And I think we may well be able to prove that, far from witnessing someone carrying a can to the wood yard, that actually it was you who did that, and having started the fire you took the can and placed it in Dave Goddard's shed. I'm sure, for instance, that we'll find your grubby little fingerprints on the can and all over his shed.'

'I didn't do it.'

'Mr White we have more than enough reason to arrest you. If you choose to cooperate with us it would be to your benefit.'

Even in the half light they could see that he was trembling and sweating.

'It was that Callum Stecher! I had no choice. If I didn't do this he would see to it that I lost my job. If I agreed to do it he said they would pay me £5000 and I would be in line for promotion.'

'You work at Walkers?'

'Yes, I've been there for years.'

'Who is Callum Stecher working for?'

'I don't know. He never told me and I never asked.'

'Have you heard of Granville Thompson?'

'No.'

'Okay, Darren White, I'm arresting you for conspiring with others to set fire to a wood yard and lying to the police. We are taking you to Regent Street police station where you will write a statement and be questioned further.'

It was late by the time they had finished with Darren White consigned him to a cell overnight to await an appearance before a magistrate in the morning. On the face of it their day's work was over. They were preparing to leave.

'So, boss, are we going after this Callum Stecher?'

'What do you think?'

'We need at least a statement from him.'

'All we really need from him is the identity of Granville Thompson.'

'He may tell us if we arrest him.'

'I doubt it.'

'So, what are we going to do?'

'How about a drink?'

'I thought you would never ask.'

They drove to the Earl Grey.

'This is a long shot, Collins, but either way we'll get a well earned drink.'

The bar was crowded and noisy. There was a young man and a young woman serving behind the bar. He ordered their pints and McClean showed his badge to the man. 'Is the landlord around?'

'I think he's in the Saloon. I'll get him.'

The landlord was a large bald man who seemed none too pleased to have officers of the law on his premises.

'I'm looking for one of your regular customers, a Callum Stecher. I just need to have a word with him. Is he in here tonight?'

The landlord scanned around the room. 'Yer, he's over there - at that table - in the blue tee-shirt.'

'We'll just have a very short word with him and that will be it.'

Stecher looked up apprehensively as McClean showed his badge. 'We just need a short word with you, Callum. Shall we step outside for a moment so that we can hear one another?'

'Okay.' They went out onto the pavement.

'I hoped you might be able to help us. You see, in our investigation of the fire at the wood yard we came up with your name as manager of a wood yard in Shotley Bridge that went up in smoke in 2005. Now, we have been informed that the wood yard in Church Road is owned by a Mr Thompson, and that he also owned the one in Shotley Bridge. I was hoping you might be able to tell us about him or how we might make contact with him.'

'I'm afraid I can't. It was a long time ago. I had dealings then with a guy who called himself Thompson, but I don't think that was his real name. I don't know anything about the wood yard here.'

'Can you remember anything about him?'

'As I say, it's a long while ago. He was of medium height, with a tooth-brush moustache. I think his hair was brown. I didn't see him often.'

'Mm. Okay Callum. Another thing. When we spoke to you just now you were sitting alone. Right?'

'Yes '

'But Callum I couldn't help noticing that there were two half drunk pints on your table. Who did the other one belong to?'

'A mate of mine.'

'What happened to him, or was it a her?'

'He had to rush off like. His missus phoned.'

'I see. Who was that mate, Callum.'

'Just a guy I see here sometimes. I don't really know him.'

'What's his name?'

'I don't know. Maybe he's called Frank.'

'Really. I see. Callum, just now I was standing at the bar enjoying a well earned pint and waiting to speak to the landlord when I saw someone leaving. A big bloke with ginger hair. Now I could swear he was a guy called Kevin Haas. Is that the person you were having a drink with?'

'No, I don't know him.'

'You're sure of that?'

'Positive.'

McClean sighed. 'Well, thanks for your help for now. We'll need to talk to you further, Callum. I need to see you down at the station in Regent Street tomorrow.'

'What for? I've done nothing.'

'Well in that case you've nothing to fear. Eleven o'clock tomorrow. Okay?'

'I've got work.'

'I'm sure they can spare you.'

'Everyone knows that useless Goddard bloke did it.'

'No stress then. See you at eleven.'

Stecher went back in.

'I never finished my pint, Boss,' said Collins.

Nor did I, but we have something a little more important to do.'

They walked to their car that was parked a hundred yards down on the opposite side of the road. They got in but McCean showed no inclination to move.

'We'll see what he does.'

'Won't he just phone Thompson or send him a text?'

'Maybe, but calls can be traced.'

'So?'

A couple of minutes later the door to the public bar opened and Callum Stecher came out. He looked up and down the road and then set off walking briskly away from them. He disappeared behind a parked lorry.

'Quick Collins, see where he's going.'

'Sir?'

'Get out of the car, man! Get across the road!'

The constable ran across the road. 'Okay Boss, he's still going. No, he's stopped.'

'Make sure he doesn't see you, man!'

'He's getting into a car. He's about 300 yards down the road.'

McClean started the engine as Collins jumped back in. They could see Stecher pull out and drive away from them. McClean, without turning on his lights, eased the car out and followed.

Collins was consulting his phone. 'Okay Sir, this continues for a few hundred yards to a T-junction.'

McClean hung back, still with his lights off.

'Okay, he's indicating right. That direction leads out of town towards Butterly.

They turned right and could see Stecher's lights in the distance. A car coming the other way flashed them, but still McClean kept his lights off until the street lights ran out and they were in black countryside, illuminated only by a full moon, still low in the sky.

Stecher was driving fast and as the road was winding and undulating their view of his tail lights came and went.

'There's a turn to the right coming up.'

They flashed past a narrow lane. There were a couple of cottages. They drove on fast for another thirty seconds.

'I think we've lost him,' said Collins.

'We'll go on a little further.' McCean was driving as fast as he dared. They reached the brow of a hill. There were the lights of a village below, but no tail lights.'

'Okay. I guess we know where he's gone, said McClean, turning the car with difficulty in the narrow lane. They drove back and took the turning to the left.

'According to Maps this is a dead end after about half a mile.'

The single track lane climbed between fields and then into a wood. At the top the land opened out on the left. There was a driveway leading to iron gates, beyond which in the moonlight they could make out a large white house with a tiled roof and dormer windows, framed by dark trees. Several lights were on and there was a black car parked in front.

'I guess this must be it, Sir.'

'An impressive pile,' said McClean. 'Let's see if they will let us in.'

There was a button and an intercom at the side.

A man's voice. He sounded annoyed. 'Who is it?'

'Police, Sir. Please let us in.'

'It is not convenient, officer. Please come back in the morning.'

'We need to talk with you now, Sir. It is important.'

'Oh very well!' The gate began to slide back. They walked up the drive.

'Look Sir!' At the side of the house, under some trees a car was parked.

'Well done Collins.' They walked over, photographed the vehicle and McClean felt the bonnet.

'This is it. It's still warm.'

They banged on the front door, waited and then banged again. At last they heard footsteps and the door was opened by a tallish middle-aged man with black hair. McClean noted that he bore no resemblance to the man described by Callum Stecher.

McClean introduced himself and his colleague and showed his badge. 'Perhaps we could come in, Sir.'

The man stood aside and they entered.

'May I know your name, Sir?'

'Yes, I am Henry Walker.'

'Anything to do with the company of that name?'

'Yes, I am co-owner with my brother William, who is currently the chairman. I am a director. May I know what all this is about, Sergeant?'

'Yes Sir. As you will be aware there was a fire two days ago at the wood yard on Church Road. We have been investigating the cause of the fire and in the course of this, just a few minutes ago we had a brief chat with one of your employees, Callum Stecher. Immediately after that interview your Mr Stecher got into his car and came straight here, driving at high speed. We followed him and now find his car parked outside. So, Mr

Walker, we would like you to confirm that Callum Stecher is here in your home.'

'Yes, Sergeant, he is here.'

'May I ask why?'

'You may not, Officer. As an employee of my company he reports to me on various aspects of the running of the company. These matters are confidential.'

'Is he reporting to you about our interview with him this evening?'

'That is of no concern to me.'

'Or about the wood yard fire.'

'That also has nothing to do with me.'

'Mr Walker, I want you to understand my line of thinking. Our investigations suggest the fire was started deliberately and that Callum Stecher is involved. This evening he was having a drink with Kevin Haas, the manager of the wood yard. Following our conversation with him he has come straight here, and you have felt unable to explain why. I therefore want you to come down to the Regent Street Police Station tomorrow afternoon for an interview under caution.'

'What do you think?' McClean asked the Constable as they drove back to town.

'He's the mysterious Grenville Thompson for sure.'

'I agree, but I doubt we will be able to prove it. His name won't be on the deeds. It'll be a holding company of some sort, and that'll be owned by another and another. Maybe the insurance company will want to look into it, but we won't be able to afford the time and trouble and probably we don't have expertise.'

'So, he'll get away with it?'

'Probably. He'll turn up tomorrow with a smart-arse obstructive lawyer and will avoid answering anything that might incriminate him.'

'What about Stecher?'

'Ditto, I imagine. Walker will see he comes with a lawyer and we won't get far. He won't be convicted on Darren White's evidence alone.'

'Bit of a waste of time really.'

'Not at all. We can at least take Goddard off our list of suspects. That's the worst aspect of this case, that these scrotes have tried to blacken the name of an innocent man. That's the sort of people we're up against.'

It had been a busy morning, with interviews and statements and decisions, so by 1.30 pm Det Sergeant McClean decided he needed to get out and get a bite to eat. He also needed to pay a call.

Dave Goddard was in his bedroom with the curtains drawn and door shut when he heard a knock on the door. He was not inclined to answer. He curled himself up and pulled the bedclothes over his head. They were knocking again. He was certain the police had come to get him, to throw him in gaol. They knocked again, very loud. He was shaking with fear, sweating and breathless.

Then his mobile rang.

'Hello?'

'Dave Goddard, this is Sergeant McClean. If you're in there you might like to come and open the door. I have some good news for you.'

Dave suspected a trick.

'Can't you tell me over the phone, like?'

'Well, I suppose so. We've excluded you from our enquiries.'

'How do you mean?'

'We don't think you did it and we've made an arrest.'

'Oh. So I'm off the hook, like.'

'Yes Dave, you're off the hook. They were trying to set you up, but they failed.'

Two weeks later, Dave was feeling better. Dr Ali had started him on antidepressant pills, but he was still secretly drinking most days. That morning he came downstairs later than usual. The pills were making him sleep better. To his surprise Beryl was still there.

'Put your best clothes on, Dave. We're going out to find you a job.'

'Why aren't you at work?'

'Because I've got something very much more important to do.'

'Where are we going, Beryl?' She was striding ahead of him down the road.

'Come on Dave, we've got a bus to catch.'

'So where are we off to?'

'To Walkers, you daft git. Where do you think we're going?'

'But why?'

'Why do you think? To get them to take responsibility for what happened. That's what.'

'But you can't just go there and demand.'

'Can't we? Let's see.'

Dave had always entered the place through the goods entrance at the back. He had hardly ever been to the management office where they were now heading. He held back, frightened and embarrassed. His wife was out of control.

They went in. A receptionist in a neat blue uniform was sitting behind a counter.

'I want to see Mr Walker?'

'Which Mr Walker was that? There's Mr William and Mr Henry.'

'I need to talk to the one who's in charge.'

'That'll be Mr William. He's the chairman. May I ask what it's about.'

'You may!' said Beryl, putting on airs. 'It's about my husband here, David Goddard, who was dismissed and victimised by this company. I want justice.'

'I think, Mrs Goddard, that it would be best if you wrote to the Company Secretary about this, and we can take it from there.'

'No, dear. That would not be best. Best would be for me to speak to Mr Walker now.'

'That's not possible. Mr Walker is currently chairing a meeting of the Board.'

'So he's in the Boardroom, is he?'

'Absolutely.'

'That's upstairs I suppose.'

'Yes.' And she immediately regretted this confidence, as Beryl, grabbing her husband, made for the stairs.

'You cannot go there, Mrs Goddard.'

'Get lost!'

They shot up the stairs to a carpeted landing. Opposite were double doors conveniently labelled 'Boardroom'.

'Beryl, we mustn't!' Dave held back, horrified.

She ignored him and made a bee line for the doors. She yanked one open and walked into the room, with Dave standing sheepishly at the entrance. At one end of a large table an elderly gentleman was seated with a woman with a hairdo and a lorgnette seat next to him. Around the table were seven other middle aged and old men. All gazed at the intruders with surprise and apprehension. The woman got to her feet and came towards them.

'I think you've come to the wrong room. This is a private meeting.'

'No,' said Beryl. 'I think we're in precisely the right room.'

She stepped forward.

'Mr Walker, we've come here for justice! This is David Goddard, a man who worked for this company without complaint for 15 years, only to be thrown out on the say-so of a man who has subsequently been shown to be a crook.'

'Mr Walker,' said the secretary, turning to the Chairman, 'Mr Goddard was dismissed for fighting.'

The Chairman shook his head. 'We cannot overlook or tolerate any form of violence.'

'I wasn't fighting!' shouted Dave. Adrenalin was coursing through his circulation. 'That Callum Stecher insulted me then grabbed me. I just pushed him away and he fell over.'

'That's not the version we heard,' said the Secretary. 'Shall I call Security, Mr Walker.'

'No. Let's hear what they have to say. So this man Stecher is one of those under investigation about the fire.'

'Yes. And he, and another one of your employees, Darren White tried to set my husband up. They gave false evidence and my husband was interviewed by the police.'

'I'm sorry, Mrs, err Goddard. I hadn't realised this aspect of the case.'

'Well you or someone here bloody well should have. Between you you've made him a nervous wreck. He can hardly leave the house because of fear and panic. He's on pills from the doctor.'

'Chairman,' said a large bald man. 'This is all very irregular. They must take their case through the proper channels.'

'Here, here!' said several of the seated gents.

'The proper channels!' screamed Beryl. 'If you ask me the proper channels are the local press, the local radio and TV. They will be very interested to learn how Walkers have dealt with this. This is a scandal!'

'This company will not be intimidated by such threats,' said a short, overweight bald man, getting to his feet. 'This matter may need looking into, but we will not respond to threats.'

'You'll see!' screamed Beryl and was about to make an exit as dramatic as her entrance when a dark haired man stood up.

'Please Mrs Goddard, if you would just wait a moment. Chairman, I am acquainted with several aspects of this case. Please don't ask me how I know, but I am. I hope the Board will take my word on this. Mr Goddard has been very badly treated. I believe his dismissal was unjust, and the company should have taken much more notice of his exemplary conduct over many years. Subsequently employees of this company tried to pin a crime on him. This must all have been a terrible stress for Mr and Mrs Goddard.' He looked round at his colleagues.

'May I say one other thing, Chairman. I do not believe this company can afford to face condemnation in the local media. We depend on the good will and support of our community. So I propose we expedite matters and treat this request for justice with the respect it deserves.'

'What would you have us do, Henry?' asked the Chairman, quietly.

'I suggest you ask Mrs Goddard what she wants.'

'Well?'

'I want you to reinstate my husband into his previous job, better still make him a foreman, and I don't want him anywhere near that psychopath Callum Stecher. Secondly I want you to pay him compensation for the two months of mental distress and mental illness that this company, and several of its criminal employees have caused.'

'You make a powerful case, Mrs Goddard. I am distressed that I personally was not informed that your husband had been victimised in the way you describe, particularly as others seem so well informed.' He looked at his brother.

'You did not bring this matter to our attention, Henry.'

'I apologise, Chairman. I have had much on my mind.'

The Chairman looked around at his colleagues. 'It's probably best for all concerned if this could be resolved as soon as possible. Perhaps, Mr and Mrs Goddard, you could wait outside while the Board discusses our course of action.'

'By all means discuss, but we're not leaving until you've come to a decision, and I'd like to make it clear that we will not accept less than a four-figure sum.'

'That's preposterous Chairman,' said the bald man.

'I think we need to take advice and evidence, Chairman,' said a rotund man with red cheeks. 'I do not deny that we may owe this gentleman his job back, or even compensation, but these things need to be properly considered. It is really a matter for HR.'

'Tell me, Mr Goddard,' asked the Chairman. 'This incident with the foreman, err Stecher, were there any witnesses?'

'How do you mean?'

'Was there anyone around who saw what happened?'

'No, Sir we was alone in Packing.'

'So it's his word against yours.'

'Yes, but I'm telling you the truth. I wasn't fighting.'

'And since Mr Stecher's name is under a bit of a cloud, and I believe he is suspended from work, I think the Board could reasonably take your word rather than his, particularly bearing in mind your exemplary work record up to that point.'

'But Chairman, we have procedures for this kind of thing.'

'It seems our procedures have failed Mr and Mrs Goddard, Tom. Okay, I suggest, subject to the agreement of HR, that the Board recommends that Mr Goddard is reinstated as of today, and HR can decide whether promotion is appropriate. Can we agree to that?'

There was a general nodding of heads.

'Carol can you note my reservations in the minutes?' said the bald man.

'I'm not sure, mind, that he's well enough to start right away,' said Beryl.

'Yes,' said the Chairman. 'He can be eased back in slowly, but on full pay from now.'

Dave began to feel most peculiar. He went pale and came out in a cold sweat. 'I need to sit down.'

Beryl grabbed a chair from the table and he collapsed onto it.

'Perhaps we could call the nurse,' said the Chairman.

Someone brought him a glass of water.

'I think I'm okay, like.'

'Are you sure, Mr Goddard?'

He nodded.

'Okay,' said the Chairman. 'We must consider compensation.'

'No, Chairman, we cannot consider compensation,' said a small man in a tweed suit. 'We just do not have the information to do this at this time. Setting aside the question of possible wrongful dismissal, we need information about the damage to Mr Goddard's mental health. He has also suffered because others, men who work for this company may have tried to pin a crime on him, which must have been distressing, but these individuals are yet to be tried in a court of law. At this stage we have no basis to fix a sum of compensation fair to Mr Goddard and to this company.'

'I agree with you, Jim. Matters need to be sorted.'

'So we have to sit on our fannies and wait and see?' said Beryl.

'Mrs Goddard, I really want to help you, but it isn't simple. As Mr Finch says, there are things we need to know to make a fair assessment.'

'And when you've made that assessment and you offer Dave compensation, what if we don't think it's enough?'

'Well yes, I see your point. You really need a lawyer to look after your interests, and you need an expert doctor of your own to look at your husband independently of our work's doctor.'

'But we don't have that sort of money, Mr Walker. We have no way to do that stuff.'

'Right, then we need to help you, as the evidence points to us being responsible for your husband's problems. Carol, an *ex gratia* payment. Can we let them have £1000?'

'Yes, Sir, if you think that's in order.'

'I do. Mrs Goddard, *ex gratia* means 'no strings attached' It doesn't imply that we accept responsibility. It is to help you with any legal or medical expenses. You understand?'

Beryl nodded.

'When can they have that Carol?'

'I could write a cheque now, Sir.'

They went to the Earl Grey to celebrate. The landlord gave Dave a look, but said nothing as he was with Beryl.

'I can't believe I've got my old job back, Beryl.'

'The thing wrong with you Dave Goddard is that you've no imagination.'

'You know Beryl, I think I could start tomorrow. That's what would make me feel better. I don't need those bloody pills. I need work. I need to earn a living again.'

'Are you mad, Dave Goddard? That's just what they want you to do. They want you to get over this, to get well.'

'So then we'll all be happy.'

'Gawd! Are you really that stupid? They're going to have to pay you compensation, right? And the more you are ill and the longer you are ill, the more compensation you're going to get. Right? They've agreed to pay you anyway. You can stay at home and twiddle your thumbs knowing that every day you're off work with sickness, the more money they're going to have to pay you. We'll get a good lawyer and we'll make a bloody fortune!'

'But Beryl, I don't want to be ill when I don't have to be and I don't want to pretend to be ill when I'm not. I've seen it with fellows at the pit. They get injured and claim compensation. They pretend to be worse than they are. They get lawyers and doctors and they argue on and on and they begin to believe they are still disabled. They don't want to get better, or feel they can't, so's to get more money. No Beryl I want to get back to normal and to my old life. What's the use of money if you have no life?'

'I didn't call it a life when you were working. It was dull. It was monotonous. We didn't have money to do anything.'

'Well, we're going to get a bit of money now, aren't we?'
'Not enough to make a difference, unless we box clever.'
'We'll be fine, Beryl.'
'You go back to work and I'll leave you. Do you understand?'

It was still dark when he woke the next morning. Beryl lay snoring gently at his side. Silently he got out of bed. His overalls were still in their usual place. He dressed in the bathroom and crept downstairs. He shut the kitchen door and made a cup of tea and a bowl of instant porridge as he had a thousand times before. He filled his thermos, put it in his bag, found his cap and with joy in his heart stepped out into the still dark street and set off to walk to work.

The Solicitors' Benevolent Fund

Coal Miners' Compensation

Coal dust is definitely bad for your breathing tubes - the bronchi, and almost all coal miners had a productive cough that continued for years after they left the pit. This was very unpleasant. More important however, was the question of whether long term inhalation of coal dust narrows the airways in the way that cigarette smoking does. This is important because airway narrowing causes shortness of breath that can lead to severe disability and death.

Until recently whether long term exposure to coal dust caused airway narrowing was controversial. Some studies suggested it did, and some that it didn't, so it was almost certainly not a big effect. In fact, some have suggested that coal mining could indirectly protect the airways because while underground, miners were banned from smoking cigarettes. In 1998, the National Union of Mineworkers brought a case in the High Court involving a handful of miners with airway obstruction, some of whom were cigarette smokers. The court ruled that on the balance of probabilities British Coal Corporation was negligent in respect of coal dust causing airway narrowing and emphysema (COPD - Chronic Obstructive Pulmonary Disease). In the light of subsequent epidemiological studies showing a causative link between coal dust and airway obstruction, this was a reasonable conclusion.

What happened next was perhaps not quite so reasonable. The Blair government immediately accepted the verdict and set aside £4 billion to provide compensation. If they had thought about it a little longer they might have considered whether this problem was of significant magnitude to warrant this level of response, and whether it would be possible, in individual, miners to decide on an appropriate level of compensation. This latter point arises because in a majority of miners there were other uncontroversial factors that could have narrowed their airways. These are cigarette smoking in most and asthma in some.

The court judgement covered the period from 1954 onwards. Over this period most miners were cigarette smokers. Whether a smoker develops COPD depends on many factors including the number smoked daily for how many years, the manner of smoking, type of cigarette and individual susceptibility. These things are difficult to define. If a miner was found to have COPD but was also a smoker how would it be possible to apportion that airway damage to cigarette smoke or coal dust? It would be difficult even if the amount smoked and the level of dust exposure were accurately known. If there was no record of the miner's smoking habit, and he underestimated or denied his smoking there would be a severe risk of awarding compensation where it was not warranted. It was necessary to define a small and controversial possible effect (of dust) in the presence of a large, but undefined, uncontroversial possible effect (of cigarette smoke). Similar arguments can be put forward for asthma which predictably would be present in about 5 - 8% of miners.

It was therefore necessary for each claimant to be thoroughly assessed with regard to their lung function, medical symptoms and diagnoses, past history with particular respect to cigarette smoking and asthma. Medical notes, sometimes going back to the 1940's were obtained from GPs, and reviewed in detail by a doctor, with particular reference to cigarette smoking and respiratory symptoms. Current smokers have a few percent of carbon monoxide in their breath. This was therefore measured to check on current smoking.

I was involved in this assessment work for several years. It was interesting work, but at the end of it I was unconvinced that coal dust alone caused significant COPD. I did not see convincing evidence of it. Many had airway obstruction but most had smoked or were asthmatic. Compensation was awarded according to a formula that allotted some of the obstruction to coal dust and some to smoking etc, but it was usually impossible to know for sure whether coal dust had actually contributed to the obstruction.

Compensation was also available to the families of dead miners. As you can imagine, the assessment of the respiratory status and smoking history of a dead person is even more problematic.

Solicitors involved in this process have come in for a great deal of criticism, much of it deserved. The system of compensating miners was basically a legal one. Each miner effectively sued the Department of Trade and Industry (DTI) for compensation, and this process was managed by solicitors. At the outset a team of lawyers' representatives negotiated a rate of payment with the DTI that was extremely generous. The High Court subsequently criticised these payments as excessive. For each successful claim (and most were successful in some regard) solicitors received approximately £2000 from the DTI and many charged extra from their clients' settlements. Several lawyers were struck off by their professional body, many were reprimanded and many had to repay money to their clients. One struck-off lawyer made £13 million in a single year! I am not clear what they were doing for this money. I suspect not a lot. The majority of claimants earned less from this exercise than their solicitor.

By contrast, doctors received just £250 for assessing a claimant and their lung function results. Unlike the lawyers, the doctors were senior specialists in respiratory medicine. Even this rate of pay was generous as each case only took about one hour. Still, we weren't in the same league as the lawyers.

At the time of writing, roughly three quarters of a million miners had been assessed. The minority of miners with COPD received a median award of £1500, but the average was about £3500, reflecting the fact that most miners got a small payment for chronic bronchitis (chronic cough with sputum) and a few got a much larger payment for COPD.

Coal dust, it seems, can cause COPD, but it is usually a minor effect, as must have been obvious from the fact that previous studies had failed to show a significant effect. So the alacrity with which the Blair Government agreed to pay out £4bn was surprising, and I guess this reflected the considerable clout that miners and their trade union wielded over New Labour. Moreover, the Department of Work and Pensions already had a scheme to compensate long term coal miners for COPD. Chronic Bronchitis and Emphysema (= COPD) in coal miners was already a prescribed industrial disease. Thus,many miners were compensated twice for damage to their airways that was in all probability caused by smoking or asthma.

An expensive shambles from start to finish and a grotesque misuse of taxpayers money.

Private Care; Public Care

What's good for patients is bad for doctors
What's good for doctors is bad for patients

This adage was often quoted by Prof Hugh de Wardener, my first boss after I qualified. He would explain that the NHS and other forms of social health care were excellent for patients, who generally got a good standard of care free of charge, but not so good for doctors who had to care for too many patients in poor facilities and on lower wages than they could earn privately. Conversely private medicine was good for doctors who could earn a great deal more with better facilities and greater freedom, but private medicine was generally bad for patients, who had to pay through the nose, and often got lousy care in a relatively unregulated system from second-rate practitioners.

Of course the adage was not always correct, and it's not that simple. Good medical facilities for investigation and care, and efficient organisation are good for both patients and doctors as are advances in medical understanding and treatment.

If you have a non-urgent problem the NHS can keep you waiting for months or years. The problem may be non-urgent, but that doesn't mean it's not unpleasant or worrying. You want an answer; you want treatment. You have to be a patient patient. If you belong to a private scheme you may be seen in days, but it's not cheap and many cannot afford that route. The glory of the NHS is that it treats everyone, however ill they are, and however long it takes. The NHS takes on the chronically sick, the aged and the insane, and everyone (more or less) has equal access. The rich or influential don't jump to the front of the queue, or get better treatment, at least they are not supposed to. The NHS is also excellent in dealing with emergencies.

The need for medical care is more or less infinite. The NHS cannot possibly deal with every cough, pimple or headache. Where care is limited, the overall *quality* of care for the population, and the overall *quantity* of care are in many ways the same thing. The more care that is given, the more problems solved, better overall is it for the population. So, in order to reach the whole population the NHS cannot afford frills. It has to be evidence-based and efficient. If your doctor doesn't seem to spend long enough with you, it is likely he has another dozen or so waiting. The health service cannot cherry pick what is easy or cheap, and it may not be able to afford some expensive treatments that are judged to be poor value for money.

The NHS has to continuously strive for efficiency. It seems to me that in this regard it still has a long way to go.

One aspect of this is that the NHS will frequently go for the cheaper option - physiotherapy and pain killers, rather than surgery; older, cheaper drugs rather than the latest more expensive ones, old run-down hospitals rather than new, modern ones. In private systems opposite pressures apply. I am writing this in Malaysia. Here practitioners and hospitals have to earn lots of money to survive. Over the years I have witnessed the best and the worst. Frequently people are recommended unnecessary and dangerous investigations, as well as treatments that are excessively expensive, but not clinically justified. An elderly relative was recently recommended major surgery, for which there was no clinical indication that I could see. It could have killed her. Doctor friends of mine here tell me the same thing.

The question constantly arises, but is of course rarely voiced:

'Is this treatment/ investigation for my health, doctor, or for your wallet?'

On the other hand you can phone one day and see a highly qualified practitioner the next day at reasonable cost, and usually the advice and treatment is good, and of course, the majority of practitioners in Malaysia are ethical and honest.

Financial reward is a great motivator to practice good medicine as well as bad. Practitioners in the NHS do not have this motivation. Doctors are in demand and so they don't have to compete for patients or for their patients' approval. Their standards and diligence are down to training and selection, personal motivation, ambition and ethos, guidelines, regular validation (with its demands for evidence of good practice, self reflection and continuing training), fear of reprimand or legal action, and audit. But the system is still undoubtedly let down by lazy, complacent, ignorant and unmotivated practitioners. Standards fall when practitioners are overworked and when facilities are poor.

Private systems, like that in the USA, give a proportion of the population (those who can pay or are covered by a scheme) superb care, while the rest get something that may be far inferior. It is inevitable that the exorbitant cost of health care will discourage folk from seeking the help they need. Life expectancy of babies born in 2015 was 78.6 in the USA, as against 81 in the UK and 82.3 in Canada, which, like the UK, has a scheme of universal access to publicly funded health care. In the same year the US spent 17.9 % of its GDP on health care. The UK spent 9.5% in 2016 and Canada 11.6% in 2012. I suggest that the difference in health care systems and their population coverage may be one reason for the differences in life expectancy.

Whatever the rights and wrongs of different systems, in my long experience of working in NHS hospitals I have observed that the staff pretty well universally approve and support the system, while most lament the way it is run, and that it is underfunded and abused by politicians, patients and occasionally by staff.

North and South

I worked for seventeen years as a consultant physician in a London Teaching Hospital before I was appointed to a Chair in Medicine in the University of Newcastle upon Tyne. Although I had important educational roles in that great city, my clinical work was as a consultant physician 40 miles south on Teesside.

I had not heard many good things about medicine in the North. A friend had done his house posts on Teesside, in the eighties and he was appalled. I assumed that, compared to my London ivory tower, standards would be low. I saw myself, arrogantly and inappropriately, as a sort of missionary of medical excellence. I was not inclined to change this view when I first visited the hospital situated in a large and rather dreary council estate to the north of the town. A grey concrete tower block that reminded me of places I had seen in Russia and Eastern Europe.

But, appearances aside I couldn't have been more mistaken. The place was clinically wonderful, and the contrast to London was as stark as it was surprising. There were several reasons. My fellow consultant physicians were of very high standard, and this was not just that over the years the hospital had managed to attract the best, but was also because the hospital had a tremendous throughput of patents, and they had therefore seen everything. They were enormously experienced. In addition they dedicated themselves solely to the hospital, as opportunities for private practice were few. There was no Harley Street and no wealthy Arab patents to treat.

Hospitals in Central London have many problems not experienced away from the Metropolis. The biggest difference is demographic. Central London Hospitals would admit patients who lived alone in bed-sits, in doss houses or on park benches. Few had local family or social support. So, though their medical treatment may have only taken a few days, it often took weeks to arrange discharge to suitable accommodation. So convalescent or entirely well patients occupied beds on wards that were staffed and equipped to care for the acutely sick patients. On Teesside, patients invariably had adequate accommodation, a daughter round the corner or a supportive neighbour. As a result, in acute

267

Medicine alone, my hospital would admit more than 30 patients daily, and of course discharge a similar number. This was more than three times more than in my London Teaching Hospital, which was far better equipped and staffed.

Another thing, Teesside hospitals had far more stable staffing at all levels, than in London. If you were a nurse or a radiographer living on Teesside you have no alternative but work in one of the three Teesside hospitals, and you might stay there the whole of your working life. You would have a continuing commitment to the hospital and its patients. The place was a bit like an extended family. A nurse or radiographer in London has an enormous choice of where to work and is less likely to stay put. Health care workers would arrive in London from all over the world and would get employed for a few months in a London hospital. Lower paid staff could not afford to live locally. Staff turnover was high. People were not always committed to the place. Senior staff in London were more stable, but, at least as far as senior doctors were concerned, their commitment was often diluted by the fact that many were part-time, often with private medical work elsewhere in the metropolis.

The spectrum of disease was also quite different. For several years before I left London in 1993 some of our most challenging work was with young men dying from AIDS and its complications. AIDS was almost unknown on Teesside. In London, many patients were from abroad and one experienced cultural and language barriers. Almost all my patients on Teesside were British. Social mobility was much less and therefore there was more social cohesion. Teesside is about 220 miles from London, but the trip seemed to involve time-travel! It was as if I stepped back about two decades to a more traditional, stable, monocultural England, like the one I grew up in.

At the Fringes

Faith, Placebos and Charlatans

As a clinical student I became interested in spiritual healing, though I never believed in it. One evening, walking back from medical school I came across a spiritualist bookshop and went in. At this stage in my life I was still a Christian believer, so I had a certain sympathy for this sort of thing. The proprietors explained to me that spiritual healing was done by doctors who had 'passed over into the spirit world', working through an earthly healer. They claimed to have seen many cases of miraculous healing and suggested that I travel down to Shere in Surrey to witness the work of the famous spiritual healer, Harry Edwards. After many years of peripatetic and public healing demonstrations Harry was famous, and was able to establish a Healing Sanctuary in a large house, Burrows Lea, in the village of Shere.

So, sometime later I went. Me and a gaggle of sufferers were picked up by minibus from the station and taken to the Sanctuary. It was a slightly spooky place with overgrown gardens and a lot of dark wood panelling. The large room they used for healing was sombre and churchy with its stained glass windows. Harry and his acolytes were dressed in white coats, mixing the metaphor. Their 'patients' had varied conditions. Those with back problems were manipulated and massaged. One middle-aged to elderly lady of a nervous disposition had a number of problems that one of Harry's assistants addressed one by one with her. The last thing she mentioned was a mole on the front of her chest that had increased in size and had begun to weep. This was almost a classic description of a malignant melanoma. The healer laid his hand in the middle of her chest, just above her bosom and through several layers of clothing pronounced that 'there is no anger there'. Wonderful!

Another woman had what appeared to be Turner's Syndrome (a chromosomal abnormality where a woman has only one X chromosome rather than the normal female complement of two). She was short and had the characteristic 'webbing' of the neck -

a skin fold running from the top of the shoulders on each side up towards the ears. The skin folds were massaged, but on the minibus back to the station she was complaining that the folds were much the same as they had been before.

Harry Edwards was a healer of high repute. Many believed he had a gift for it, but quite what that involved is hard to fully understand. He is reputed to have cured advanced cancer and tuberculosis, but I wonder what documentation there was for those claims. An elderly friend of mine who was a Christian told me how he was in a chest ward with a lot of men dying of lung cancer. He, the only one who was praying, was the only one who survived, but that was because, as it turned out, he didn't have cancer.

Later, as a final year medical student I was on my GP attachment in Battle, Sussex. One evening, with nothing better to do, and out of curiosity I went to the nearby Crowhurst Christian Healing Centre. There was a short evening healing service at the conclusion of which members of the congregation went up to the front for the priest to lay his hands on their heads and utter a set prayer. As everyone seemed to be availing themselves of this ministry, I too went up and had the hands laid on me. His hands shook as he said the prayer and it was easy to imagine some divine healing power flowing into me.

After the service, I introduced myself to the minister, and on hearing of the medical school where I was studying, he told me there was a lady doctor from my institution who had cancer, but was cured after a spell at the Healing Centre. I later found out that he was mistaken. He was referring to a medical student that I knew. Hers was a truly tragic story. During her first term at medical school she was taking part in a practical class, the aim of which was for the student to make a microscope slide of his/her own blood and examine it under the microscope. She pricked her finger and put a drop of blood on a slide and stained it. When she examined it she found her blood had far more white blood cells than should have been there. She was promptly sent over to the hospital where leukaemia was diagnosed. Leukaemia is a disease of relapses and remissions, and it seems that after going to the Healing Centre she went into remission, and this is what the minister took to be a cure. Unfortunately it was only a temporary remission and she eventually died of the condition.

My Christian faith was challenged when for a weekend I stayed with a friend with advanced breast cancer. She and her husband were devout Christians, and despite the fact that she had secondary deposits of the cancer in her liver, and was severely jaundiced, they continued to be joyfully optimistic that the Lord would intervene at this late stage, and allow her to see her two small children grow up. They had faith, though I guess it must have been very difficult. I was caught up by their belief, so I too began to think a miracle could happen. I prayed for it, but of course it didn't happen. The inevitable happened instead.

'God moves in mysterious ways, his wonders to perform...'

In the end I entirely lost my Christian faith. It had been undermined by the suffering I had witnessed in hospital. My faith had been naive. But for me the real clincher had been the question of assumptions. I learnt with force when I started doing medical research just how dangerous assumptions are, and how often, even in relatively simple situations one's assumptions are shown to be incorrect or unfounded. Think of the number of assumptions involved in being a Christian, or a member of any other religious group. The Apostles' Creed involves more than twenty assumptions about history and metaphysics. Nowadays we are suspicious of authority and rightly demand evidence.

Spiritual and faith healing are but one part of a whole galaxy of complementary or alternative therapies that are outside modern medicine because they have little or no scientific basis, and usually have only subjective evidence of benefit.

We are learning more about the placebo effect. Many people will respond positively to a pharmacologically inactive medicine (like a sugar pill). This is best shown with pain relief. Somehow the treatment, and expectation of benefit cause the brain to dampen the pain, possibly by endogenous release of opioids (beta-endorphin, enkephalins and dynorphins) that act as

273

neurotransmitters to produce pain relief. In the past we would sometimes give sterile water injections to people complaining of pain, particularly if we felt their complaints were bogus or exaggerated, and they usually got relief. Better, we thought, than giving them a potentially dangerous opioid drug.

Today it is rightly considered unethical to give a placebo when the patient believes or is told that an active medicine is being administered.

Homeopathy is entirely placebo medicine. The dilution of the active principle is so extreme that nothing but water is administered. I guess that this is ethical because the practitioner thinks he or she is giving something effective, not just a placebo, and the patient can reasonably be expected to be aware of the nature of the therapy. At least it does no harm, unless its use is delaying the prescribing of effective treatment. The vastly lucrative multivitamin trade is similar. People believe the hype, and charlatans and pharmaceutical companies get rich.

Naturopathy takes stupidity several stages further by setting itself against most practices of modern medicine. In arguing against vaccination they oppose one of the most potent and safe tools in combating infectious diseases. They soak up every bit of fake news about the risks of vaccination. They avoid drugs that have been tried and tested and prefer to take 'natural' treatments with only anecdotal evidence of efficacy and safety. Hemlock, botulinum toxin and strychnine are 'natural'. They basically do not understand science or have problems with it, and feeding them with nonsense are journalists and opinion makers who are equally prejudiced and ignorant of science, of the scientific community and of scientific methods.

274

Living with the Chinese

I married a Chinese doctor many years ago and at various stages have lived with her family in Malaysia. We have many Chinese friends. Most have had some Western education, but all believe in their Chinese traditional medicine (TCM), of which they are proud. They point out it has a history going back thousands of years. In my experience, belief and pride in TCM is virtually universal amongst the Chinese, inside and outside China. They bleep over the lack of evidence of efficacy or safety. Belief has been instilled in them from an early age and is reinforced by anecdote.

As you may have guessed already, I am not a fan of treatments for which there isn't decent evidence of effectiveness or safety. Chinese herbal remedies generally lack this evidence, though scientific studies of acupuncture have shown that it is mildly effective in some people with pain. TCM believes in qi (energy) that moves about the body in meridians, but this is nonsense. You cannot find or measure qi, neither can anatomists find meridians. TCM's use of animal parts has decimated many wild animal populations, including tigers, pangolins, sharks and rhinoceroses and involves gross cruelty. It may be the root cause of the SARS epidemic and the Covid 19 pandemic.

I must be fair, for there are exceptions.The Chinese have, for thousands of years, used a herb they call qinghaosu. This is a type of Artemisia. During the Vietnam war, when the Vietkong were being laid low and killed by malignant (Falciparum) malaria, the profound antimalarial effect of the herb was discovered by a Chinese scientist, Tu Youyou who was awarded the Nobel Prize for this discovery in 2015.

Of course in the West many people believe in alternative or complementary medicine. Pseudoscience practitioners convince us to take vitamins that we don't need, and promote expensive detox therapies for which there is no evidence of efficacy. I believe the problem is greater amongst the Chinese because they are still widely influenced by Confucianism. Confucius taught the Chinese to respect their elders, the authorities and their traditions. The influence of Confucius is waning, but the Chinese still grow up with more deference for their elders and traditions, and obey great many rules and regulations about health and diet. They are much less likely to question these than would be the case in the West.

A relative told me:
'I had this sore knee so I went to the doctor and tried all kinds of drugs, but my knee was no better, so I went to the Chinese medicine man. He gave me these pills and my knee got better at once.'

I've heard this sort of thing on numerous occasions. I suspect that if we knew the details, things might appear different. Either way, things get better by themselves, and it is easy to ascribe a spontaneous resolution to something you've done or eaten. In this way many 'remedies' have gained an undeserved reputation for efficacy. If you treat a common cold with TCM you will always get better. So TCM is good for colds?

A few years ago a Chinese friend, an intelligent man in his early 50's developed cancer and was advised by his medical advisers that he needed immediate surgery to eradicate it. Instead he delayed so that he could take courses of herbal TCM, that he believed in. His condition worsened and the tumour became inoperable and killed him.

Recently I was chatting to an elderly Chinese lady about how her sister's hepatitis C viral infection had been eradicated by a course of Interferon injections. I was saying it was a modern medical miracle.
'Oh no,' she said. *'She was cured by a Chinaman she consulted in the market. He gave her herbs and she was cured just like that.'*

In a world where experts and scientists are increasingly ignored and distrusted I guess this sort of nonsense will increase. We are all experts now. The fact that my wife and I have spent lifetimes studying and practising medicine seems to count for virtually nothing in this parallel universe. Chinese relatives are completely unabashed as they tell us about some bullshit theory for which there isn't a shred of evidence. Their view of health and medical science is as valid as ours, even though they have never bothered to open a medical textbook.

You may be able to persuade someone to take a particular course of evidence based treatment, and you may explain the scientific reasoning, but this will likely be overthrown by the ill-informed advice of a friend or an auntie:

'Oh, I was taking that medicine too but my doctor told me to stop it,' says the friend.

So the medicine is stopped.

Anecdote rules!

A few months ago some relatives went to see a Chinaman who professes to cure things with a stick, and they took their granddaughter who has poor eyesight. My wife was with them. The man massaged the granddaughter's forehead and temples with his magic wand.

'Is that better?' asked the man,

'Not really,' said the girl.

'Of course it's better!' said her grandmother.

'I suppose so,' said the girl.

You really couldn't make this up!

On a slightly different tack. A couple of years ago a Chinese relative developed a crushed vertebral fracture - a very painful condition. She phoned me in England.

'Douglas. I want you to go to the cathedral and pray to Jesus for my recovery.' She was actually a Buddhist.

'But, Auntie, I don't believe. I'm an atheist.'

'That doesn't matter. You have to go.'

So being a good family member I toddled to the cathedral for Choral Evensong and prayed as she had commanded. It felt strange after all these years and I apologised to the Almighty for failing to be in touch for so long. A week or two later she phoned again:

'Douglas. I'm a lot better.'

'That's excellent! Of course, I prayed for you in the cathedral.'

'Yes, that's it. Jesus must have heard you! You must go back to the cathedral and thank Him.'

She had been in hospital, had a small operation and was taking powerful painkillers, but it was all down to divine intervention!

'Surely Jesus already knows about your recovery and gratitude.'

'No. It doesn't work like that. You must definitely go.'

So I did as I was told.

Neurology and the Soul

I spent two enjoyable years as a postdoctoral fellow in the Cardiovascular Research Institute of the University of California San Francisco. It was a large research outfit that took about 30 fellows annually from all over the world. There was a weekly meeting addressed by distinguished outside speakers, and as it was such a large and prestigious outfit it could attract the best, including three Nobel laureates while I was there. Of these the one that sticks in my mind was Sir John Eccles, the Australian neurophysiologist.

His was no conventional physiology lecture although it was billed as 'The Control of Voluntary Movement'. He described the conventional aspects of this subject at the outset, just to dismiss them.

'Of course you all remember about the pyramidal cells in the primary motor cortex that send their long axons down the spinal cord in the corticospinal tracts. These synapse with the anterior horn cells that in turn send axons to skeletal muscles that they stimulate at their motor end plates.'

'Of course, you know all that - it's old hat and not too interesting.'

He had a very direct, unaffected way of speaking. At the time I didn't know he was Australian and I guessed that like myself he came from the East End of London.

'When you want to move your arm the appropriate pyramidal cells fire, the nervous impulses pass down the corticospinal tracts and in turn stimulate the anterior horn cells which in turn stimulate the muscles of the arm via the release of acetylcholine at the motor end plate. A wave of depolarisation spreads through the muscle causing it to contract and move your arm '

'Of course, you know all that - it's old hat and not too interesting.'

'Now, it gets more interesting when you consider what makes those pyramidal cells fire. What leads to their depolarization? It's not in the physiology textbooks, but it's rather important. We think "I would like to move my arm" and somehow the mechanism I describe kicks in and does it for us. How does the intangible will cause a tangible movement? This, I think, is far more interesting.'

We all agreed with him.

He then went on to describe experiments by the great American neurophysiologist Roger Sperry who showed that the intention to move causes activity in the much smaller nerve cells of the supplementary motor area in the frontal lobe approximately 0.2 seconds before the large pyramidal cells fire.

'So, this shows that intention acts not directly on the primary motor cortex but via cells in the frontal lobe that synapse with the pyramidal cells and cause them to fire.'

'But now,' he continued, *'what you really want to know is what makes these frontal lobe cells fire, isn't that right?'*

We all did indeed want to know the answer to that question, and I don't think many of us would have predicted his explanation.

Eccles won the Nobel prize for Physiology or Medicine in 1963 along with two British scientists, Andrew Huxley and Alan Hodgkin, basically for figuring out how nerves work. That year I did a biophysics course at University College, London and had tutorials from the donnish and rather down at heel Andrew Huxley. He was the grandson of Darwin's 'bulldog', TH Huxley, and the younger brother of Aldous Huxley, the writer and Sir Julian Huxley, the biologist. While I was there the Nobel prize was announced and a celebratory drinks reception was arranged in one of the large teaching labs. This was chaired by the zoologist, JZ Young who years previously had discovered (or rediscovered) the giant nerve fibres in the squid that Huxley and colleagues subsequently used in their groundbreaking experiments. Squid nerve fibres are maybe a hundred times the diameter of the largest mammalian fibres. They could insert electrodes and even use a little roller to squeeze out the cytoplasm of the nerve and replace it with different artificial solutions to decipher its ionic mechanisms.

At the reception Andrew Huxley gave a little speech. Rather diffidently he said:

'The thing that gives me the greatest pleasure is...err..'

'THE MONEY!' shouted his audience.

Eccles was a lifelong Catholic. His science, it seems, did not diminish his religious faith. Christianity teaches that we have a soul, something apart from the body, but able to communicate with it and able to survive death. So it was natural for him to conclude that the mystery force causing frontal lobe neurons to discharge was this soul. For many years he had worked with the philosopher of science, Sir Karl Popper and with the quantum physicist Friedrich Beck to develop a 'dualist' theory of mind and brain. The 'soul' he thought was immaterial, or made of a stuff we do not understand, but that was able, perhaps by quantum methods to stimulate neurons to cause thought and action.

Though this was a logical conclusion for a Christian, it must have taken courage to advocate a mechanism outwith science that was based on religion or even, some would say, superstition. For his part he did not believe it was good enough for science to vaguely promise to find a mechanism for consciousness at some unspecified time in the future.

Neurophysiologists view consciousness as the 'hard' problem. I suspect it's more than hard. My reading suggests that despite many eminent minds addressing the problem little, if any progress has been made. But science cannot take Eccles' solution seriously either, because it can neither be proved nor disproved by experiment. Christians have faith in what they believe to be divine revelation; truths from God. They are assumptions. You must make scores of assumptions to be a Christian.

About this time I witnessed two other Nobel laureates mouthing off about subjects distant from the area of their primary

281

expertise. We had a couple of lectures from the great Linus Pauling, the man who won a Nobel prize for chemistry and then another one for peace - both of them unshared - an achievement that has never been equalled. But in retirement he had devoted himself to the beneficial effects of taking large doses of vitamin C for its ability to suppress the symptoms of the common cold. It was odd to hear such poor science from such a great scientist and human being.

At the same time there was a series of programs on the US National Public Television in which William Shockley was interviewed by the acerbic William S Buckley. Shockley had won the Nobel prize for physics for his work developing the transistor. He was one of the founders of Silicon Valley, but was now obsessed with eugenics. He argued that because unintelligent people have more children than those who are smarter, the average intelligence of the population will gradually decrease. He advocated offering financial incentives to people with an IQ below 100 to be sterilised, and he set up a sperm bank for Nobel laureates and other gifted men to spread their superior genes. He also opined that the lower levels of intellectual performance of African Americans was racial and genetic so America's policy of affirmative action was pointless.

His ideas were generally felt to be offensive and unacceptable. Subsequent studies have also shown that he was wrong at least with regard to intelligence, for in a study in 48 countries published in 2015 IQ was found to have risen by an average of 20 points since 1950. This is known as the Flynn effect and was particularly marked in developing countries.

The End

Printed in Great Britain
by Amazon

68267221R00163